DARKSIDE

'Don't go near the Darkside.'
The anonymous warning appears in your mailbox. A stone,
marked with an ancient symbol, is hurled at your door. And
your daughter creeps out of the house in the dead of night.
The horror has begun.
You have stepped into a terrifying nightmare. You are walking
on the razor's edge of death. But it is too late to turn back.
You have entered the Darkside – and there is no escape . . .

DENNIS ETCHISON
Darkside

Macdonald

A Macdonald Book

Copyright © Dennis Etchison 1986

First published in Great Britain in 1987 by
Futura Publications, a Division of
Macdonald & Co (Publishers) Ltd
London & Sydney

This edition published in 1987 by
Macdonald & Co (Publishers) Ltd
London & Sydney

The prologue was first published in slightly different form in *Night
Cry* magazine, Summer 1986 issue. Copyright © 1986 by TZ
Publications.

The excerpt from the poem on p. ix is copyright © 1982 by the
Estate of Philip K. Dick. Quoted by permission.

British Library Cataloguing in Publication Data

Etchison, Dennis
    Darkside
    I. Title
    813'.54[F]   PS3555.T35

    ISBN 0-356-14746-0

Printed in Great Britain by
Redwood Burn Limited, Trowbridge, Wiltshire
Bound at the Dorstel Press

Macdonald & Co (Publishers) Ltd
Greater London House
Hampstead Road
London NW1 7QX

A BPCC plc Company

The author wishes to thank Reverend James E. Brown, Margaret Coleman, David Gibney, and D'Arcy, Brooke and Cory for their help.

To
Elliot Gilbert

Keeper of the Gate and much more . . .
fine writer and fine friend.

Rest in peace, buddy.

For
D'Arcy
With My Love

This is an obscure and fantastic case, a contemporary case, something that could only happen in our day, when the heart of man has grown troubled, when people quote sayings about blood "refreshing," when the whole life is dedicated to comfort.

—*Fyodor Dostoevsky*

The landscape stiffens. This might be death.
But further, in a new, whiter heart
Which no one sees, a dear unkilled portion overlooked
Harps on. She will not die. Not ever.
We knew her once.
And, kissing her, have scraped the wall that hides us,
each from the rest . . . .

—*Philip K. Dick*

I would not believe such a thing possible had I not been shown.

—*Terence McKenna,* True Hallucinations

prologue

His name was Shaun and he worked at the Stop 'N Start Market, the afternoon shift. It was only thirty hours a week but it would be enough to pay his first year at Santa Monica College—as long as he could take living at home, that is. Somehow he managed to schedule all his courses before noon, no mean feat in itself; that left him exactly one hour. He would bolt from his last class at the bell, skipping lunch in order to stop by the campus library, then hoof it down Pico to 26th Street, where he had to change clothes and be ready for the counter at one o'clock sharp. Raphe needed all the help he could get ringing up the Twinkies and Monster Slurps and microwave burritos before the rush was over, and as long as Shaun clocked in on time and made sure that what he put in the safe matched the register tape, the job was his. He couldn't afford to blow it, even if the pay was only two bits over minimum wage. Where else could he hope to land a job this close to the junior college?

Today the noon crowd was no better or worse than ever, with the usual crush of school kids dodging petty businessmen in the parking lot, littering the tarmac with beef jerky wrappers and half-empty potato chip bags that crunched under the tires of parking cars like sacks of small bones. Inside he recognized a girl from his freshman English class, about to pay for an avocado-and-sprout sandwich and a can of Tab. He ducked into the storeroom and put on his uniform; by the time he came out she was gone. He was relieved not to have to face her in his cap and smock.

"No more calls on Company time," Raphe told him right off.

"Sure, I know that," said Shaun, snapping open a bag big enough to hold the string cheese and six-pack of Olde English 800 on the counter. "I never use the store phone. When do I have time? Hi, Raphe."

"Six ninety-one," Raphe said to the surfer waiting in line. Then, to Shaun, "You better tell your buddies to cool it. This one, he kept ringin' all morning. The District Rep was even here. It was embarrassin'. We got work t' do, kid, you know?"

"I know." *He*, thought Shaun, and got a funny feeling. He tried to ignore it. "Did they say who it was?"

Raphe rang up a carton of menthol lights and a *Playgirl* for the next customer, a long-necked account-ant from across the street. "No message. If there was I couldn't make it out. Bad connection. But he wouldn't give up."

"Well, he'll call back, I guess, if it was important." *Don't*, Shaun thought, *please don't* . . .

"He better not," said the manager. "You tell him it's Company policy. No personal calls."

"You got it."

By two o'clock the line had thinned out. It would be awhile before the first afterschool wave came rolling in, piling up bikes and skateboards at the entrance. Raphe doffed his red-white-and-blue cap and started counting down the drawer for a last cash drop before heading out.

For the moment there was no one else in the store. Shaun took a bottle of sparkling apple juice out of the case and one of Mrs. Chippie's oversized cookies from the jar on the counter, adding the exact change to the drawer before Raphe finished with the bills. As he ate, the boy leaned against the newsrack and idly straightened the stacks of stroke magazines and cheap horror novels with metallic cut-out covers. He never bothered to read the books anymore. They were always the same, about possessed children or possessed houses, one or the other, sometimes both. Who had time to worry about stuff like that? He tipped the bottle back and drained it. This was the first break he'd had all day and the apple juice tasted like gold.

"Hey, Raphe?"

"Ninety-three, ninety-four, ninety-five . . ."

"I was wondering."

"Ninety-eight, ninety-nine, a hundred bucks. Yeah?"

"What'd be my chances of getting in some overtime?"

Raphe frowned. "You seen the rubber bands?"

"Next to the *TV Guides*."

"What do you mean, overtime?"

"Well, I was just thinking. I'm finished with my midterms, and Easter's coming up. I could use the extra money."

"I got Craig down for seven-to-midnight. He never misses, you know that. He needs the money, too."

"I know. But what about the late shift? I could do Fridays easy. No classes on Saturday, so I could sleep in. Unless you already have somebody regular."

Raphe paused with the bundle of bills, staring out at the gray pavement and the battered cars rippling past on the other side of the glass, the mix of faceless strangers jerking along the dirty sidewalk. He raised an eyebrow tiredly.

"How old are you now, kid?"

"Sev—" Shaun caught himself in time. "Eighteen. So?"

"So you don't want the late shift," said Raphe. "The kind that come in here then, they belong in a zoo. Take my word for it. Plus there's always holdups. I don't wanna lose you that way, boy. You need the money that bad, get it from your folks."

"Well, see, I can't do that. They don't even want me in school. My old lady's divorced. She thinks I should go to work full-time."

"You got the rest of your life to worry about full-time. Take my advice. Don't drop out. You still got a chance." He deposited the wad of bills, reset the timelock on the safe. "You forgot something."

"I did?"

Raphe reached into the drawer, took out a dollar and some change and slid it across the countertop, then made it up from his own pocket.

"What's that for?"

"Don't worry about it. The Company can afford to buy you lunch once in a while. Those guys they give me for the late shift, if you knew what they get paid . . . I don't know where they come from. Wetbacks or somethin'." He stopped before he said too much. "Anyway, this time it's on the house."

"Aw, no, man, I can—"

"Don't argue. It's Stop 'N Start policy." Raphe made his way back to the storeroom. "See you tomorrow, kid. And if Craig is late, I want to know. Got that?"

"Yeah, sure, Raphe. And thanks. I really—"

The phone rang.

Shaun waited for Raphe to pick it up. But the manager was all the way in the back room. What if it was the main office? Raphe would want to know. The boy hesitated, then answered.

"Hello?"

"Hello, who is this?"

He fell back into his role. "Stop 'N Start, We Never Sleep. May I help you?"

"Well, I'll be gonged. I finally got a live one." A chuckle. "And I even recognize your voice."

The line swirled away in a static wind, as if the call were coming from a long way off, then reformed. Now the voice on the other end was close again, the tone so intimate that Shaun's ear twitched as though it had been touched by lips he did not know. He held the receiver an inch away from his face. "You do?"

"Sure. Did you think we forgot?"

Shaun felt a grabbing in his spine. He couldn't shake it off.

"Sorry, but I'm real busy right now. If there's nothing I can—"

"We never forget. We don't like to lose track of our own. You had us lookin' in all the wrong places. What did you have to go and do that for? But I wanted to let you know. *It won't be long now.*"

Shaun ducked down and pretended to restock the cigarettes, taking the phone with him. "Listen, I can't talk. I've got a customer." It was true; he heard the blue dinging of the electric eye at the door. "Besides, you have the wrong person. If this is some kind of joke . . ."

"Joke?" A chuckle. "Is that all it means to you?"

"I don't know what you're talking about."

"Don't you? Well, you didn't think it was a joke that night. Or have you forgotten that, too?"

Shaun peered out between the disposable lighters and the display of Hostess cupcakes and Mickey Banana Dreams. The refrigerated cases were cool and still, with no movement reflected in the misty glass doors. Had someone come in or not?

"What do you want from me?" he said.

"Nothing that you don't want to give. A guy's only as good as his word. And I always keep mine."

As Shaun stood up he almost lost his balance. His temples throbbed, his kidneys ached, like that afternoon in the seventh grade when he had gone out to fight Billy Black at the edge of the park after school. All that day he had tried not to think about it. But when it was finally time there was nowhere to run. He had wobbled then, too, going out to meet it.

"When?" he said into the mouthpiece.

"Hey, I can't tell you that, now, can I? It would spoil everything."

The line broke again, crackling like cellophane peeled off a pack of cigarettes. Then it steadied and cleared, so near that it might have been coming from inside his own skull.

"Where are you?" said Shaun. "At least tell me that much."

"Close, Shaunie. Closer than you think."

Then there was only the chuckling.

The boy slammed down the phone, missed the cradle the first time, fumbled it back into place. He stood. The seals on the cold cases must have been leaking. The air inside the store was suddenly so chilly that he could hardly breathe.

He leaned out into the aisle. "Can I help you? Is anybody—hello? Is anybody there?"

The long, jagged rows of packaged goods fanned out before him. He couldn't see into more than one row at a time.

There was a rumbling.

He turned. In the parking lot outside, a spotted Chevy Malibu circled the store and dipped out into traffic. Raphe's car.

The manager had walked right by while he was on the phone. He hadn't yelled. He hadn't said anything. Shaun saw him now through the window, hunched resignedly behind the wheel, taking his leave as quietly as a father who has been betrayed by one of his own children. Sorry, Raphe, he thought. It won't happen again, you'll see. The next time that white-haired son of a bitch calls I'll tell him to—

Tell him what?

Give me one more chance, thought Shaun. *They've got to. Oh God, please . . . !*

"Shit," he said to the empty rows, the echoing store, "I really don't fucking *need* this kind of shit right now, you know?"

He stood there stiffly, one hand on the bundle of *Penthouse Variations*, the new April issue with the girl in the mask and leather bondage suit on the cover, and the fingers of his other hand wrapped around the axe handle on the shelf below the counter, waiting to see who would come into the store next.

*   *   *

At a quarter past seven he caught his regular blue bus eastbound on Pico. As he climbed up, the driver pretended not to know him, as usual. Then the driver said, "Hey there, Willy! What you got for me tonight?"

Shaun glanced back at the stepwell and saw a pale man hauling a plastic trash bag onboard. A white hand wriggled out of a dirty coat sleeve, reached into the bag and came up with three oranges.

"Well now, Willy, I don't know. That'll get you to Rimpau, but if you want your transfer . . ."

The pale hand felt around under the coat and emerged dangling a Lady Timex wristwatch.

"Good! That's right, you did good." The driver took the watch and laid it out on the dashboard, next to a box of Bic pens, a brand-new pair of men's deodorant socks, a Mexican wrestling magazine, an Atra razor with the price tag still attached, and a copy of a book entitled *How To Profit From Armageddon*. "For that, you can ride anywhere you want. Go on an' sit down. Your friends are here already."

Shaun stepped aside. The pale man shuffled to the back and sat between a shopping bag lady and a young man with no eyebrows.

They were all here, the derelicts, the misfits, the outpatients from the VA hospital who had spent the day at the beach and were now returning to voluntary lockup for the night. They were always the first on at Ocean Avenue, filling up the seats in back as the sun turned bloodshot beyond the end of the pier; the Chicana maids and undocumented restaurant workers boarded farther along the route, next to gremmies with skateboards, students on their way to Westwood, pensioners with senior citizen passes and even the occasional businessman or teacher whose car had broken down one time too many. Until he could afford wheels of his own Shaun was forced to ride this last daylight run with them; the Whammo Express, he called it. Again he wondered where some of the ones in back went after dark,

what they would do to shelter themselves if they ever
missed the final buses from the beach before the fog
rolled in. Sometimes he could imagine himself burning
out and turning into one of them like so many other kids
he saw, and at such times he was almost glad to have the
job and school to keep him busy. With a shudder he
dropped a token in the fare box and tried to locate an
aisle seat.

Tonight the charity cases took up more space than
usual, occupying at least a third of the vehicle and forcing the paying passengers forward into every available
spot. They're multiplying, he thought. Like coathangers.
Like the garbage on the streets. Nobody pays any attention, that's why. And nobody will till it's too late and
there's no room for anybody else. Then what?

He found a place next to two dwarfs wearing identical
polyester leisure suits and too much after-shave lotion.
The twins smiled sweetly at him as he wedged in on the
edge of the seat. Across the aisle an old soldier stared
straight ahead as the light changed and the bus moved
out.

Shaun gripped his knees and tried not to think of
anything but the patterns of color sweeping by outside.
Fuzzy neon signs were coming on everywhere, bright lettering and beckoning doorways and unreadable bill-
boards, swollen tubs of fast food thrust skyward like of-
ferings to unseen gods, and through it all the moving
crowds, heads down and faces hidden. The bus passed a
group of curiosity-seekers knotted around a dark,
elongated shape at the curb. The boy tensed and braced
his back against the seat. It could be any one of them, he
thought, as the bus slowed at the intersection. *He* could
get on at any time, without warning. Would I even notice him before he works his way back to me and—but
the bus driver shifted and rolled past the corner without
stopping.

The old soldier began mumbling into a CB micro-
phone. Shaun noticed that the cord dangled in the aisle,
unattached.

"Passing Thirty-third Street. Green light. Counted

fourteen telephone poles. I forget how many more. Do
you have that information? Over.''

The boy drew inward, squeezing his hands between
his legs. At least this part of the trip was short. If he
could make it through the next few minutes he'd be
halfway home. Next to him the dwarfs whispered and
giggled. He shut his eyes.

Something touched him on the shoulder.

Closer than you think, he remembered, and jumped
forward to get away.

A hand pressed him back into the seat. Behind him, a
voice spoke directly into his ear.

"Which one?"

He freed himself and half-turned. A male human of
indeterminable age was leaning over him, breathing
hotly.

"Come on, which one do you want?"

Shaun watched a creased and worn slip of paper
unfolded by blackened fingernails.

"My name's Logus. What's yours?"

"Excuse me," said Shaun, "but I have to get off
at . . ."

"How about 'Anti-Matter: Does It Matter?' Or 'Heat
Death of the Universe.' You look like the type of person
can appreciate that one. Are you a scientist, too? You
look like a scientist."

". . . the next stop," said Shaun. The dwarfs were
watching him. He scanned the interior of the bus. There
was nowhere else to sit.

"Got ten of 'em. Take your pick. Each idea is
guaranteed to make you a million dollars. I don't have
time myself. Too busy. Right now I'm studying the
Heisenberg Principle. Do you know what a Klein bottle
is?"

The bus lurched over railroad tracks. Shaun looked
out and saw a Polynesian bar, weathered tiki heads
guarding the front like relics from a lost civilization,
and then the illuminated ideographs of Chinese and
Japanese restaurants. Farther on, the marquee of a
movie theater and the bloated tenpin sign of the

Picwood Bowl, nakedly white and ready to be knocked
down. He grasped the back of the seat in front of him
and stood.

"Wait," said the voice, "I've got eight more. How
about 'White Holes'? That's a good one. You can give
me a down payment. I trust you. No checks, though.
You'll make a million dollars, I personally guarantee
it!"

Even though a shadowy clot of bodies already waited
at the next corner, Shaun yanked the cord. The bus
braked with a sound like chalk on a blackboard and
they started to force their way in. He saw them pressing
onboard, eyes averted so that he could not read their
faces. Without waiting he swung across the aisle and out
the rear exit.

He hoped the connecting bus would not be late
tonight. He didn't have his schedule—With a deadening
feeling he realized that he had left his book bag. Where?
Back at the library, maybe, or at the store. Or on the
bus. He couldn't remember. He pictured the dwarfs'
small hands pawing through his personal effects. But
there was no time to worry about that now. Where was
the #8?

He stood apart from the crowd and looked south
down the dark tunnel of Westwood Boulevard for a
sign. But the approaching headlights were all too small
and too low. One set caught him full in the face, blinding him momentarily as it yawed around the corner,
spotlighting him as clearly as a jackrabbit on a mountain road. He stepped back. But the side of the building
offered little protection.

He could join the others at the bench, try to blend in
. . . Who were they? He couldn't be sure. Their faces
were concealed behind turned-up collars. One, a drive-
thru cook from the Weenie Wigwam, was munching on
a barbecued pork rind. The smell of it blew on the wind.
Shaun started to gag.

A dumpy, tattered woman waddled over. Shaun
turned away, trying to penetrate the approaching
headlights.

"Have you read *The Way of the Wach*?" she said, her voice already rising to a harangue. "It'll help you get a new job. Do you need a raise?"

Shaun ignored her.

"Well sir, you'll get it. Here, read this. It'll help you. Yes, it will. There's always room for one more at the cross!"

He refused the book and hurried across the intersection. He didn't need any of it. He didn't even need the bus. He hadn't remembered to ask for a transfer. But it was just as well. He could walk for now. Besides, this way he would be able to make one more stop.

It wasn't far.

The gas station on the corner fired a volley of soft bells at him as cars wheeled past the pumps, their lights wavering coronas through a descending mist. At the Apple Pan customers were lined up three deep behind the stools for pie and hot coffee. He smelled the warmth blowing out the open door as he passed, thought of eating but knew he wouldn't be able to hold it down, not now. He cut left at the first sidestreet and pressed north through a residential neighborhood, moving away from the open boulevard and the traffic.

He crossed Olympic, then the tracks at Santa Monica Boulevard, moving up Glendon so fast that his ankles began to hurt. As he drew closer he felt less protected than ever despite the darkness, with the Mormon Temple to his right as brightly lighted as a movie set, its golden angel with trumpet raised as if to announce his passage. By the time he hit the alley behind the Club he could no longer be sure that he was not being followed.

There were only a few cars behind the building at this hour, making him even more conspicuous as he crunched over gravel to the rear entrance. But at least it wouldn't be crowded inside. They would hear what he had to say. He opened the door beneath the circular sign, the one that was like a clock face with permanently frozen hands, and forced himself to go in.

It was so early that there were only three or four college couples slumming against one wall; otherwise the room was empty except for Big Vivian and a solitary waitress who sat smoking a cigarette. The turntable in the corner was unattended. There was not even a bouncer at the door to collect admission.

The one with white hair wasn't here yet, either.

Vivian was drying soft-drink glasses and setting them out behind the bar with anal-retentive determination.

"Any table," she said without looking up. "The music don't start till nine o'clock. You got ID?"

"I'm not here for the music."

"You got to have ID."

"I don't want to stay. I only came by to talk to . . ."

For the first time it occurred to him that he did not know the name of the person he had come here to see. He knew only the image: the hair, the clothes, the voice. The face was unclear in his memory, if he had ever gotten a close look at it. Or had he blocked it out of his mind along with the rest?

"You remember me, don't you?"

"I don't remember nobody," said the owner. "Four dollars."

"I don't want to go down," he said, pointing at the fire door. "I just want to talk to—to him. It's important."

"Still cost you four dollars."

"You don't understand. I have to talk to him. *I have to*."

The big woman pressed a button. A red light bulb went on. A bald bouncer came out of the hall, picking his teeth.

Shaun hooked his fingers over the bartop and hauled himself closer.

"Look," he said, "this is private. It's a matter of—" *life and death*, he thought, but couldn't say it. "It's between him and me. Are you gonna let me talk to him or not?"

"Who?"

"You know who I mean."

The bouncer started over.

"Ain't nobody here yet." The big woman reamed out another glass with her towel and eyed the boy. She sized him up, then waved the bouncer off. "Go on home, come back later when—"

"I can't. Don't you get it? I have to talk to him first. I—I have to tell him something."

He couldn't give up. He considered rushing the fire door. But the bouncer had moved over, blocking the way. It was too late. It had always been too late.

"Give him a message, then. Can you do that for me?"

The woman stared him down.

"Tell him it's off. The whole thing. Here." He grabbed a cocktail napkin, started to scrawl a note with his felt-tip highlighter, the only pen he could find. But the letters came out faint and the napkin was wet; the ghostly letters bled and ran together. "Tell him Shaun was here. S-H-A-U-N. Say that I changed my mind. Do you understand? *Please*?"

She nodded in a way that might have meant anything. One thing was clear. He had been dismissed. She did not look at him again as she returned to her fragile, spotless glasses.

He left the room exactly as he had found it. Nothing was changed. The couples against the wall were sipping something green and flirting with each others' dates as if there was all the time in the world. Maybe there was, for them. They did not notice him leave. Nobody did. He might not have come in at all.

A fine mist had settled in the lot, coating the stones with slime and turning the trees into giant mushrooms grown up out of the ground while he was inside. At the end of the alley the mist thickened into a fog, masking the traffic that passed on the boulevard as if it did not exist. A distant stoplight blinked its warning at him, winking like a red eye behind spun glass.

Anyone could be out there, waiting. The fogbound street was white as an ice gauntlet, a glacial tunnel where nothing would survive except the most primitive elements. How was he going to get home now? The bus would never see him standing at the corner, and it only ran to Sunset and Beverly Glen anyway. He would still have to walk up the canyon. Even tonight.

He could call somebody.

But who? Who did he know with a car who would come out and get him on a night like this? He gave up on that line of thought. If he had any real friends he would never have gone near the Club the first time.

His mother? No way. She would be dead drunk in front of the TV, as usual. And God only knew where his father was.

What do people in the movies do at a time like this? he wondered.

They . . . they take a cab.

Yes!

He opened his wallet and rifled it for his emergency ten dollar bill. *Be there*, he thought. But it wasn't. He had had to spend it on a book for class yesterday. And he didn't get paid again until Friday.

Now I really am up shit creek, he thought. I am totally, royally screwed.

He felt deep down in his pockets. A couple of dollars worth of change, some bus tokens. How far would that get him? Not far enough. Unless—

There might be a way.

It wasn't much, but it was the only way he could think of. He had never done anything like it before. But it was worth a try.

He couldn't see but he made himself keep going through the fog until he hit the car wash a block down. He didn't look to his right or left but kept walking, watching his tennis shoes and the suction-cup prints they made on the cement. He practically bumped into the phone booth. It was where he remembered it. He rattled the door shut and started leafing through the directory.

The yellow pages were soggy and smelled like laundry that has been left in the washing machine too long. Half of the page he was looking for had been ripped out. The only listing he could read was for the Beverly Hills Cab Company.

He kept slugging in cold coins and dialing until he got through.

It took the cab thirty-five minutes to find him there behind the booth, out of sight of the other cars that whispered past like U-boats on patrol. He only showed himself when he saw the yellow beacon on top. As soon as he got in he locked the door, then told the driver to take him up North Beverly Glen.

The cabby didn't try to fake conversation, which made it easier. Shaun wasn't sure what his own voice would sound like snow; it was hard enough to get out the name of the street without stuttering. Judging by the unpronounceable name on the operator's permit, the driver probably did not know more than enough English to get by, anyway.

For the moment the boy was relieved. It seemed so much safer this way, with the windows rolled up and the heater on, the milky colors of a fogged-in Westwood slipping by on the other side of the glass like a faded mural from a circus sideshow. The driver lowered the volume on his squawk box and didn't ask any questions, whipping around corners as if shortcutting a maze he knew by heart. Shaun couldn't get a clear shot of his face in the mirror, but he didn't care. He only wanted to be home.

Not until they had turned up the Glen and were swinging past the market, tires howling, did he remember what he had to do.

"You tell me where, yes?" said the driver.

"Uh, yeah," said Shaun.

He counted the curves as they pressed higher into the canyon, the few weak streetlights streaking past like melting stars, the untrimmed branches of wild oaks and elms clawing at the car doors. He let the driver pass Chrysanthemum Lane, ready to speak up only when the Cafe Four Oaks came into view. The signal at Beverly Glen Place would be set on rest-in-red so he knew they had to come to a stop.

"Take a left here," Shaun told him.

"Here?" The turn forked away in three directions, each as dark as a mine shaft.

"Here. See the sign? My house is—is over on
Scenario Lane. The one with the porchlight." It was the
neighborhood rec center, a converted private residence,
but the driver wouldn't know the difference. "Yeah,
that one."

The meter totaled as much as Shaun made in three
hours at the Stop 'N Start. He got out right away and
went into a routine with the wallet. He held the billfold
open in front of his face and pretended to count.

"Wow," he said, "I thought I had more than that."

The driver cleared his throat.

"Look, I'll go in the house and get the rest of the
money. It's in my other pants. I'll be right back, okay?"

The CB speaker came on again with muffled directions to a long-distance fare. The driver checked his
watch. Then he leaned his head out and took a good
look at Shaun.

"Can't wait very much long. Right?"

"Right." Shaun flashed a phony smile that still had
enough of the old high school charm left to do the trick.

Nod, stuff the wallet in your back pocket and start
walking like you know where you're going, he told
himself. He felt the headlights on his back as he took
out his keys and disappeared around the side of the
small house. Immediately he cut across the lot and
through the next yard. Presently the sound of the idling
taxi was only one more cricket in the night.

He didn't like stiffing the guy, but what else could he
do? He would worry about it later, inside. He could
mail him the money. Yeah, sure, address it to the cab
company with the driver's name, if he could remember
it. A weird name, not from anywhere around here,
African or Asian or something like that. They would
know who he meant.

After a while the cabby started in with his honking,
then packed it in when somebody opened a bedroom
window and made an impossible anatomical suggestion.
A minute later Shaun heard the car gun through a J-turn
and roar back down the canyon, radials screaming.

His heart finally began to slow down.

He came out onto the lane and backtracked to the

signal. All he had to do now was make a right onto
Beverly Glen and walk about two hundred feet and he'd
be home. He smiled, relaxing. The paranoia he had felt
earlier dissipated with his breath on the air as he smelled
the night-blooming jasmine, felt the familiar cracks in
the sidewalk under his rubber soles, the same sidewalk
he had run up and down so many times as a kid, the
sidewalk that never failed to lead him to his house and
his room and all the things that kept him safe.

He came to the sign at the corner, the one with the
cartoon of a burglar inside a circle with a diagonal line
across it and the words *WARNING*: *This Area Pa-
trolled by Neighborhood Watch*. That made him feel a
little bit better. Even the traffic light showed him a
reassuring yellow glow. Suddenly he wanted to run the
rest of the way, through the cafe lot and around the last
curve, no longer motivated by fear but eager to be home
so that he could put everything that had happened behind him.

He started down Beverly Glen Boulevard, silent and
empty of traffic, the foggy tops of the peach trees and
Chinese plums blurry as Christmas firs draped with
angel hair.

And stopped.

There, in the restaurant patio, next to the Four Oaks
sign, was a tall figure.

"Huh," he said to himself, remembering that it was
nothing more than the stunted remnant of the massive
oak that gave the cafe its name. It had spooked him
more than once as a child. But not anymore.

Just the same he walked rather than ran, stepping
lightly so as not to make too much noise, reminding
himself all the way how foolish he was being. He tried to
see it for what it was. A game, nothing more serious
than those Halloween ghost stories he used to tease
himself with, the shiver that was only fun when it got
out of control. But there was no time for any of that
from now on. There was nothing in the dark that didn't
show. He knew that, he knew it was true.

He tightrope-walked the curb, whistling in the dark, a
few bars of "Missing You." He had almost made it to

the fence when he heard the song completed for him by a whistling that was not his own.

It was an echo, yes, that was it, the way sounds bounced off the hill behind the reservoir, especially with the canyon so quiet right now, and the fog—

No way.

The tree was still there in the patio. It hadn't moved.

"Hi, Shaunie!"

"Who's there?" he said, backing off the curb.

"It's only me," said the voice. And giggled.

He looked back as the tree changed shape through the fog, crossing the patio, coming this way.

He needed to get past the fence. Then there would only be another hundred feet to go. He could make it in seconds.

"Shaunie," said the voice again. It was small, girlish. It was coming from the other side.

"Melissa? Is that you?"

Yes, he knew that voice. It was the little girl from next door. She wouldn't leave him alone. She and her friends. The tree was in the patio, after all.

"God damn it, Melissa, where are you? Get out here where I can see you!"

"We can't come out, Shaun. We're in our nighties." More giggling. "We're having a slumber party. Do you want to come?"

"Stacey? Jennifer?" He tried to remember the rest of their names. "Go back to bed, all of you. Stop bugging people. Don't you have anything better to do?"

"No."

A head appeared at the top of the fence, freckled and supported by folded elbows.

"Stacey has something to tell you. *Don't* you, Stace?" Melissa was jerked from below, as if by an angry dog. "Cut it out, you guys! What are you, a bunch of queers? Sorry, Shaun, but some people around here are very immature. Anyway, Stacey? she likes you."

"I do not!" said a horrified voice.

"Never mind her. She lies like a rug." Melissa's face

seemed to hover disembodied, angelic in the floating mist. "Anyway, we're going in the hot tub later. Do you want to come o-ver?"

"Why don't you pick on somebody your own size?" he told her.

"I'm thirteen."

"You're eleven."

"Well, I'm almost twelve. I got a new bathing suit, a two-piece. Don't you want to see it?"

"Good night, little girl. Your mother's calling you."

"Fuck you, Shaun!"

"You wish. Now go back to bed where you belong, like a good kid."

He walked away.

"Melissa's the one who likes you!" a voice called after him. "She says you're cute! She wants to—"

"I do not!"

He heard them squabbling like cats. Kids, he thought. That Melissa . . . maybe in three or four more years. But not now. No way.

He rounded the last stretch, saw the lot full of weeds, his mailbox leaning precariously by the driveway, the relentless growth of bamboo blocking any view of the house from the street. The growth was so dense that it formed a solid barrier; no one passing by would have any idea that a house was there unless they knew where he lived. That was the way his mother wanted it. And tonight he didn't mind.

As he crossed the driveway, dry leaves broke underfoot. He kicked to shake them off.

But there were no leaves in his driveway.

He hesitated at the bottom of the stone steps, listening. The fog blew, moving patches of light and darkness across the glen, the vacant lot, the hillside behind the bamboo, just as it had back in the patio. He was being followed, all right—by smoke ghosts. Nothing more than that. The sound of leaves? That would be the raccoons coming down to forage under cover of nightfall. He heard them all the time. He had always heard them. So what?

The fog drifted, leaving a patch of white so clear against the dark that it looked like a human figure at the top of the steps. He waited for the shape to blow on.

It did not.

"Mom? What are you doing out here? You'll catch cold. What's the matter? I'm all right. Sorry I'm late. Mom?"

No answer.

It was the kids again, then. One of them. It had to be Melissa. He could tell by the long lines of the night-gown, solid white in the darkness.

"All right, who told you you could come over here? I'm tired. I don't have time for your games. Didn't anyone ever tell you about private property? If you don't go home right now I'll—Melissa? Do you hear me?"

"Shaunie?"

The voice was not high-pitched this time. Not at all.

A car sped around the bend, its tires making a tearing sound. Headlights swept the driveway and the wall of bamboo with twin high-beams, cushioned by the fog but bright enough to outline something at the top of the steps. Then the car was gone. But not before Shaun had time to see what was there, what was really there.

A tall figure dressed in white, arms outstretched.

As Shaun gaped, unable to move, the figure raised a forefinger and made a cutting motion across its throat.

Then it smiled, eyes flashing with a light of their own that shone coldly down the steps and over the boy's startled but unsurprised face, freezing him where he stood.

Later, when the moon was high, the fog continued to hang over Beverly Glen like a shroud.

It remained especially thick in one back yard where, behind a fence, a new vapor was rising in a circular cloud.

The little girls had come out to play.

Just now a hand, a very small hand, was reaching out of the misty streamers, feeling for the valve that would release more steaming water into the hot tub from the

column of pressure that the girls believed ran all the way
to the center of the earth. But the valve would not
budge; it was so corroded with mineral deposits that it
required more strength to turn than Melissa had in both
of her hands.

"Leave it go, Melissa."

"It's not hot enough."

"It *is*. It's a hundred-and-five degrees, that's what the
dial says. Me*lis*sa!"

Melissa's hand disappeared as she drifted backwards
through the warm current. It was almost cool at the surface and yet too hot deep down, though tonight not one
of the girls had yet dared to touch bottom. They had
changed into their bathing suits and slipped in as quietly
as possible, staying close to the edge.

And now the vapor parted as Melissa moved through
it, allowing a brief glimpse of the lightly rippled surface.
A bubble formed and floated out of sight; they heard it
pop in the darkness. Then the steam closed over and
there were only the sounds: distant traffic and the click-
ing of squirrels in the trees, a deep gurgling and, if you
listened very closely, a steady hissing that seemed to be
near and far away at the same time.

"Is he coming, do you think?" (The voice of Dawn,
the ten-year-old.)

"Is who?"

"You know. Shaun."

Melissa sighed, or was it only the hissing? "Whose
toe is that? Stay on your own side, will you?"

An acorn fell and struck the ground nearby as the
mist drifted unexpectedly, revealing the face of the
moon and their thin arms floating on the water. Here a
kneecap that was round and white as a cup of snow
broke the surface, bobbed and resubmerged; there
strings of wet hair flowed out at the waterline around a
skinny neck and open mouth.

"He is, I think. I feel like somebody's already
watching us."

"Shh," said Melissa, "you want my mom to hear?
We're supposed to be asleep, remember? If she finds
out we won't ever get another sleep-over." Her hand

made a nervous figure-eight in the water.

"I don't care if he comes or not," said Stacey. She arched and floated, paddling in a slow semicircle. "He thinks he's so big."

"I know you do," said Melissa.

"Stacey doesn't mean that," said Jennifer. "She's just having one of her moods."

"Yeah, her stuck-up mood," said Dawn.

"Her mood of getting a period," said Melissa.

They tried to stifle the giggles. A stream of noisy bubbles blew from their mouths.

Melissa said, "Who got out?"

There was the sound of bare feet slapping on the deck.

"Shh! Did you hear that? If my mom—"

The slapping came closer.

The four girls dunked underwater.

After a few seconds a head ventured up, wet hair clinging.

The slapping had stopped.

One by one the others came up for air. Melissa pinched her nose to clear it, still holding her body in to the chin as if hiding under a bedsheet. She looked around as the circles of hair on the water drew upward like flowers closing. She listened, then laughed.

"My gosh," she said, "it's only my baby sister!"

"How did she get out?"

"She's lonesome for me. Aren't you, baby?"

"She's afraid the Lost Ones are gonna get her!"

"There's no such thing," Melissa said. She caught the pudgy two-year-old and swung her over the lip of the hot tub.

"Well hi, baby," said Jennifer in that special singsong voice small girls reserve for dolls and smaller children. She and Dawn and Stacey coasted over to Melissa's side. "Where did she come from? She's getting so big!"

"She's so pretty," said Michelle.

"Have you been bad, Farrah?" asked Dawn. "Have you?"

Baby Farrah started to whimper.

Melissa lifted and coddled her. "I think my sister came out for a swimming lesson."

"Can I hold her? Please?"

"Maybe we'll let you and maybe we won't. Isn't that right, baby? If nobody pokes us with their toes."

"I never touched anybody," said Dawn.

"Me neither," said Jennifer.

"Well, don't look at me, you guys," said Stacey.

"Sure, I really believe that." Melissa shivered and lifted her sister all the way in. With a practiced move she skinned the training panties from her sister's legs. The elastic snapped, shooting away into darkness. "I'll dry you off after and Mom'll never know. Okay?" Cradling the baby, she moved to the center. She dunked several times. Her teeth chattered. "I said s-s-stop kicking me, Stacey!"

"I'm *not*."

Melissa drifted to Stacey's side and reached around the baby's body for the valve.

"But it's hot enough al—"

"Is not," said Melissa. "Anyway, it's my tub. I have to make it hot enough for my sister. Then I'll turn on the Jacuzzi. Help me, somebody, will you?"

Stacey added her hands to the wheel. They buoyed together, tugging until it began to move. Then Melissa found the whirlpool switch.

A hiss of tiny bubbles clouded the water.

From across the yard, the sound of the back door opening.

"Quiet," said Melissa, "it's my mom!"

They waited for the door to slam.

Melissa waved in the thickening steam, motioning everyone down. Three heads plopped out of sight. She kissed her sister, took her deepest breath and ducked with the others, holding the baby's face above water.

"MELISSA?"

The spring on the screen door tightened, creaking open another notch.

Melissa struggled to keep her sister's face clear. The

baby slipped through her wet hands, surfaced with a splash and began to choke. Melissa pushed her higher, her hands showing above the water.

"FAR-RAH," called the mother.

The cloud of bubbles increased as the jets swelled the pool. A mound of aeration foamed at the center.

The baby slid lower. Melissa's hands gripped tighter.

The water gushed and hissed. Steam snaked into the air. The screen door creaked, creaked again as if ticking the seconds.

At last Melissa came up gasping, hugging her sister against her, flinging water from her hair.

One by one the other heads came up.

"All right, who did that?"

"Shh, Melissa! Your mother—"

"I don't care! It's too late, anyway. Who's doing that? If you don't stop pushing me, Stacey, I'm never going to invite you—"

"But I didn't, Melissa. Somebody's touching me, too."

The hissing grew louder. The water churned in the middle of the tub. There was a leaf, bouncing on the surface. It skimmed the waves like a silvered insect. And then—

There.

A shape.

A dead-white mound came floating up from the bottom, oily bubbles rolling off it. It was solid, moon-bleached, smoking.

"Oh my God," said Melissa, "it—it's Shaun! *He's already here . . . !*"

And then the baby was crying at the top of her lungs and the others were screaming and the back door slammed and more feet came running and it was, it really was too late, after all.

Part
I

The Tunnel

one

Friday night

It was all right to be afraid.

Erin lay with the covers up to her chin until the sliver
of light under her door disappeared like the sweep of a
knife blade across the carpet, cutting her off completely
from the rest of the family. She heard the faraway click
of the latch to Lori's room, then the whistling of water
through the pipes in the walls, the muffled thud of feet
overhead as Mom and Doug shuffled out of the TV
room and into bed. The moon rose behind the trees and
cold blue shadows fell across her desk, spilled onto the
floor and crept up the end of her quilt, a relentless advance that she did not want to stop. The hands of the
alarm on her dresser sliced through another hour and
closed the gap, merging straight up. Still she waited,
listening intently for unexpected footfalls on the stairs
outside her room. But there was only the faint insect
grinding of the electric clock, the distant humming of
the refrigerator in the kitchen, and then—at last!—the
whispering of oversized tires passing slowly on the street
in front of the house.

She took a deep breath, held it, slid out from beneath the bedclothes, and padded silently across the floor.

She eased the window open, nudged the screen impatiently.

It did not give.

Oh my God! she thought in a panic. *Now what do I do?*

She felt for her manicure file and pried the metal frame, but it would not budge. She raked her fingernails across the mesh. She could snip the screen with her scissors, but tomorrow Mom would spot the cut for sure. And then—

Busted!

She pushed at the screen till white moons shone on her thumbnails, but it was no use. Her eyes stung with tears of rage. *I should've made sure after school. Lame! No, it's not my fault. It's this house. It's like a tomb. I have to get out of here this one time—I have to!*

She hammered the sill with the heel of her hand, no longer caring whether anyone heard her or not. It was too late. Her friends wouldn't wait. They'd go on without her. Angie and Justin and Damon would laugh if she told them why; it was bad enough that they already knew her mother wouldn't let her go out on a real date. She'd never be able to face them again. She'd have to stay home from school, get Lori to answer the phone—

The window frame creaked, and the bottom edge of the screen popped up.

She couldn't believe it.

She squeezed her eyes shut and cradled her head in her arms, a tendril of moonlight catching in her hair as it tumbled forward, each pale strand crosshatched by the pattern of the screen, and waited one last time for the clumping of slippers on the floorboards, the worried knock at her door. But she was safe. There was only the steady pulse of crickets in the flowerbeds, the crisp falling of dead leaves, the secret shiftings of unseen life in the mulch of the garden below the retaining wall.

At first such sounds had frightened her, but not

anymore. The Lost Ones were nothing more than an invention to keep children tucked into their beds and out of mischief. Now, after three weeks, the canyon was familiar to her; she had lain awake night after night until the yelping of the coyotes and the strange configuration of the yard and the shape of the hills were no longer intimidating, until her fear became a tingle of excitement. There was life, so much more of it than she had ever known, just there on the other side of her window, and it would not let her sleep.

She went into her bathroom without turning on the light, pulled on her black Levi's and sweatshirt, toed into her white flats, and crawled out through the open screen.

The only thing she forgot was her wristwatch. But with any luck she'd still make it through the canyon in time.

"Doug?"

"Mmm."

"You awake?"

Douglas Carson's eyes popped open. He continued to breathe evenly, hoping Casey would go back to sleep. The topmost branch of a pine scraped its needles at the bedroom window like fingernails against the glass. He lay there on his side, staring at the illuminated numerals of the digital clock. He had managed an hour and twenty-three minutes this time; some kind of record.

She rustled under the comforter. "Doug, I really think I heard something."

He rolled onto his shoulder blades. "I heard it, too. That damned tree. I'll have it topped next week." He reached out for her. "You okay?"

She didn't answer.

A silhouette of the branch, projected by the mercury vapor streetlight at the corner, wavered and flowed like a snake across the ceiling. His arms sank into the mattress as though encased in cement; he doubted that he could free them if he wanted to. Through slits he saw the room begin to invert, so that now he was gazing down at a kind of grotto, the crossbeams becoming the timbers of a sunken ship, the tentacles of floating plants blurring in the blue-gray currents, beckoning him deeper. His eyelids drooped.

A swishing of sheets and the mattress shook, a coil in the box springs twanging his spine. He turned his head in time to see a twist of satin as she jackknifed up and swung her legs down, thumping for her slippers.

"I'll go," he offered.

"Well," she said abruptly, a sentence unto itself. She fumbled for her robe, stabbed her arms into it. A car passed. Across her back a displaced reflection ricocheted like the beam of an usher's torch. "They're your kids now, too, you know."

I know, he thought. I wouldn't have it any other way.

She swept to the door, but slowly enough for him to catch up.

"It's okay," he told her. "You get some sleep."

If I'm not back in five minutes, send in the Marines.

The hallway was easy to follow under the skylight, but the floor might have been a gaping pit. The pile of the carpeting stuck fungus-like to the soles of his feet. He stopped at the top of the landing, one hand securely on the wall.

Below, the dining room was shrouded in darkness. The remains of a log sizzled in the fireplace, releasing a last ember to float like a red eye up the chimney; he glanced outside and watched it rise into the sky, a shooting star in reverse. In the kitchen the dog tested its chain, sniffed the air and clicked its paws on the linoleum, circling for position. Crickets resumed a sawing chirrup out on the patio. Somewhere radial tires screeched past a curve and rushed away into the night. The house settled and the canyon closed around it.

At the base of the stairs he navigated right to the living room, dodging a mine field of unopened packing cartons, and checked the front door. Then he turned left to Elizabeth's room. The sound of her breathing was deep and regular, with only the suggestion of a snore left over from the bronchitis. He gentled the doorknob

like a hair trigger and peered in at the tangle of curls and
the open triangle of her mouth sucking the pillow. A
Dappy the Duck doll leered at him obscenely from the
headboard. He eased the door closed and moved on.

In the room next to hers, all of Lori but one arched
foot was mounded under a white cloud of covers. The
door to her closet stood ajar, the string from the light
bulb hanging straight as a plumb line. He stepped in
long enough to leave a kiss on her temple, just below the
delicate, translucent convolutions of her ear. She sighed
and smacked her lips.

"Daddy . . . ?"

"No," he said softly. "But that's all right."

He left her room and crossed the kitchen. Towser
wrinkled golden brows and gave him a rheumy, mourn-
ful look. Doug passed between the microwave and the
sink, rechecked the back door, made sure the fireplace
screen was closed, fingered the catch on the sliding door
to the patio, and headed back to the stairs.

He paused in front of Erin's room.

There was no light showing. So she wasn't going to
read till dawn again tonight. He started to reach for the
doorknob but decided instinctively against it. Instead he
pressed an ear to the wood. Nothing—no TV, no stereo.
That was good. She was sleeping at last, lost in a fantasy
of quick, furtive graspings in shadowed places and
words whispered into the tender skin of her throat. And
why not? He saw what her mother refused to acknowl-
edge: that there were now two women in the family.

Enjoy yourself, sweetie, he thought. *I'm on your side*.
But he did not open her door.

Erin walked the retaining wall as if it were a tight-
rope, being careful not to look down. The mortared
rocks were glistening with dew, and even the thought of
the house, squatting behind her like some huge, malev-
olent animal half-hidden against the hillside, was nearly
enough to cause her to lose her footing on the slippery
stones.

She found the path and drew herself up through a

maze of foliage, moist branches skidding off her face, until she came to the first plateau. Below, the surfaces of heated swimming pools winked at her like azure eyes through the trees. She caught her breath and glanced ahead for the drainage tunnel, her shortcut to the other side of Beaumont Canyon.

How much easier to have let herself out the back door, scramble around the garage to the sidewalk . . . but then Mom or Doug might have spotted her from the upstairs window. Mom slept like a cat—no, more like a spider in the center of a web, an extended nervous system that spread with the electrical wiring through the floors and rooms of the house—keeping one eye open even in the darkest hours of the night. Doug would not have cared; at least he would never say anything to blow her cover. He was only six months younger than Mom, but he seemed light years closer to reality. Without him there life in the new house would be—what? Unreal. Really unreal.

She felt something crawling over her face, going for her eyes. She snatched a twig from her hair and brushed it away, shuddering. It skittered down the incline and caught in one of the soft footprints she had left behind, a brittle dowsing wand painted silver by the moon. She pressed on.

Ahead, less than ten feet from her and yawning like the black, hungry maw of the earth itself, lay the entrance to the tunnel.

But what was that pounding?

She had never noticed it during her daytime explorations. It was like the beat of surf—but the beach was ten miles from here. Some sort of power generator? Or a pump that brought water to the homes on this side? No, the reservoir was up high, above Beverly Glen Circle; she passed it every day on the way home from school. There was no need to pump water downhill, was there? Something to do with the sewer, then, cesspools, septic tanks, whatever they had here. Or a turbine of some kind. It sent a deep, nearly subaudible throbbing through the soles of her shoes. It couldn't be coming from the tunnel, could it?

She came to the end of the path and stepped in.

The drainpipe was at least six feet in diameter, more than enough for her to stand upright so long as she walked heel-to-toe. But it was impossible to remain centered. She sidestepped a line of melting newspapers that littered the bottom like a cauterized vein, bracing against the concave sidewall for balance. The sweating concrete felt unnaturally cold against her palm.

She spread her legs and straddled the refuse, one hand on the side for support, and inched deeper into darkness.

The throbbing did not go away. It grew louder, more insistent. Now it was overlaid with a hollow rushing, as if the sea itself had broken through and was about to crash over her in a great tidal wave that would carry her back down the hill, helpless as a piece of driftwood. But it wasn't real; it couldn't be. Her breath came fast, faster, reverberating in the enclosed space, folded back on itself the way the ocean is amplified within the hollows of a seashell.

The pounding, she finally realized, was the beating of her own heart.

One of her shoes clipped something hard and misshapen and she cried out involuntarily, a piercing scream that bounced deafeningly off the curved walls. She slapped the cement with both hands to keep from falling as a collapsed beer can chattered into the shadows, its bends and creases stained with rust the color of dried blood.

She stood panting and tried to see the rest of the way.

A thin, circular glow became visible some thirty feet ahead, tinting the walls farther along the tunnel with rings of soft, aquatic light. Between here and there the floor of the cave fell away into absolute darkness. She could barely make out an angular shadow at the end. She squinted. Was it moving?

She remembered the stories about the Lost Ones and considered turning back. But they were only stories. At a time like this Lori and Elizabeth would break and run home to the waiting arms of their mother, which was where they belonged. Her sisters would never have dis-

obeyed Mom's rules in the first place. And they didn't
have friends like Damon waiting at the other end. Their
new playmates, spoiled Beverly Hills clones of the plastic doll variety, had a spaz every time Dappy the Duck
so much as stubbed a toe. But it was too late for Erin.
She wasn't a child. She was fourteen years old, for
God's sake. No, this was real life. Starting here, starting
now.

A surprising drop of perspiration ran down between
her breasts, puckering her skin. She tossed her hair back
from her face, screwed her eyes shut (what difference
did it make? it was too dark to see anything, anyway)
until shards of gray light sparked on her retinas, and
frog-marched a few more paces. Then a few more.

After what seemed an interminable number of steps,
she felt a gust of cool air in her lashes.

All right! she thought.

Her eyes feathered open.

The end of the tunnel was only a step away. She
lunged over the concrete lip to the safety of the grass
beyond and raised her face to the open sky.

Which was no longer there.

A tall, very tall shadow fell across the opening as a
black silhouette flowed over her, growing long append-
ages that reached in and snared her wrists, and then she
was yanked up and off her feet and the shadow enfolded
her and would not let her go. She pushed out in an attempt to lock her elbows but strong arms held her close
enough to press the life from her body. She kicked—
tried to kick, but there was no leverage. She let her
muscles go limp for an instant, contracting into a wiry
ball, and then arched her back, driving her knee up into
the middle of the shadow with all her strength.

"Her, Er—*unh*!"

She flailed away, stumbling backwards. The cement
rim cut her across the spine. She sprang forward again,
fists flying.

"Shit," said the voice, "what'd you have to do that
for?"

Her wrists were caught again, and this time they were

locked to her sides until she stopped struggling.

"*Damon*?" she said. "My God, I didn't know! Y-you scared the *fuck* out of me! How was I supposed to—?"

He doubled over at the waist, his knees knocked grotesquely, and let go, clutching himself. As she moved closer the stars behind him became the lights of the San Fernando Valley below the ridge, twinkling like Christmas tree bulbs through a heat mirage. She stifled a laugh.

"When you didn't show," he said hoarsely, "I came lookin' for you."

"Well, th-thanks. I guess." She wanted to touch the highlights in his hair, bend over him from behind and hug him to her like a teddy bear. But she had not known him long enough to do anything like that. Instead she came around in front and rolled her open mouth over his for a few seconds. He pulled away, shaking his head.

"God, Erin," he said, "remind me never to try to rape you, okay?" He let go of his crotch and took her by the hand. Much more gently this time, but still demanding. "Come on. We gotta jam. Everybody's waitin'."

He got back into bed.

"The hatches are battened," he said. "Now you can get some rest."

She studied the ceiling with him, as though trying to find a familiar pattern in the contours of an alien landscape.

"I don't know what's wrong," she said.

"I do. Moving's always a trauma—one of the biggest. But try not to worry. It's all going to come together, I promise. Are you still taking those pills?"

"You think I need them, is that it?"

"I didn't say that." He leaned across her and snagged his cigarettes from the top of the clock. Her body stiffened under the nightgown; only her breast moved, shifting warmly when his arm brushed it.

He struck a match. It flared in front of his face.

She winced. Then she threw off the comforter and went into the bathroom. He heard a plastic bottle cap bounce like a roulette ball into the sink. Water running. She wiped her mouth and came back.

"I'm sorry," she said. "I know it's me."

"It's the house," he told her. "It'll take awhile to get used to us. The kids on the stairs, the weight of the furniture. The way we fill the space. That's why the boards creak when no one's walking around—it's a big adjustment on both sides."

"I'll get the rest of the boxes unpacked in the morning," she said quickly.

She was missing the point. "I'm not criticizing you. Am I criticizing you? Why would I do that?"

She sighed. "I guess I'm not very good at this. It's been sixteen years since—since Geoff and I bought our first house. I'd forgotten what it's like."

He reached for her hand. It was cold as a rubber glove. "Give it time."

"But you can't spare any more time. I know that. You don't even have a proper place to work yet. I was thinking. If you want to buy that new desk . . ."

"I've got a desk. And the attic room's perfect. It's bigger than my old studio. Tomorrow I'll get the keyboard hooked up and—"

"I'm not criticizing you."

He turned onto his side and propped up on one elbow. In this light and without makeup she appeared years younger, her eyes kind, her mouth as shy as a Botticelli virgin's.

"Don't be so hard on yourself," he said. The cigarette tasted bitter. He stubbed it out and leaned in, combing his fingers through her hair.

She curled against him, burying her face in his shoulder.

He touched her tentatively at first, his hands smoothing the tension from her back, easing her legs. He nuzzled her collarbone and started to undo the ribbon.

Then he felt the deep, regular cadence of her breathing.

The sleeping pill, he thought, and tried to be grateful.

Erin had lost all track of time, but she knew it was late. The gaunt face of the moon had been eaten away by the chaparral; now only a chipped wafer glowed behind the oaks and pepper trees, hovering like a damaged flying saucer. She heard the gunning of an engine and twisted around for a last wave. Was it Damon's car? They had let her out where they picked her up, just below Mulholland, hadn't they? She thought that had happened; she couldn't be sure. Whosever car it was, it was already withdrawing up the fire road, throwing gravel and spinning out as it went.

Her eyes weren't working right. The vodka in her system didn't make the going any easier. The road narrowed to a trail that snaked downward into pitch blackness. She took several deep breaths to stop her head from spinning, but that only made her throat hurt more. What had happened? She couldn't remember. She hesitated at the plateau and tried to get her bearings.

A steely, protective haze hung over the Valley on the other side of the ridge, turning once-bright chains of traffic signals into a broken necklace of dusty jewels. The smog had stratified into a vast horizontal layer that spread to the northern horizon, transforming the diffused lights below into an iridescent vision, a wide and opalescent stage bathed in an unearthly radiance. The swishing of tires drifted up to her, muffled and distant as a receding memory. The world she had known only a few minutes ago was slipping away, the coordinates of a time and place already lost to her like the rapidly dissolving membrane of a dream. The fine hairs on her arms stood up as a sudden chill passed through her. She glanced blearily at the spot on her wrist where her watch should have been. At least the sun wasn't up yet; she would not have to face its accusing red eye. She hugged herself, rubbed her arms, and turned back to the firetrail.

The canyon contracted around her. The shrubbery moved on all sides, rustling and ticking, marking every step. Tiny serrated leaves picked at her scalp as she passed under a bower of dead wood. She yanked free and descended deeper.

She smelled the dank, moldy scent of standing water, and then heard the bullfrogs at the bottom of the gully; the natural amphitheater of the canyon magnified their throaty song into a thrumming chorus. Crickets rang in the thicket as if hastening her on her way. They grated her ears until her nerves were raw; she wanted to grind them underfoot if she could but see them. For a brief moment they grew louder, their voices synchronizing in a series of notes as singular as the tolling of a bell. Then the ringing separated again into an indistinct trill that seemed to be coming from every direction at once. She suctioned her hands over her ears and tried to concentrate on the murky footpath ahead.

The ground broadened and leveled. Eventually she caught another glimpse of the pearly stratum of the Valley through a break in the trees, then of the houses staggered like headstones down the eastern slope of the hill, and knew she was almost home.

From this side the tunnel was one of several irregular patches of darkness. She chose one and shuffled forward.

As she approached, two pointed ears rose up in the opening. She froze. She saw the outline of a sharp, bushy tail, and then two unblinking yellow eyes trained on her.

A cat?

No, it was much too large for that.

She stopped breathing and began counting her heartbeats.

To her left she heard a plaintive wailing that choked off into a whimper. The eyes in the tunnel went dark. She saw a paw lift, then heard a splashing as the creature moved out fast, its claws scratching the concrete. She couldn't tell whether it was running back through the tunnel—or coming for her.

Then it was gone.

There was a thrashing in the shrubbery to her left.

This time the lonely wailing was joined by another voice; the cries became a single yelp that was halfway between a sob and a laugh.

She relaxed and allowed herself to breathe again.

Coyotes must be beautiful, she thought. Like the rarest breed of dog in the world. What color? Gold, she thought, like the sun, with faces that are unbearably handsome, too terrible and too perfect to look at except in flashes out of the corner of the eye.

Someday I want to try, she thought. *I want to see one up close. I really do*.

As she closed the distance to the passageway, one of the coyotes in the brush gave out a last sound that was so pure it reminded her of a timber wolf howling at the sky, crying for the moon to come back.

Doug heard something this time.

He had been dreaming that he was conducting a recording session in an enormous studio—the clock next to the projection screen was as big as Frank Morgan's head in *The Wizard of Oz*—laboring to match the click track on a sequence from an absurd exploitation film. He sliced the air furiously, wielding his baton as if it were a saber as the metronome ticked like a time bomb, forty musicians raised gleaming instruments and waited for him to signal the downbeat . . . but every time a streamer slashed across the screen to mark a cue there was a thunderous pounding on the soundstage door. The red warning light would go off, the projector shut down, the timer reset and he would tap his music stand and raise his baton again. Then—the knocking. Another take ruined. He knew he would have to start again. And again. Forever.

He lifted his face from the pillow, listening.

Had someone really been knocking? No, of course not. And yet—he had heard something. Hadn't he?

He left the warmth of the bed, carefully so as not to wake his wife, tiptoed to the window and gazed down, rubbing his eyes.

A mist had settled during the night and the street

below sparkled as if coated with radioactive dust. Above the treetops the sky was fading to the color of milky ink. He pressed his face to the glass and shivered.

No one on the front porch.

The back door?

He could go downstairs and check.

He waited for the sound to come again, but it did not.

Forget it, he told himself. You're getting to be as bad as Casey. He had—they both had—more than enough to worry about without looking for trouble. Seek and ye shall find. His nerves were going fast. Shaking his head, he went back to bed.

Farther along the block, near the corner, a car downshifted. He heard the brakes squeal like drowning mice, and then a newspaper struck the door of the house across the street.

A minute later another newspaper landed on his front porch. *Thwack*.

That was all.

But he was wide awake.

He'd never get that cue laid down. At least not tonight.

Well, he thought, I can try, can't I?

He closed his eyes.

Still, there was something else that would not let him sleep, *something* . . . .

two

Saturday morning

Elizabeth was head-over-heels for Dappy the Duck.
The attachment had begun innocently enough, with
the first appearance of his dashing likeness on a box of
Kwackles, the Cereal That Stays Kwisp No Matter
What, progressing from casual acquaintance to in-
timacy under the spur of his constant presence on early-
morning and after-school television. By Thanksgiving
of the first year he was featured prominently on every
package of breakfast cereal manufactured by Federal
Foods; by December he had landed a starring role in
the Kwackles Christmas Special, featuring Goodbye
Kitten, Fudgy McNutly and the precociously seductive
Bluesberry Cheesecake, who was Elizabeth's primary
competition. By the end of winter Dappy's jaunty
countenance had penetrated the all-important notebook
and lunchpail market and, fame being the instantaneous
phenomenon that it is today, an Animal Kwackers com-
ic book, a Punk Duck record album and a Saturday
morning cartoon series followed in rapid succession. In
a few short months, thanks to shrewd and aggressive
career management, Dappy had achieved that pinnacle

of success known only to the very few: he had become a
household word, something that took merely mortal
stars salty years to accomplish.

On this particular Saturday morning Elizabeth awoke
reflexively, as if to a call to prayer, precisely in time
to dress herself, pour out a vitamin-enriched dose of
Kwackles and ascend the stairs, the bowl held in her
hands as reverently as a religious offering.

She set the bowl carefully on the coffee table, closed
the doors to the hall and to the bathroom that adjoined
Mom's and Doug's bedroom, and flipped on the TV.
She made sure the sound was low enough to go
undetected, then got her drawing paper and marking
pens out of her toybox in the closet while the set warmed
up.

She did not need to consult the *TV Guide*. On channel
7 the Floppy Friends Hour would be ending. As the picture tube brightened, she adjusted the rabbit ears and
saw a dog with super powers being pursued across the
surface of a chartreuse planet by an army of rabid ger-
bils in space helmets. According to the timer on the
videotape recorder below the set it was 7:55. There was
just enough time left for Floppy to signal his super pals
for a super rescue before the station break. Then there
would be commercials for Bitchen Wheels, Bad Baby,
Taco Time Home Video Game, Spider-Man Shuttle
Shoes and Gee Your Teeth Are Delicious toothpaste.
Then a Pre-Teen Newsbreak with Cyndi Lauper,
followed by the opening strains of Dappy's very own
theme song, sung—or quacked—by the star himself.
She laid out a sheet of paper on an extra-thick issue of
Los Angeles Magazine, the one with Phoebe Cates on
the cover, uncapped a yellow marker, and tried for the
thousandth time to draw a picture of her favorite duck.
She had the head and perky beak down pat by now, but
the feathers on his fingers were always a problem.

She heard feet dragging into the bathroom, and then
the door to the TV room glided open. She did not glance
up.

"Hi, Mom." And at once an unreasoning panic
gripped her heart. With the self-control of a criminal

hiding evidence, Elizabeth picked up another sheet of drawing paper, reached casually behind her back and covered the cereal bowl. "How are you?" she asked innocently.

"Mom's still asleep," said a deep voice. "Keep it as low as you can—we don't want to wake her up, do we? And you'd better not let her catch you bringing food upstairs. You know the rules."

Elizabeth's heart began beating again. She spun around and extended her arms. "Da—Doug, I mean!" she crooned. "How come you're up?"

"I had a bad dream." He knelt and hugged her. His pajama bottoms sagged comically low on his hips. He hiked them up with one hand as he patted her back. "Why do you have to watch that thing so early in the morning? It rots your brain, do you know that?"

"Does not."

A close-up of a duck flashed onto the screen, centered in a halo of spiked pinfeathers to focus attention on his blindingly cheerful smile, as a chorus of electrified kazoos began bleating out the famous overture.

"Yea!" she cheered, clasping her small pink hands to her chest.

"I don't suppose you're going downstairs for any reason," he asked without hope.

"Well . . ."

Resignedly Doug made for the hall, head down.

"Oh, watch it with me?" She contorted her features in a desperate appeal. "Please?"

"Hang on," he said. "I gotta get some water boiling. You can tell me what happens."

He opened the door to the hall.

Lori stood there, yawning. "I'll do it for you," she said. "Why was the phone ringing?"

"I didn't hear it."

"I did. The last time, I answered it. But there was nobody there."

"Lo-ri!" cried Elizabeth. "Get out of here—you'll wake Mom!"

"I can come in if I want to," said Lori. "It's a free country."

"Morning," said Doug. "I have to make some tea."

"I'll make it in the microwave," said Lori, hugging him sleepily around the waist. "It's easy."

"You don't have to do that, angel. Besides, I don't like you messing around with that thing. I'm not so sure it's safe for little girls."

"It is," said Lori. "Mom says . . ."

"No!" Elizabeth saw another perfect Saturday morning slipping tragically out of her grasp. "You're going to watch TV with me! Lori, *get out*—you're ruining everything!"

"Hey hey hey," called a drowsy voice from the other room. "I don't like to hear my girls talking to each other like that. Lori, leave your sister alone, for godsakes."

"I *was*! I didn't do *any*thing!"

Doug hooked an arm around the ten-year-old's neck and walked her down the hall to the big bedroom.

"Sorry," Elizabeth heard Doug say to Mom. "We didn't mean to make so much noise . . . ."

She slumped before the television set, sniffling. Dappy was singing and dancing with furious abandon, but she couldn't make out the words. She turned up the volume. Through a veil of tears she saw the duck wink at her. The bluriness in her eyes cleared like morning mist lifting through the trees and soon she was giggling wetly, then chortling at his irrepressible antics. If Doug didn't come back right away she guessed that would be all right. After all, it was an hour show. For now she'd just have to watch Dappy and company by herself, the way she did every weekend.

Without taking her eyes off the screen she stretched out her left foot until her big toe made contact with the hall door. She kicked it shut.

The first commercial was for the Weenie Wigwam fast food chain. This month they were giving out free space shuttle drinking glasses with every large Coke, Tab or Sprite. That sounded pretty good, though Dappy glasses would have been better. Then there was an advertisement for the phone company, urging her to reach out and touch someone; this one showed a little girl telephoning her daddy at work for an intimate, heart-warming conversation.

Elizabeth sat staring at the unconnected telephone next to the bookcase while she waited for Dappy to come back on. She couldn't call her dad, her real dad, she realized, even if the upstairs phone were working. It was long distance and Mom would yell at her. Besides, she didn't have his new number.

"Sorry," Doug was saying. "We didn't mean to make so much noise."

An idea for the new score ran through his head. *Ta da da da ta da da da*, he thought.

His wife kicked onto one side, then slithered her legs eel-like beneath the covers. "What time is it?"

"You don't want to know."

"Couldn't you sleep? Do you want me to—?"

"We've got it under control." The sun was already firing yellow bolts onto the balcony and through the windows. Doug flinched; his eyes felt as though they were peeling burned skin. Got to get the curtains up, he thought. *TA da da TA da da*? "Lori and I can handle everything just fine."

Lori took a tentative step into the big bedroom. "Um, Mom? Do we have any more croissants?"

"In the drawer," said Casey. Her hair was bunched like shiny copper wire over her forehead and her eyelids were puffed shut. She groaned. "My back hurts. Don't know why it should. No time to lay around when there's so much work to be—"

"Will you come off that?" Doug told her. He placed a knee on the bed and massaged her shoulders. But her back was stiff and unyielding, armored like a protective carapace. "Stop pushing yourself."

"That's enough." She seemed not to want to relax. "Is Erin all right?"

"Why shouldn't she be?"

Lori dove onto the bed. She rolled and rolled. She fanned her fingers, the tips diamond-bright in the sunlight. "Look how long my nails are getting," she announced.

Casey drew the hands closer, as if trying to read fine print without her glasses. "Very pretty, darling. You're getting to be so big . . . ." She kissed the smooth, tapered fingers and resealed her eyes.

"Mom, can I have some clear nail polish?"

"As soon as I unpack it."

"No, I mean my own. Plus I need some new shoes, you know, those white ones with the little strap? And—"

Doug withdrew, tapping out a time signature on the door jamb as he left. *TA da da da da TA*? he wondered.

Downstairs, Towser was wiggling to be let out. Doug removed the chain leash and opened the kitchen door. It was already unlocked. If Lori or Elizabeth had been outside, why had they left the dog tied up? The cocker spaniel bounded out, ears flapping, and shot after a sparrow in the oleander. Got to get that cut down, he thought. It's poison. If the dog starts chewing the leaves . . .

TA TA TA TA?

Maybe. That might work as a secondary theme. Of course he couldn't really get going till the final cut of the film was ready. But it would help if he had a head start on the main title before then.

As the water heated, he shuffled listlessly between the counter and the open carton of pots and pans, the lids nested like silver hubcaps in last month's crumpled newspapers. The cupboards stood open, many still in need of shelf paper, empty sets waiting to be dressed. Like most of the house, the kitchen was part of a half-finished soundstage, an uncompleted interior not yet ready to be inhabited. He fished in the flatware drawer and set a spoon next to his cup; the sound of metal striking the tiles rang hollowly from the freshly-painted walls.

Soon, he thought. The apartment in Santa Monica, though well-furnished, now seemed only a rented rehearsal hall. It had been time to move up. Soon the rest

of their personal effects would be in place and the
rooms of the new house would resonate with possibilities. It won't be much longer, he told himself. Then
it would be time for their life together to begin in
earnest. Soon it would be real. He would see to that.
With Casey's help it would be easy.

The teakettle steamed and began to whistle. He
turned the fire down before the whistling extended into
its highest register like a shriek of downbow har-
monics, poured sputtering water, melted a spoonful of
granulated honey into his cup, and headed back to the
stairs.

The door to Erin's room stood out starkly with its
new paint. He smoothed his disheveled hair and listened
for the bass-heavy heartbeat of rock music through the
wall. But there was only the jingling of Towser's collar
out on the patio, the squeak of birds flying a merry
chase on the other side of the sliding glass panels, the
tremolo of Lori's laughter from the bedroom above his
head. Erin would probably sleep peacefully through
most of the morning, and why not? Why should she be
in any hurry to drag herself out of bed? She saw her
mother as an unsympathetic authority figure, her sisters
as hopelessly immature children. It would be years
before she was ready to rejoin the fold. For now, obli-
vion was undoubtedly much more appealing. And who
could say she was wrong? Not Doug.

He was tempted to open the door a crack and look in
on her, to reassure himself that she was all right—that
she had not been parboiled by her electric blanket, say,
or smothered by the mountain of down pillows. He
placed his hand flat against the wood grain, as if to
detect her pulse through the skin of the enamel.

Then he remembered passing the open door to her
bedroom one night last week, catching a glimpse of taut
flesh and incredibly pendulous breasts; for an instant
he had wondered why Casey was undressing in her
daughter's room. But it was not his wife. Shocked, he
had immediately moved out of range. Erin was not the
little girl he had wrestled with on the living room rug in

the house where he had first met them all only a few seasons past. She was the image of what her mother had been years ago, and that was a vision that must be forever lost to him, something he had no right to know. Feeling vaguely ashamed, like a trespasser in sanctified territory, he unstuck his palm from the slick, warm wood and carried his cup upstairs.

The door to the second floor bedroom was closed and Lori had stopped laughing. She must have crawled into bed with her mother the way she used to before I came along, he thought. I'd better leave them alone. She doesn't get that kind of attention often enough, and pretty soon she'll be too old for any of it.

He sidled into the TV room and plopped down on the couch. Elizabeth was pie-eyed in front of the set, where just now noisy animals with abilities no creatures on earth have ever needed were battling it out in a two-dimensional war, complete with arcade-game sound effects.

"Those are the Space Spirits," Elizabeth explained. "They're always trying to catch Dappy. But they can't! 'Trouble rolls off my back!' he says. Listen, he's going to say it now!"

Doug studied the mock conflict as he sipped his tea. May as well check it out, he thought. No telling what the breakfast food companies are filling our kids' heads with nowdays. Does anybody over twelve monitor this stuff? It could be a communist plot. Or a fascist one; same thing in the long run. A conspiracy to turn them all into mindless consumers. By the look on Elizabeth's face right now—and the bowl of cereal on the table— they're winning. Hell, they've already won. And right under our noses. In our own homes. Their little minds have been washed and hung out to dry while we were asleep, and nobody ever bothered to notice.

"When you finish your cereal," he said, "take the bowl downstairs. You remember what Mom said, don't you?"

"Yes." She sighed, her narrow shoulders drooping as if under the weight of the world's sins, and sat back as a promo came on for the ABC Blockbuster Movie. Tonight it was to be the world premiere of something called *Diana Ross: A Life Supreme*, starring Michael Jackson. She folded her legs under the table and clacked a spoon into her Kwackles, which by now resembled a bowl of congealed chicken fat. She didn't seem to notice.

Doug nearly spat out a mouthful of tea as a sharp *crack!* sounded at the front of the house. The framed collection of Player's Cigarettes duck cards came loose from the wall and fell straight down to the floor like a guillotine. It was a miracle the glass didn't break.

Elizabeth looked up, her spoon suspended in midair, as though distracted in the middle of a dream.

He put down the cup and went to the window.

From here he saw the empty street through the high branches, the mottled pavement clean and gray as a snakeskin, the sun mirrored hotly in the windows of houses on the other side. No cars, no pedestrians. Nothing.

What? It had been as loud and clear as a handball lobbed at the front door. And yet—the porch was clear. Nothing down there but the welcome mat, the newspaper and a few dead leaves.

Something had struck the house and moved on. Something he was too blind to see.

It could have been a tree limb breaking, he supposed.

Elizabeth scraped her bowl calmly, methodically.

"You heard it too, didn't you?"

" 'Course." She tipped the bowl to her lips and drank the sweet milk from the bottom. "I always heard it. Mom says it's pinecones."

"Honey," he said, "I don't think so."

"I know. It's the Lost Ones."

"The what?"

He could get dressed and go outside for a closer look. From the loudness of the report he would not be surprised to find a divot gouged out of the wood between the first and second stories, maybe even a cracked beam. His clothes were in the bedroom. Should he disturb Casey? Even if she had gone back to sleep with Lori at her side she would be awake now. If she had heard it. Apparently she had not stirred. And yet if there was any damage to the house . . .

"Sit down," said Elizabeth. "Dappy's back!"

Pinecones. It was a cinch no falling pinecone could strike with such force. But—had he really heard it? He began to doubt his own senses. Had the picture frame fallen accidentally? It hadn't been up long. The hook could have come unstuck. The house was silent again except for the high, nervous squalling of cartoon stock music.

Dappy's synthesized fanfare blared out of the tinny speaker, assaulting his eardrums like colored needles. He stood in the middle of the room, disoriented.

Is there something wrong with my hearing? The tension, the late hours—could I be that far gone and not know it? Pinecones, he thought. Rocks from the sky. Next thing you know it'll be raining frogs, lightning coming out of the ceiling to split my skull. When do I start feeling those crawly things all over my body, start seeing bats nailing rats to holes in the plaster? And I haven't touched a drop this morning. Maybe Casey's pills aren't such a bad idea. My nerves are shot.

He sat on the couch and rubbed the bridge of his nose, shaking it off. Now there was only the yammering of the cartoon characters, like barnyard animals force-fed a diet of methamphetamines. That and the persistent theme in his own head, hammering to be let out.

TA TA TA TA . . .

The door to the TV room opened.

He lifted his cup shakily in greeting. Erin was wearing her extra-large James Dean T-shirt, the silk-screened face imprinted with sleep wrinkles like those on her own full cheeks, the short sleeves bunched up at her shoulders so that her long arms appeared thinner and more frail than usual. *Back from the Dead and Bigger than Ever*, proclaimed the shirt. "Morning, Lazarus," he said.

"What?" Her eyes were slits, her skin pale and

bloodless, her tongue thick. Her mouth was swollen and distended, as if she had been abused repeatedly through the night by a pack of crazed perverts.

"Glad you decided to join the living."

"The gardener woke me up," she mumbled contemptuously. "That dick."

So that was it. Yard work, equipment—maybe it was a branch, after all. Wait a minute, he thought. "We don't have a gardener yet."

"Whatever." Her lips expelled a short, disdainful burst of air. "He was standing outside on the patio. Trying to see into my room."

Doug was confused. "I was just down there. I didn't see anyone. He doesn't start till next week."

She collapsed on the other end of the couch, as far away from the bare windows as she could get. "Well, *some*body was outside. He even scratched on the window to get me to turn over. The creep."

"Are you sure?" She could have been dreaming.

She hugged her sides as though her ribs hurt, cradling her breasts on her forearms. James Dean's face folded in half. She looked for all the world like someone with a bad hangover. That was impossible, of course. "I don't know why I bother to say anything." Her voice cracked. "Nobody in this house even listens to me."

"Er-*in*," said the seven-year-old, rocking closer to the television set. "You're ruining it!"

"Oh yeah, right, sure," said Erin. She made the hissing sound. "You always get everything your way, don't you, Lizzy? Why don't you go out and play in traffic? Why don't you take your Dappy the Duck doll and—"

"That's enough," said Doug. "Erin, don't talk to your sister that way. It's ugly."

"Well, she's about the ugliest person I ever saw. Why did you have to be born, Lizzy? Mom and Lori and I were doing fine before you came along."

Elizabeth bolted from the room, crying.

Doug flushed. His hand shook, with anger this time, as he set down the cup. He touched Erin's shoulder roughly, turning her to him. He wanted to—

She grunted and fell sideways onto his lap.

His hand slipped to the back of her neck. He tightened his grip and started to shake her. Her head lolled, her muscles gone slack. He loosened up.

"What's the matter with you?" he said gruffly. She looked miserable, like death warmed over. "Look, I know you're sleepy. And bored. And fourteen. But is that any excuse for—?" He looked down at her, at the mass of tawny hair in his fingers, at the bruise on her white, hyaline neck. "Are you all right?"

She flopped over tiredly so that her face was pressed to his chest and buried her hands between his back and the cushion. Her warm breath filtered through the lapels of his robe.

He lifted her hair away from her neck. The bruise was on the side, below the jawbone. It was purple and black, the handiwork of someone—or something—larger and stronger than herself. He suspended his hand near the mark, superimposing his own long fingers. They didn't fit. Something other than a human hand had gripped her there in an attempt to—what? Strangle her? No, of course not.

"How did you get that?" he asked calmly. Then he understood. Oh Jesus, he thought, now I remember. It had been a long time since he had seen one. "Is that a hickey?" he asked, laboring to hide the disappointment in his voice. "Is it really?"

She looked up at him with weary but mischievous eyes. The incipient freckles around her nose might have been painted by a sable brush; a cat would have tried to lick them off. Then her eyes widened, flicking nervously between his. She sat up abruptly and staggered to the bathroom.

"Oh my God," she said from in front of the mirror. She returned and slumped on the edge of the coffee table with her long legs at an uncomfortable angle. "When Mom sees it . . . oh, *shit*! I'll be grounded for a month!"

"You're learning."

She searched his face for an answer. "I won't be able

to go anywhere with my friends after school. I'll have to stay in my room . . ."

"I didn't know you had any friends here yet, except for that one kid down the block. But I see I was wrong."

"Buddy? That weirdo, the one who's always trying to follow me? He's no friend of mine! I wouldn't be caught dead with him. He's a creep."

Her expression tensed as she pulled back. He felt the distance between them increasing as she considered for the first time the consequences of growing up. She was weighing them against the benefits, a new and frightening equation. His heart sank with pity for her. But in the long run no one would be able to keep her safe; she was ultimately responsible for herself. The sooner she realized that the better, or so it seemed to him.

"Do you at least have a scarf?" he asked.

"Oh sure, I'll walk around with my neck all wrapped up like a mummy! Perfectly normal. Why didn't somebody tell me?" She pounded her temples and her flaxen hair fell over her hands, capturing the backlight from the window in a burnished wave. "I don't even remember when . . ."

Doug touched her wrist. She set her jaw and glared at him, recoiling exactly as her mother would have, but with a fierceness that surprised him.

He said, "You should have been more careful."

"I didn't know!"

"Well, you do now. Didn't you think what you were doing?"

"It wasn't what you think."

He tilted his head and examined the bruise. It was so large and dark that he almost believed her. He couldn't imagine the animal capable of marking her so. The thought of a slobbering mouth fixed under her chin for so long repulsed him. He closed his fingers around her wrist and attempted to draw her closer. "Come here."

"No."

Anger welled up in him again and he snatched at her more firmly. "Come here, I said. I want to see. Is this what you do with your friends after school? When did it happen?''

She began gasping in short, shallow breaths. Then, astoundingly, she took a swing at him.

He caught her wrists and pulled her fists down to his knees. "You think I'm going to hurt you?" He saw hot tears slip out of her eyes. "I'm not supposed to care what happens to you? Is that the way you want it?"

Outside, a blackbird cawed across the disc of the sun, sending a shadow winging over the deck. The feral wildness faded and she blinked wet lashes and focused her eyes on the dust motes in the air in front of her, then on his face as if seeing him clearly for the first time this morning. Along the block the voices of children at play rang like beaten silver through the back yards of the canyon.

He loosened his grip.

"Why are you so mad at me?" she asked.

"I'm not mad at you."

"Yes, you are."

"I'm sorry."

"Me, too. I guess."

She leaned her head on his shoulder. The TV continued to blare kitschy music. An intolerably cute caterpillar was cavorting onscreen now, tossing Shirley Temple locks and blinking seductively long false eyelashes, singing lasciviously through a puckered red gash in her segmented face. That, Doug realized, was the infamous Bluesberry Cheesecake he had heard so much about from Lizzy. He was appalled. It was a blatantly sexual come-on aimed directly at the pre-pubescent set. If I were a few years—quite a few years—younger, he thought, I could get pretty turned on to something like that myself. Those legless, pneumatic curves . . . He pictured little boys all over America running through their houses with tiny erections like ballpoint pens in their jeans, rubbing up against their mothers' legs and begging them to bring home the latest Federal Foods breakfast cereal. The thought was horrifying.

"Why are we watching this crappy show?" said Erin.

She yawned, spacing out. "I hate this kind of shit."

"You and me both," said Doug. A majority of two, he thought, and felt closer to her than ever. They were cut from the same cloth. A couple of outsiders from way back. We would have been co-conspirators in high school. She felt uncannily like the daughter he had never had—until now.

Lizzy never came back for the end of her program. He was sorry, though it was good to have time with Erin; since the move he had missed her late-night confidences. Above the ersatz music he heard the big bedroom door open, then three pairs of footsteps in the hall. Then the front door to the house opened and, a minute later, the mailbox clanged at the curb. Casey and her helpers were at it already. Got to get moving, he thought. On TV, an idealized two-dimensional hero wrestled jerkily with featureless invaders from another world.

"It's just as well she didn't see it," he said, meaning the seven-year-old. "It warps kids' brains. Did it warp yours, sweetie?" He put his arm across the back of the couch and tousled her hair.

"I never watched stuff like this," said Erin. She pulled thoughtfully at her lip as a trashcan-sized robot set about abducting Bluesberry Cheesecake. "What do you mean? The violence?"

"What violence? There isn't any. It isn't real. Nobody ever gets hurt. What does that teach you? It's all a game. It makes it easy to shoot down anything in sight, as long as you know they're going to bounce right back. As soon as you put in another quarter. Or another commercial comes on. Same difference. Am I right? Say right arm."

"Right arm." Erin hissed. "You're so corny. Didn't Mom ever tell you that?"

"She's corny, too. Why do you think I married her?"

"So you could be close to me. I saw *Lolita*, you know."

"You did? When?"

"Well, part of it, anyway."

"You should have seen the end. It turns into a real tragedy."

"You're the only tragedy around here. You're gonna be forty years old next month. Ha ha. D'you know how old that is? When are you gonna get a lifestyle, Doug?"

"Cool it, kid."

"Who are you calling kid?"

"Who do you think? Do you see any other punks around here?"

"What do you know about punks, *grandpa*?"

"That's enough."

"Eat it."

"What did you say to me?" He tightened his arm playfully around her neck. "Hm?"

"Eat it raw."

"Where did you learn to cuss?"

"I cuss better than you, old man. Look at all those white hairs . . ."

"Why, you disrespectful little—"

"Grow up, Doug, before it's too late!"

He grabbed her in a mock headlock. She struggled, laughing and screaming curses, pushing off the end of the couch with her strong legs. As usual she didn't know when to stop. It was like trying to hold a forty-pound tuna in the bottom of a boat. Downstairs, the front door slammed. He wrestled Erin's head around so that he could see her, but he was careful to avoid the bruise on her neck. That was his downfall. She got hold of his little finger and bent it out of position.

"You think that doesn't hurt because I'm bigger than you, because I'm a grown man? How would you like *your* little finger broken?" He heard footsteps marching up the stairs, heading this way. It was time to finish it. But Erin didn't want to quit. If they weren't interrupted she'd go on until one of them got hurt. That was her way. She never gave up. "All right, I guess I'm going to have to teach you a lesson. You fight like a girl, do you know that?"

He turned her over and wrenched her forearm up into a hammerlock. He keyed it into a chicken-wing and pulled it a little bit higher than usual to get it over with.

"Give up," he suggested.

She wouldn't, though she couldn't move.

He let go and stood up. "There," he said in his most hardboiled voice. "That should teach you a lesson, little girl." He knew she hated that, hated it and loved it. Her real father must have played that way with her. Or was it that he never played with her at all? Unfortunately Casey's playful side, the child buried within her, had apparently been locked away since the onset of puberty.

He flexed his little finger to be sure it was not broken. It wasn't—but there, looped around his hand, was a swatch of Erin's hair. Not just a few strands but a formidable lock the thickness of a small rope, yanked out by the roots. She had made no sound. Hadn't she felt it? When had that happened? He had scarcely tugged on her hair at all, or so he thought.

"Jesus, sweetie, I'm really sorry. You should have said something. I didn't realize what I was . . ."

"What?"

Ashamed and chastised with guilt, he sat quickly in the chair by the window and hid his hand, as the door to the hallway burst open.

"Doug," said Casey, "I want to talk to you."

"What's the matter?" He played dumb, feeling for the moment more like one of the children than their stepfather.

Casey would not meet his eyes, the eyes of a subversive in her own house, a revolutionary in collusion with her own flesh and blood.

Erin raised to her elbow and feigned interest in the television broadcast. It was Hal Linden at the station break, oozing through another FYI. This time he offered advice about designing a bright and breezy repast with a flair by dressing up a card table. Erin was breathing hard but trying not to show it. She knew her mother didn't approve of horseplay in the house.

"What's this?" Casey said.

"Lizzy isn't still crying, is she?" asked Doug. "I had a talk with Erin about that. It wasn't really her fault. It wasn't anybody's fault. It was all a misunderstanding. But she says she's sorry. Don't you, Erin?" Don't fail me now, kid, he thought. I'm giving you a break; don't blow it.

"I'm sorry," said Erin. Whew. "But Lizzy's such a little princess. Sometimes she really gets on my—"

"Doug, what is this?" repeated Casey.

Now he saw that she was holding something in her hand. It was an envelope. There was something funny about the way it was addressed. It had been torn open.

"I found this in the mailbox. And this was next to the front porch." She held up her other hand. It contained a rock about six inches in diameter, with something painted or written on it.

"Let me see that."

"I don't like this," said Casey. "I don't like it one bit. *What is going on*?"

three

Saturday afternoon

Lori was almost finished making the roast beef and chocolate sandwich when the doorbell rang. She kept working, piling thin slices of meat over the buttered halves of the croissant, hoping that someone else would get to the door first. She had a steady, efficient rhythm going in the kitchen and hated to break stride.

The floorboards creaked on the first landing, and then the door to the attic room unstuck with a splintering crunch. But she didn't want Doug to have to come down—that would spoil the surprise. Where was Mom? Elizabeth had sneaked up to Lester's pool and Erin was asleep again. What else was new? She exhaled wearily, put down the Ghirardelli semisweet bar and wiped her hands.

The doorbell rang again. Twice.

She gave up. "I'll get it!" she yelled, beaten.

A tall man with a handlebar moustache stood on the porch, rocking impatiently from one foot to the other. He was younger than Dad, younger even than Doug, and he was wearing a jumpsuit with a name sewn on the pocket. The way he was moving around she couldn't read it.

"Um, yes?"

The tall man smirked down at her and twirled his moustache. The ends curled like antennae. "Are you the lady of the house?" he asked.

"Um, no, I'm not." He must put something on the whiskers to make them stay pointed like that, she thought. Glue? They were sharp as crochet hooks. She wondered if he got kissed very often. "What is it you wanted?"

There was a quick thumping on the stairs and then in the living room behind her. Before Lori could turn around, Mom put a hand on her shoulder and leaned in front of her to open the screen door.

"Mrs. Carson? ConCable here."

"Why today?" Lori heard Mom mutter.

"You called in an order for an additional outlet?"

"Two, actually," said Mom. "Come in."

She held the screen wide and Lori saw the van with the ladder on top parked at the curb. Mom looked scared, like the time Grandma was dying in the hospital and she kept putting off going to visit. She had looked that way almost since she got up. Why?

"Excuse the mess. I'm afraid we're still not quite moved in."

"Not to worry," said the man. "I know how it is." He doesn't, thought Lori. How could he?

She went back to work. The cable TV man lumbered through the house, heavy tools swinging from his belt like the weapons of an occupying soldier. When Mom led him into the dining room the dog went apeshit out on the patio, barking and jumping at the sliding doors until the glass was streaked with saliva. At least they weren't coming into the kitchen. For now it was still her domain.

"Towser, cool it!" shouted Mom. The dog snorted and loped away. She turned back to the cable man and addressed him with her best stewardess's smile. "One of the sets is in here. My oldest daughter's room." She knocked on Erin's door.

Lori unwrapped the foil from the chocolate, separated some of the squares and inserted them between the layers of roast beef. She rewrapped the other

half of the bar and put it in the refrigerator, a snack for
later.

Mom knocked louder. "Erin, are you in there?" She
twisted the doorknob and stuck her head in. Lori heard
her say something in a deceptively conversational tone.

"Can't you see I'm trying to sleep?"

"It's one o'clock in the afternoon, young lady," said
Mom more firmly. "What are you doing back in bed at
this hour?"

"I don't feel good."

"If you want your TV hooked up you'll get up and
get dressed right now, like a normal person."

"Who wants to be normal?" moaned Erin. "Go
away."

Mom faced the cable man with a tight, forced grin.
"Why don't you start with the one upstairs?" she tried.

Lori added a green lettuce leaf, popped open the
bottle of Noche Buena beer she had stashed in the
freezer, got out the individual serving of Fritos she had
saved from her school lunch the day before, and folded
a napkin under the plate. Balancing it all, she carried the
tray around the counter and walked as if on eggs toward
the stairs. At the first landing she stopped in front of the
attic entrance.

Below, the doorbell rang.

Oh no, she thought, not again. She looked around,
frantic. Mom was all the way upstairs by now. Lori had
no choice. She set the tray on the landing and started
back down.

Someone put a hand on her shoulder.

"Whoa . . . *Mom*! You scared the—you really, really
scared me!"

Mom continued to press her shoulder as she said,
"You stay right here." The way she said it Lori knew
she meant business. What was going on? The beer
would get warm and Doug would be pissed off; he
wouldn't say so but she'd be able to tell. Desolated, she
sat on the step and waited.

This time it was the telephone man. *It never rains but
it pours.* That was what Grandma used to say. At last
Lori understood. Erin would be glad, though; she had

been wanting her own extension for a long time.

"Erin," Mom called hopefully from the dining room, "the telephone company is here."

In the room below the stairwell, Erin threw something and cursed. "Okay, all right, fine! Do what you want! I don't care anymore!" Erin's bathroom door banged shut and the water started running.

"It's in here," said Mom cheerfully. Lori saw a plastic handset dangling like a strangled doll from the repairman's web belt. As soon as she could, Mom came back up to the landing.

"Lori, listen to me closely. This is very, very important." Mom kept glancing up and down the stairs, probably afraid that the cable man or the phone man would hear.

"What?"

"From now on, I don't want you to open the front door unless you're absolutely certain who it is. Do you understand?"

"Why?"

At the top of the second landing, the cable TV man cleared his throat. Lori saw his thick arm on the railing and the razor-end of his moustache twitching the air.

"Ma'am, where exactly did you want that outlet?"

"Just a moment. I'll be right with you." Mom pressed Lori's shoulder tighter than ever and put her mouth over her daughter's ear. "I'll explain later," she whispered. "For now, do as I say. Make sure you let a grownup answer the door. Promise me."

"I promise."

Mom kissed her on the cheek and left her there.

"Where's Elizabeth?" Mom asked from the top of the stairs.

Lori told her.

Mom's eyes went wide and her jaw jutted out in that way that meant she was mad. *I wonder why?* thought Lori.

The way Doug held the rock, it might have been a meteor fragment from another world.

It was a little larger than his fist, quite ordinary

granite, worn smooth as the stones that were cemented into place along the retaining wall in the back yard. Nothing at all unusual about it. Except for the symbol painted across one surface:

It appeared to be a misdrawn peace sign.

And what of the one on the other side? He turned the rock over:

That reminded him of—what? *Something*.

Below, the doorbell rang again. Why hadn't Casey let one of the girls answer it instead of running out in the middle of their conversation? She was obviously wound up tighter than a violin string and needed to talk. Now that would have to wait. He couldn't tell her what she wanted to hear until he knew the rest. Was she going off the deep end? Not likely, knowing Casey. But she needed answers.

He set the rock on his music paper and tipped back from the desk. He switched off the gooseneck lamp—no matter how he adjusted it the high-intensity bulb seemed to sear through the hood, the filament vibrating like a luminous moth, beating feverishly against his face—and closed his eyes. He couldn't get them out of his mind. Patterns of lines crisscrossed inside two circles . . .

There was a great and continuous commotion on the stairs. The dog barked endlessly. He tried to block it out. He needed to think before Casey came back.

Did she know what the markings meant? No, he was sure she didn't. She took things at face value, which was her strength, he supposed. It was a stone that had been hurled full-bore at the house for no good reason—what reason could there be?—and she had to know why. Now. It could have broken a window or worse, especially if one of the kids had been outside. What if it happened again? And so on. There was no room in her mind for randomness; she had to have everything in its place, even things she could not see. And though she was as different from him in her way of thinking as anyone could be, that difference was precisely why he treasured her so. Without her sense of organization and direction he would probably still be playing for tips in a piano bar somewhere.

The doorbell rang yet again and there was more tramping on the stairs. Doug decided to stay put. He convinced himself that he'd only get in the way.

He had listened to her here in the privacy of the workroom as she weighed the distasteful object in her hand. And there was more. She had reeled off the details. She assumed that he had been too absorbed in his work to notice any of it until she pointed it out. She did not blame him—she, too, had been busy, overseeing the reconstruction of their lives to too great a degree, in fact, for him to feel anything but guilty. Despite his protests she claimed to be happy with the division of labor.

But now, this morning, there was the rock. And the strangely-addressed letter in the mailbox with no stamp on the envelope. Today was the last straw. Because there had been—other things.

The footprints in the flowerbed outside Erin's room.

The marks on the tree outside their bedroom window.

The phone downstairs that rang with no one on the line.

Doors that did not stay locked.

And, also today, the chalk-mark emblem on the driveway: a three-foot circle with a crisscross of lines inside it.

Casey could deal with almost any obstacle that life placed in her path, with the myriad details making up the mountain in labor that she embraced as her lot. But for the things that didn't add up, for the mystery parts, she needed his help.

Was she losing her grip, breaking under the stress of the last few weeks? For his own sake as well as hers he wished that he could so easily dismiss the flinty reflection of fear and anger in her eyes. But it was not that simple. Not if there was any danger to the children.

They now had material evidence that added up to a pattern of escalating threats, and that could not be ignored.

He reached for the envelope, the one that had arrived without benefit of the mail truck, to examine it one more time. Even if it was part of an elaborate prank it was still up to him to find that out and put a stop to it.

He heard Erin yelling, a door slam, the pipes running water in the walls. He tried not to listen.

If he could piece together the clues . . .

There was a knock on his door.

Why not? he thought. Let the chaos in. Try to keep it out and it will start seeping in through the cracks, anyway. The music score would simply have to wait a bit longer. Either that or he would have to learn to work in the midst of the madness. Perhaps that was not such a bad idea. It would make him stronger, more disciplined, would build his character. Enter, life, he thought. Come into my garret, said the fly to the spider. I may be tougher than you think.

"Yes?"

"Um, Doug?"

He tugged to unstick the plywood panel. The door frame was warped, skewed a few degrees so that it did not fit properly. He couldn't leave it that way. Some night soon, when he took to working instead of trying to sleep, he'd have to kick it to get it open and the shock waves would wake everyone else in the house. The dog would bark, the dishes would rattle, the side of the hill would shake loose in an avalanche and his attempts to get his own work done would bury them all . . . . He'd chisel it and sand it down before then. Soon.

If he could only get a few measures written first.

"Hi, angel. Why, what's all this?"

With the tray protruding like that, Lori reminded him of a concession girl in a nightclub. The plate was sliding against her tummy and the beer wouldn't stay upright for long; a rising tide sloshed inside the neck.

"Um, can you help me?"

He took the heavy tray and set it on his desk. Beneath

the music paper, a Rapidograph pen snapped like a breadstick. "What do you have here? Cigars? Cigarettes?"

"What? Um, no." She was as literal as her mother. "Mom said you're busy working and I'm sorry to bother you. I know you never eat breakfast. But I thought you might be ready for some lunch."

He shook his head in wonderment. What did I ever do to deserve this kind of special treatment? I must have gotten something right somewhere along the line. I never knew it. And now my cup runneth over. He poured the beer. It foamed up and over the lip of the glass.

"Thanks, angel. You know you didn't have to do this."

"I know."

"What's going on out there?" He took a bite of the sandwich. "I thought I heard swords rattling in the living room."

"It's only the repair man. Men." She was out of breath and blinking too fast. Something was bugging her. "Um, can I ask you a question?"

"Shoot."

"Why can't I answer the front door?"

"You tell me. Why can't you?" The sandwich was delicious, sweet and especially rich. What had she loaded it with this time? "Is this a riddle?"

She came closer, past boxes of tapes and the serpentine of wires patched into his mixing board and recorders. "Is this a bad neighborhood or something?"

"Don't you like it here?" Naturally, he thought. I work for three years scoring pictures I wouldn't even wish on Roger Ebert so we can afford to move up in the world, and the kids don't dig it. Just my luck. He tore open the Fritos and stuck a few into his sandwich. She saw that and smiled wistfully, but her face remained clouded over.

"I like it fine. Only . . . never mind." She bellied up to the desk, traced her finger over the rock, over one of the circles with the lines in it. "Where did this really come from?"

"I wish I knew." He bit down and chewed. The sandwich was perfect now. He stared with her at the rock. On an impulse he asked, "Do you remember that movie I worked on last year, about devil worship and all that nonsense?"

"You mean the one that made me throw up? The one where they put the kitty in the microwave oven?"

"That's the one. See that box over there, next to the electric piano? It's full of old posters. See if it's in there. I think it was *Beyond Redemption*."

She dropped to her knees, eager to do her part. I'd better appreciate it while it lasts. She won't have time for grownups much longer. In a couple of years she'll start thinking of me as a jailor, or worse. But for now she's still proud to be her stepdad's helper, bless her face.

Chocolate, he realized, licking his teeth. Well, god damn. She sure knows the way to a man's heart. Like her mother. Suddenly he wanted to tell her that he loved her. But he was embarrassed.

"Thanks," he said.

"For what?" She riffled through the carton and came up with a folded one-sheet. "It's not hard. I remember what it looks like."

"I mean for being such a swell kid."

She *tsk*ed, an imitation of her big sister. "Oh, Doug, you're *so* corny. Is this it?"

He unfolded the lobby poster. Mint; it had never even been tacked up. I could get it framed, he thought. It wasn't much of a picture but at least my name is in the credits. I could start a rogue's gallery of my work, such as it is. Casey would never stand for such lurid artwork out in the open, but it might help me in here when the going gets rough. Like now. Of course that would be pretty egotistical. Wouldn't it?

"Here, let me help you." Together they spread out the glossy paper on the floor. A disembodied eyeball glared up at them, dominating the garish design. In the center of the eye, in place of the pupil, was a circle containing lines in the approximate shape of a star.

He set the rock to the left of it.

"It's not the same," said Lori.

"No." He felt oddly relieved. "Thank God."

"Why?"

"Because people used to use the one on the right for black magic, crazy things like that. For a minute there I thought . . ."

"What?"

"I'm not sure."

"It almost is, though." She picked at the image on the rock. "If you draw two more lines, like this—" She ran her fingernail from the right end of the horizontal to the bottom of the left vertical, from the left end of the horizontal to the bottom of the right vertical. "—Then you'd have the same thing, just about."

His spine locked as a chill went up his back. Lori was right. It could be an incomplete pentagram. If the person who made the drawing (it looked like Day-Glow highlighter from a felt-tip marker, the kind he had used in college) had been interrupted and left the design unfinished . . . . It was possible. But why?

"I've seen that before," said Lori.

"Where?"

"I can't remember."

"Try, angel. If somebody around here's into that sort of thing I want to know about it." Black magic, he thought. Jesus H. Christ. And in Beaumont Canyon. Who'd believe it?

"And do what? Call the police?"

"Maybe. If you see any more . . ."

"No, the ones I saw, they weren't finished, either. Like the rock."

"Then they weren't pentagrams," he said. And neither was this.

"So what are they?"

"Help me figure that out and I'll buy you a pair of Shuttle Shoes. How would you like that?"

"Oh Daddy," she said, "I wouldn't let anyone see me

wearing Shuttlers. They're for kids. Like Lizzy. Um,
anyway, I gotta go. I have to help Mom. 'Bye.''
" 'Bye, yourself. I'll be down soon. If Mom needs me
now, tell her—''

But she was gone. The plywood door flapped shut
and he was alone with his cassette deck, open-reel
recorder, mixing board, microphones, metronome, music stand, electric keyboard, boxes of scores, tapes,
music paper, stopwatch and his bottle of Noche Buena
beer. She called me Daddy, he thought, amazed. First
time. A slip, probably. But I like it. I like it just fine.

He pushed the tray aside and fingered the envelope
from the mailbox. He turned up one edge, cleaned his
thumbnail with the corner where the stamp should have
been, tapped it with growing impatience and finally
flipped it over.

On the front, in place of the name and address,
printed lettering cut from a newspaper had been taped
to the envelope. Each letter was of a different size and
typeface.

THEY KNOW WHERE YOU LIVE, it read.

He shook the envelope and a half sheet of notebook
paper floated out. It contained a brief message assem-
bled in the same manner as the address.

DON'T GO NEAR THE DARKSIDE.

The man with the pointy moustache finished install-
ing the cable outlets, leaving only General Telephone to
invade Erin's space. Erin refused to come out but remained barricaded in the bathroom, so Lori decided to
keep the phone man company.

She sat on the floor and sorted her sister's records and
tapes while he cleaned up.

Where did Erin get the money for so many? She
thought of her own meager collection, consisting mostly
of "greatest hits" compilations by the likes of Michael
Jackson, Duran Duran, Olivia Newton-John, David
Bowie and a smattering of other over-the-hill artists ac-
quired when her dad, her real dad, had bothered to send
gift certificates for Christmas and her birthday. How
could she possibly keep up on three dollars a week al-

lowance? She couldn't bring herself to watch MTV, wouldn't even with the new cable hookup; it made her depressed. Mom and Doug would buy her one once in a while if she made a big deal about it, but she always felt selfish. It must have taken a lot of money to make the move to Beverly Hills—just about all they had saved, probably, or else Doug wouldn't be so worried about finishing his new score in a hurry. Plus Mom wasn't even getting the checks from Dad on the first and fifteenth of the month anymore; they stopped coming as soon as she married Doug. Lori felt sorrier for Mom than she did for herself.

The telephone man peeled off a sticker with Erin's new number and stuck it on the dial, then moved the dresser back into place against the wall, leaving a snowfall of sawdust on the carpet where he had drilled a hole for the outlet. As soon as Mom saw that she would be in here with the vacuum cleaner, even though it was mostly covered by furniture; she didn't like anything that didn't show.

"So what's happening?" asked the telephone man as he rehooked tools to his belt, the pliers with rubber grips and the screwdrivers with the yellow plastic handles. He had a moustache, too, but not the devilish kind like the cable man; she liked this one better. It grew whatever way it wanted to, so low over his mouth that Lori wondered how he managed to eat and drink. Through a straw?

"Nothing."

When he stood up she saw that he had a ponytail. What Erin said was true—the sixties really were coming back. Or they never left. Now she knew what happened to old hippies, or some of them, at least. They went to work for places like the telephone company. I wonder where all the rest of them are? she thought. Would he know? Erin had been trying to find out.

"Um, can I ask you a question?"

His eyes twinkled as he got out his receipt book and leaned on the window sill. There was a crying outside and Towser jingled over to the end of the patio to see what was wrong.

"Why not?" He glanced around to be sure no one was listening. But the dining room on the other side of the doorway was empty except for the chair and sofa, the long table, the fruit bowl catching drops of crystal sunlight in its cut facets. "You wouldn't believe some of the questions I get. 'How come the numbers I call are always busy?' 'Why does it take so long for my grandmother to answer the phone?' And those are from grown people, mind you. Sometimes I wonder how this society keeps functioning at all, on any level, you know?"

Lori giggled. "I would never ask you that."

"You wouldn't, huh?"

"No. I know why my grandmother doesn't answer the phone."

"Why's that?"

"Because *she's* busy. She's *really* busy. She's dead!"

Lori broke into a hearty laugh. So did the telephone man. It started in his chest and then got his whole body to shaking. He wasn't just pretending; he really meant it, she could tell. The handset on his belt jiggled against his thigh.

It was like he hadn't laughed in a long time. When his ponytail shook loose he didn't look so old anymore. Lori lost control and guffawed till tears squeaked out of her eyes. She knew it was a mean joke but it made her feel better to talk about it, even this way. She held her sides and bumped into Erin's records; a rare copy of the first Doors album fell forward, and then the Grateful Dead and the Jefferson Airplane's *Surrealistic Pillow* followed like dominoes.

In the bathroom, Erin made as much noise as possible getting out of the shower. She wanted her room back.

The man came over to Lori. He didn't muss her hair the way grownups usually did but instead lowered himself to her level and put an arm around her as she restacked Erin's records. The way he touched her she could tell he liked her for a real friend. She imagined herself taller and older.

"That's not what I wanted to ask you," she said. "Promise you won't laugh?"

"Do I look like a laugher?"

"Um, well, what happens to people when they, you know, drop out? Into the Underground. Is that what you call it?"

He smiled indulgently and the lines around his eyes crinkled. Lori decided that he was cute. "Well, what have we here, a new-wave teenybopper? Thinking about tuning in and turning on, are you?"

"It's not for me. It's my sister. She likes, you know, the sixties."

"Does she, now? Right here in the middle of Beverly Hills? Well, tell her not to bother—it's over. The counterculture died a long time ago."

"When did it die?"

"Oh, along about the time Tim Leary had his moment on the cross, near as I can figure it. Nixon and Henry the K and the Christmas '73 bombing, sometime around then."

"But you didn't die."

"Beats the hell out of me, too." He laughed again, but this time it was a private, inside joke that she couldn't share. His face muscles went slack and he appeared to age suddenly, the way people did in the special effects scenes on some of those old *Twilight Zone* reruns. He lowered his chin from the window and his face darkened. "But you might get an argument out of me on that sometime, babe."

Lori felt sad. For a brief moment she had thought she knew him, like an instant best friend on the first day of school. But now she realized she was wrong.

The bathroom door cracked open an inch and Erin stuck her nose out. Seeing them still there, she made a disgusted sound—*chuh*, like the air going out of a tire —and banged the door shut again.

Through the open window Lori saw Mom coming down the next-door driveway, leading Lizzy by the hand. Her sister was wet from Lester's pool and crying crocodile tears. The seven-year-old resisted every inch of the way, her small rectangular feet making slapping sounds like pistol shots and her bathing suit dripping a dark trail on the blacktop. Mom jerked Lizzy's skinny arm to get her to move faster, but that only made her cry louder.

The telephone man heard the wail approaching like a siren and snapped to. When he stood up his knee joints popped. He was pretty old, after all, at least as old as Mom and Doug. He rearranged a couple of Erin's records with great respect, as though he were an archeologist handling valuable relics from a time long past.

"Your sister's got some classic sides here. If she ever wants to get rid of 'em, tell her to call Shannon at GT. I used to have every one, original pressings. *The Who Live at Leeds*! What a flash!"

"What happened to them?" Lori asked automatically, no longer listening. Mom was coming through the garage and opening the gate, dragging Lizzy to the back door.

"That is the sixty-four-thousand-dollar question. Wish I could tell you. Got melted down to make a whole lot of disco shit somewhere around the time you were born, I imagine."

Mom got Lizzy inside and tossed her a towel from the top of the washing machine. "And I don't ever want to catch you going up there without me," Mom was saying. "It isn't safe."

"Is too! I can swim! I could swim ever since I was a *ba*by!"

"That's not what I'm talking about, young lady."

"What *are* you talking about, Mom?"

"Do as I say!"

The telephone man swept his long hair up under the rubber band and tucked it inside his collar.

"How's it coming?" asked Mom, switching on her public face.

"Your daughter's plugged in now," he said. "Guaranteed."

"That's a relief. Do I pay you?"

"Yes, ma'am." He started out of the bedroom, the burden of his company tools weighing him down. He moved in short, restrained steps so as not to collide with the expensive furnishings that stood between him and the beautiful spring day outside.

Mom went for her checkbook.

He put his hand on Lori's back again the same way as before and leaned over.

"I'll let you in on a secret, if you promise not to tell your mother."

"I promise."

"There's a rumor going around that the sixties didn't die—they're only on hold." He smiled conspiratorially, squeezing her with his eyes. "Pass it on."

Then he ambled away to the living room.

In the bedroom, Erin's bathroom door opened again.

"*Is he gone?*"

"Um, yeah." Lori ducked back in and eased the outer door shut. "You can come out now. Erin, he knew you were in there the whole time. Why were you hiding?"

"I wasn't hiding. That dirty old man."

"He was not. He was nice. He was a hippie."

"There *are* no old hippies. Did he look like that? Or that?" She pointed to posters of Hendrix, Keith Moon, Jim Morrison.

"Yeah, well so what? They're all dead, if you didn't know it, Erin."

"Are they?"

"And he didn't know where the Underground is, either, for your information. I don't believe there ever was one."

Erin's eyes got glassy and her body went tense for a moment, as if she had started to remember part of a bad dream. Then she turned away from her sister and dropped the towel. Facing the poster of Jim Morrison's oversized head, which considered her as impassively as a lewd Dionysus awaiting his next sacrifice, she pulled on a T-shirt, clean panties and her tapered blue jeans. Lori saw the sides of her breasts bobbing like water balloons and was filled with awe.

"Did he touch any of my stuff?"

"Of course not."

"Good." Erin caressed her newly-connected cordless phone. She moved it over to her TV set, now also prop-

erly hooked up. "Far out. Now I can talk—in private."
She rummaged between the pages of her loose-leaf
binder and came up with a square of paper. "Do you
mind?"

"Erin, if I ask you a question, do you promise to tell
the truth?"

"Don't I always tell you everything, Lori? You're the
only one around here who knows how to keep a secret."

"Well . . . did you sneak out last night?"

"Did somebody say I did?"

"N-no. Not exactly."

"Then why do you think that?"

"Because I got up in the middle of the night. I
thought somebody was standing next to my bed. It was
weird. So I came over to your room. Only you weren't
here."

"Yes, I was," Erin snapped.

"Then why are you yelling at me?" She lined up the
edges of Erin's albums so that they were perfect. "You
should at least put your pillows under the covers so it
looks like you're there. Don't you understand?" she
added forlornly. "I only want to help."

Erin reconsidered. She set aside the phone number
and came over to her sister and stood looking down at
her. Lori felt very small.

"Yes," Erin said. "Only you don't have to. I can
take care of myself."

"What about the Lost Ones?"

"Hah. That's nothing but a story they tell the kids
around here to keep them from going into the canyons.
Like the Watchbird, the Nighthawk, the Boogyman. It's
a fairy tale, don't you know that?"

"Well, what do you do when you go out?"

"Oh, I shoot up heroin, go to work in a massage
parlor, let guys take naked pictures of me. For money,
of course. What did you think?"

"Do you really? Is that how you got that hickey?"

Erin's bloodshot eyes twinkled. She grinned and
yawned. "No, silly. Do you have to take everything so
seriously?" She tugged gently on the loose sideburns of
baby-fine hair that framed Lori's perfect oval face.

"Sometimes you're just like Mom."

I am not, she thought. Lizzy is. I want to be like you.

"So?" she said. "What's wrong with that?"

Erin dug in her jeans. "Here's that dollar I owe you. Do you need any help with your math homework?"

"You think I'm dumb. Well I'm not, you know."

"I know. That's why you're my favorite sister."

"Then why won't you tell me? You don't trust me."

"I trust you. You want to borrow a record?"

"No."

"All right, you can borrow anything you want. How about my old pussycat slippers? You can have them— they're in the closet. You're going to get everything eventually, anyway."

"When?"

"I mean if—when—I go away. This will be your room."

"Where are you going?"

"Everybody goes away sooner or later, Lori. What's the difference? When I do, you get it all. *If* you don't tell Mom."

"I wouldn't."

"You better not."

"Only why won't you tell me?"

"Tell you what?"

"*What did you do last night*?"

Erin sat down with the telephone in her lap. She stared and stared at the slip of paper in her hand as though it were an answer page that had been torn out of the back of a problem book. She held on to the telephone so tightly that her knuckles turned white.

"I don't know," she said. Her voice was frightened and came from the back of her throat, a tone she had never used before. "I could tell you, I guess. What does it matter? Only I'm really, truly not sure."

four

Erin knew but not the whole of it, and that turned out to be more dangerous than not knowing at all.

Before the alarm went off Monday morning she remembered another part. She lay in bed watching the second hand sweep closer to zero hour beyond the tented quilt at her feet. As one more bit fell into place, she heard leaves rustling and twigs breaking, and knew that someone was standing in the back yard outside her corner of the house.

She threw off the quilt and approached the dresser, hesitating a beat before opening the new blinds. She wiped cold sweat from her palms, held her breath and yanked the cord.

There was a smear of movement outside.

A squirrel perched atop the doghouse, nervously turning a seed in its nude fingers. It cocked a round, black doll's eye, bristled its tail at her and resumed nibbling. The rest of the gray patio was bare except for Towser's rubber playthings, the cement spotted with overnight moisture dark as inkblots.

The alarm buzzed, Erin jumped. She closed the blinds and slapped the top of the clock. Ten minutes to seven.

77

She blinked at the dial and tried to hold on to the disturbing fragment of memory from last week. But the thread was lost, the images slipping back into the shadowed recesses of her mind. She was close, though. It had taken her two days to recall this much of it and she had all but one last piece. But for now that would have to wait.

It was nine minutes to seven, time for Mom's warning knock.

It didn't come, but she went ahead and got dressed. While she was brushing her teeth the snooze alarm went off again. She hit the clock a second time, put on her flannel shirt, grabbed her notebook and shambled into the kitchen.

"Where's Mom?"

Lori, maddeningly fresh-faced and clear-eyed, was unwrapping a stick of butter. "Um, she's not going to be in the elementary car pool anymore. She gets to sleep in."

"Lucky!" said Elizabeth, cleaning up a bowl of her favorite cereal.

"Oh." Erin reached for the milk carton, its beaked spout open like a bird of prey. "Then how are you two getting to school? Don't tell me she's going to make Doug take you."

"Um, we start riding the bus today. Mom signed us up."

"Yea!" said Elizabeth.

"How are you supposed to get to the bus stop? I thought it doesn't come up the canyon."

"It doesn't. We're riding to the bottom with you." The toaster-oven bell went off and Lori proceeded to mash butter into her flaking croissant.

"In *my* car pool?" With people I know? she thought, panicking. "There's no room!"

"Is too," said Elizabeth.

"Um, well, that's what Mom said."

"All right, fine! Do what you want, what do I care?" Erin shook out a half-bowl of Kwackles, doused it with lukewarm milk.

"No," said Elizabeth, "that's mine!"

"Lizzy, we've got three more boxes." Lori opened the cupboard and pointed officiously, a junior homemaker with no time for arguments in her kitchen. "See? What's your problem?"

Elizabeth started to cry.

Erin hissed and dumped the cereal down the disposal. All it was was sugar, anyway. Her tongue burned.

A horn sounded, though it was only twelve minutes after seven. Lori and Elizabeth scattered to their rooms for schoolbooks and jackets. As usual, Sara's mother couldn't wait for the day to begin. Uptight bitch, thought Erin. She was the kind of woman who would lead a singalong on the way to an execution. *Keep a tight asshole, lady. I'm coming.*

Running to the car, the last part of the memory threatened to surface. Steam rumbled from the exhaust and washed forward over the landau top, forming a screen for the foggy picture in her mind. She was reminded of a smoke-filled room, demanding hands, agitated words driving her away from a table and into a hallway that led to . . . but that was all she could see before Lori and Lizzy piled in and Sara's hand extended from the mist, inviting her into the back seat.

The canyon boulevard was already clogged with a thickening stream of commuters on their way into West Los Angeles from the Valley. The relentless noise of idling engines and worn brakes set her teeth on edge. Her sisters squirmed for position in front. She chucked the door closed behind her and inserted herself in back between Sara's hard thigh and the armrest. It was impossibly crowded with Sara and Ahmet, though at least she didn't have to sit on the bump in the middle this time.

"FINGERS AND TOES," said Sara's mother. "EVERYBODY IN? THEN LET'S MOVE 'EM OUT, WHADAYOU SAY?"

The heater was on, which only served to increase the condensation of humid breath on the windows. Erin flinched at the pervasive cloud of deodorant soap radiating through the car, mingled with the smell of stale cigarette butts in the ashtray at her elbow. She closed her eyes and tried to vegetate. Cars pressed in on all sides, mostly subcompact imports that resembled over-sized Tonka toys. She heard AM radios warring traffic bulletins through the static, interrupted constantly by nauseatingly aggressive announcers of the K-Tel school of broadcasting. She hated them with a passion. Please don't turn the radio on, Mrs. Bedrosian, she thought frantically. Just this once? She dug her nails into her palms.

"HOW ABOUT SOME MUSIC TO WAKE EVERYBODY UP?" said Sara's mother.

"Great!" said Sara, fidgeting excitedly. "Gee, that sure is a neat ring, Erin! Where'd you get it?"

To silence her Erin unscrewed the ring from her finger and handed it to the girl. "Here. You can try it on if you want to." Knock yourself out, she thought.

"Omigod, it's so-o-o pretty!" Sara displayed it to Ahmet with exaggerated veneration. "Is it a real sapphire? Did it cost a lot of money?"

"Keep it." Just get off my case, she thought.

"Can I? Omigod! Erin, I don't believe it! You're so-o-o nice! Mom, look what Erin gave me!"

"Um, Dad gave you that ring, didn't he?" said Lori.

"Er-*in*," scolded Elizabeth, "you better not!"

"Are you sure?" said Sara.

"Sure I'm sure." Why can't I do whatever I want with my own fucking possessions? she thought. Besides, somebody else might give her a better one. Like Damon. If he ever took her out again. "I don't want it any-more."

"Omigod . . . !"

"THANK YOU, ERIN. TELL YOUR MOTHER THANKS. YOU'RE A NICE GIRL."

I don't want to be a nice girl, thought Erin. And what's Mom got to do with it?

"TELL YOUR FRIEND THANK YOU, SARA."

"Th-a-ank yo-u-uu!" said Sara.

Mrs. Bedrosian tuned to KJOI in time to catch the start of a Kenny Rogers medley.

"NOW HOW ABOUT SOME OF THAT GOOD WAKE-UP MUSIC?"

"Yea!" said Elizabeth, clapping her hands.

The main building was dank, row upon row of lockers set into the peeling walls like tiers of crypts in a mausoleum. Erin found hers, dialed to unlock it. It was twenty-five minutes to eight. Right, she thought, I always like to get to school almost a half-hour early. There's so much to do. God bless you, Mrs. Bedrosian. You whore.

Angie's books were wedged on top of hers, one of the inequities that resulted from transferring to a new school in the midst of the term. Of *course* she was the first one to get to the locker—no one else was even here yet. She looked up and down the corridor and had that feeling again; for a moment the very last piece of the puzzle, the one she could not quite grasp, insinuated its way into her consciousness. The empty hall, the way the light played through the frosted glass of the office at the end . . . it reminded her of her shortcut through the canyon, of course, but also of something else. What? Another hallway leading somewhere, yes, and an alley where someone was speaking to her in an urgent whisper, she was nodding yes, yes, anything to get away . . . .

The minute hand of the clock on the wall sprang closer to the eight, *ka-chunk*, a grim teacher in a polyester suit clipped out of the office, the voices of eager freshmen bounced up the steps at her back, overriding the whirring of an electric floor polisher in another branch of the hall. It was too late to remember. Or not soon enough. But it was gone. She snapped back to reality and hoisted her books.

A piece of paper from the locker fell out at her feet. It was Angie's, no doubt. It was folded and bent, as though it had been pushed through the ventilation slots in the door. She stooped and started to open it.

"What you got there, Erin?"

She stuffed the note under her flannel shirt and turned.

"Nothing," she said. "Hi, Justin. Did—did Angie get here yet?"

"Shit, how the hell would I know? I just got here

myself." He poked at the tail of her shirt. "Looks like you got another love letter, huh?"

"I didn't."

"From ol' Damon?"

"How could it be from Damon? He doesn't even go to this school. What are you doing here so early?" She tried to smile casually. But her gums were dry and her mouth wasn't working right yet.

"Oh, I gotta go to the vice-principal's office. Mr. Bledsoe wants to see me, that dork. He sent a note to my folks."

"Why?"

"I ditched wood shop again." The hand at her waist, sneaking up her back, caught her by surprise. "Hey, you wanna party? I scored some killer buds this morning. I know a place . . ."

"What would Angie say?"

"Angie ain't here. Besides, we're friends, aren't we? Remember?"

"No. I mean yes. I mean, I have to find her. She —she's got my math book. See you later, Justin."

She left him and cut through the building to the field. The morning was a typical Southern California pearl-gray. The softball diamond, the basketball courts, the lunch tables were all drab and colorless. Even the shirts and sweaters of the hyperkinetic underclassmen in front of the snack bar seemed as lifeless as seagulls huddled on an off-season beach. She crossed to the science building and back again, keeping herself as visible as a shooting gallery target, but Angie wasn't anywhere.

Homeroom was a minor irritant, English a distraction, math numbing. During nutrition break she bought an apple and some cheese popcorn and kept to herself. Unaccountably she felt that she was being watched. Was it that Buddy again, following her between classes? She hoped not. He had some kind of schoolboy crush on her, she supposed, but he was a real loser. Besides, he was only in the seventh grade. If she was lucky it was a crush; sometimes the way he shadowed her made her skin crawl.

She grew increasingly nervous through history and

put her head down for all fifty-two minutes of art class. At lunchtime she paced the perimeter of the field and wondered why she could not concentrate. But Angie would help her understand; after all, she had been there, too. Hadn't she?

Wandering by the cafeteria, she glimpsed trays of greasy fried chicken, vats of instant mashed potatoes to be topped by tureens of yellow gravy. A sad little boy at the end of the line held out his meal ticket and received a bowl containing three strips of wilted lettuce, browned around the edges and dressed with rancid salad oil. Erin shuddered and hurried past. There was some shit that even she would not eat.

She avoided the girls in Guess jeans and designer workshirts gathered together in clots at one side of the field and crossed the line to the stoner wall.

Here a loose assortment of borderline dropouts, underachievers and long-haired surfer types lounged against the sagging chain-link fence, trading drugs and tall stories to help each other through the boredom of another day. Erin felt at ease with them. She would rather sit cross-legged picking burnt grass than play games of one-upsmanship with the phonies. For as long as she could remember she had been pressured to live up to a standard she had never completely understood and which she had had no hand in devising, and she was weary of fulfilling other people's expectations. Now, at last, three-fourths of the way through the ninth grade, she was ready to get off the treadmill.

She spotted Justin with his doper friends, kicked back at the end of the fence. And, half-hidden between them, Angie's suede boots. Erin was relieved. She detoured long enough to buy a burrito and an orange juice from the hash line, then came around behind them. She prodded Angie with the burrito.

"Hey, girl, can I talk to you? How come you never call me any—"

Angie ducked, as if a bony hand had tapped her on the shoulder to tell her that her time had come. She peeked around from under a thick fall of hair.

"—more?"

Something was wrong. It was Angie and then it wasn't. One side of her face was familiar, but the other was . . .

"Erin!" said Justin, caught in the act of stretching. "Just the fox I want to see!" He rolled away from his girlfriend, grateful for the interruption. "You're comin' over Friday, right? Everybody'll be there. My folks are gonna be gone for the weekend and—"

"I'm busy," said Erin. There was no use asking him anything. She wouldn't be able to get a straight answer out of him if she tried. "Sorry."

"I'm busy, too," Angie said to him.

Erin scrunched in next to her friend and whispered, "What did you *do*?"

Angie had chopped her hair on one side and buzzed it all the way to the crown of her head. Not only that but the short side had been bleached. One outrageous earring dangled from the exposed ear; the lobe was as pale and vulnerable as a potato bug. The other half of her head remained untouched, Janus-like, the same length of straight mouse-brown hair falling to her shoulder.

"Nothing," said Angie. Not only that but her eyes were red. She stood and brushed off the backs of her legs. "Come on. Let's get away from these assholes for a while."

Erin followed her to another part of the field.

"What's going on with you two?"

"What's going on is that he's a prick, that's what. I go 'Hi!' and I take his arm, and he pulls away from me in front of everybody like I've got a disease or something. Then he goes, 'Shit, I thought I was havin' a nightmare!' *That's* what's going on, if you want to know."

"That's pretty cold," said Erin.

"Well, you know what? I don't have to take that kind of shit off anybody."

"Maybe he was just, you know, showing off in front of his friends."

"Fuck him and his lame friends! All they do is listen to heavy metal and get loaded. Like my parents. Well, fuck that."

Angie wiped her nose and shook her head violently, like a puppy dog after it rains. The last of her tears sprayed into the air and evaporated before they touched the ground. She stared out across the field, not seeing the clusters of overactive seventh- and eighth-graders and the haughty cliques of pampered Westside preppies. Then with a brave show of self-control she said, "You know, I always felt like one of those—those airplanes that fly around and around but never get to land anywhere. What do they call it?"

"A holding pattern?"

"Well, I've had it with any more holding patterns. Do you know I've been to eight schools in the last five years? This place and everybody in it can eat shit and die. I'll run away if I have to—you'll see, Erin—and find some people who'll take me the way I am. I don't have to fit in with their fucked styles. Why should I? I'll go to the Club any time I want to, with or without Justin. I can find lots of people who'll give me a ride. Just you watch."

Erin felt a surge of admiration mixed with fear for her friend.

Angie peered out from under the long side of her hair. "You want to go with me Friday?"

"I can't," said Erin. "I have to babysit." She was glad that it was the truth. She wanted to help her friend, but not that way. "You don't really want to go back there, do you?"

"Well, it sure sounds like *you* don't." Angie set her shoulders and hunkered down into herself, hiding her face behind the curtain of hair. From this angle she looked like the same lovable girl; Erin wanted to put her arms around her and comfort her. But already an invisible barrier was forming between them, or rather reforming, as it had been on their first meeting only a few short weeks ago. If it takes one to know one, then Erin had recognized her on sight, had felt the unspoken bond. You don't have to go it alone, Erin almost told her now, but found herself choking up. Why do you think you have to?

"I don't know if that's such a cool place," Erin said.

"I mean I had fun and everything, being with you guys, but—"

"But what? You sound like Justin."

"I can't remember. But something was *wrong*. I don't know. I must have been really fried."

"You were. But so was everybody else."

"That's what I have to talk to you about. What *did* happen? I remember some guys trying to talk to me, everybody pushing against us, the music, and then—did I go outside?"

"I don't know. I was talking to Justin in the car."

"Oh."

"That prick."

At least you've got a boyfriend, Erin thought. Unless you decide to dump him. And you don't really want to do that.

"Have you heard from Damon?" asked Angie.

"Uh-uh."

"Did you give him your number?"

Oh no, thought Erin. It was before I got my own phone—I must have given him the family number. He could have called and somebody didn't give me the message. Mom or—Elizabeth. That little brat. I'll bet he tried to call. I'll bet he did.

"I—I think so. There's so much I can't remember . . . ."

"Take my advice," said Angie. "Forget about it. Guys are pricks. Even if you did split on him."

"Sometimes, I guess." She picked a blade of grass that had poked its way up through the hard earth. It was rough when you rubbed it one way, smooth the other. "What do you mean, split on him?"

"God," said Angie, "you really don't remember, do you?"

"That's what I'm trying to tell you! Didn't I go home with you guys in Damon's car? Didn't you drop me off?"

Angie smirked. "I don't know who you went home with. But there aren't very many possibilities. I thought you wanted to keep it a secret. But if you don't know, well, I sure couldn't swear to anything."

Erin wracked her brain. So she really was on her own, after all. She could almost see it. "Was there a guy with white eyes, I mean really *clear* eyes that night, the kind you can see right through?"

"That's the one."

"What was his name?"

"Don't ask me."

"I can't see his face, just that look he had. He—he was hitting on me, right? Really hard. Is that it? Did I go outside with him? There was this long, long hallway and then some kind of alley and, well, the trouble is, I don't know what I did! I *don't know*, do you understand? I think he wanted to scam with me."

"Maybe. But I wouldn't say he was trying to get into your pants. I don't think that was what he wanted at all."

The warning bell rang and shattered the accumulated memories into a swirl of disjointed details. The cold sun regarded Erin indifferently from behind a scum of overcast, robbing the grounds of perspective and flattening the school buildings into a meaningless geometry of two-dimensional surfaces. How could she find her way back through all the planes and intersections? She observed her hands as they closed over the edges of her notebook, which was covered with graffiti. In the center of the matrix was her proud hand-drawn Day-Glow peace symbol.

Angie got to her feet. "Shit," she said, "I was supposed to make up that algebra test during lunch. If my mother sees another *F* on my report card she's gonna send me to a shrink."

"No lie?"

"No fucking shit," said Angie.

"I really wish we could talk some more. See you in PE?"

"Whatever. I'm not dressing, though—I'm not gonna get my hair wet. I could care less if I get another *U*. If old lady Reichert wants to fail me this time I'm splitting for good."

"Where to?"

"You must not remember *anything*."

"No! That's what I'm saying! I don't even—"

But Angie was gone. Erin watched her traipse across the lunch area, forging a solitary path through the circles of trendies who gave her dirty looks and started whispering behind her back as soon as she passed. Erin unbent her legs and used her notebook as a crutch to get up. There was another notebook on the ground. Angie had forgotten hers.

It was too late to call out. She'd have to hold it till gym class and hope that Angie showed up. Or lug it back to the locker, if there was time. Erin hefted Angie's binder along with her own, curious to decode the dense layers of phone numbers and names written across the cover, as if there might be a message there to help her understand. There was even a peace symbol, which surprised her; that was the last thing she would have expected from Angie. But no, it wasn't, after all. It was a circle with three straight lines drawn inside, but it was no peace symbol.

She stood there staring down at it, a cold wind blowing through her chest. She hadn't even remembered to ask Angie about the note she had found in their locker. Without looking she knew what it would say.

It was time to act.

Doug knew he had to do something. If what Casey believed was true, that they were being watched, in a sense quietly terrorized—and if he was ever to have the peace he needed to get his work done—then what choice did he have? The local police remained aloof, refusing to get involved unless and until he caught someone in the act. And so now, tonight, with the family tucked out of harm's way, it was finally time. He could put it off no longer.

He waited until his wife was sleeping soundly. Then he folded the sheet down, planted a kiss on the back of her neck, and got out of bed.

Ready or not, he thought, *I'm going to get you, you son of a bitch. Whoever you are. It ends here.*

He teetered before the bedroom window and gazed down at the still-unfamiliar location. Through the glass

the street below was black-edged, highlighted in platinum by the moon, as distant as a camera obscura view
of a foreign topography. The houses on the other side
had receded into two-dimensional façades; it was impossible now for him to imagine anything that lived
moving behind their flat exteriors. The squares of the
lawns shone dully, measured like the light and dark
masses of an aquatint composition. The sidewalks were
empty, the gnarled oaks and maples suspended against a
windless sky to form the permanent boundaries of an
utterly static tableau. How could any movement
threaten to disturb such a perfectly-ordered frame?

But, he was sure, something unexpected would show
itself sooner or later. All he had to do was wait.

And this time he would be ready.

He put on his robe, pocketed the cordless phone from
the nightstand, and descended as silently as possible to
the first landing. The door to his workroom was ajar, as
he had left it before going to bed. He pushed and it
swung open soundlessly on darkness. That was good.
No one else in the house would know anything till it was
over. In the morning his terse recounting would make it
only one more bad dream laid to rest.

Of course there were a few details to take care of first.

He paused, listening for anything out of the ordinary.
Above and below him his family slumbered fitfully, the
vibrations of their private dreaming interconnected by
the stairway and the skeleton beams supporting the
walls and ceilings. The atmosphere of the house expanded and contracted with the pressure of their breathing; he seemed to detect a slow pulse through the railing.
As he set foot in the dining room, Towser snuffled drily
against the rectangles of kitchen linoleum and lay back
down, hind legs flexing in a fantasy of primitive pursuit.

The lamp was off under Erin's door. Only the small
fluorescent tube in the gas range hood flickered weakly,
a nightlight for emergencies. Doug highstepped over
the dog's sleeping form and entered the kitchen long
enough to click it off.

He let himself out the back way, opened the gate and
raised the garage door. He left the gate unlatched, led

Towser to the back patio, then drew the kitchen door
shut behind him, turning the button so that it, too,
would be unlocked.

The only thing missing was a printed invitation.

He went back up to the workroom, set the plywood
door an inch away from the frame, bent his gooseneck
lamp so that only a faint corona of light escaped across
his music paper, took out the .38 Special he had bought
today and set it on his desk. Then he waited.

At 12:30, the refrigerator compressor in the kitchen
developed a wheeze.

At 12:45, a car with a bum muffler sputtered down
from Mulholland Drive and jettisoned a bottle into the
gutter as it passed through the canyon. The glass im-
ploded with the distant plash of a spring rain.

A little after one, he realized that he was in for a long
night.

He ran his fingernail down the row of switches on his
tape deck, rippling the controls as if they were piano
keys. He considered the mini-headphones. Their open-
air earpieces would allow him to keep track of what was
going on outside the room, as long as the gain was low
enough. He tapped his cassette of improvisations for the
main theme, but left it on the desk. He stretched and put
his feet up. It was too late now to think about working.

He took the phone receiver out of his pocket and
punched in a number.

"Ye-yeah?"

"Gil?"

"Dr. McClay, he died. Call back in the morning."

"Jesus, I'm sorry to wake you, man."

"Doug? 'S'at you?"

"Afraid so. I thought maybe you were still a night
owl."

The phone on the other end was dropped, then reeled
back up. "Well, if you want to know the truth, I *was*
going to watch the After Hours Movie—*Meat Girls* starring Fiona Horelick. You remember her, don't you?"

Doug felt his face unclench. "You mean the girl in
Horror House of Blood? How could I forget? You
made me sit through it three times."

"That's the one." Yawn. "Where is she now that we need her?"

"Probably pushing a shopping cart through some all-night K-Mart in the Valley."

"Naw. They train their husbands to do that kind of stuff for 'em. Hey, how's the new pad?"

"Oh, it still needs work. We're settling in. Casey's been kind of nervous, though."

"What's the problem?"

"Don't ask. She has this notion that Bev Hills isn't exactly welcoming us to its bosom. It's got her worried."

"Sure you're talking about Casey?"

"I'm sure," he said uncertainly.

"Well, you've got to throw some tenderness their way once in a while, Dougie, don't you know that?"

"I try. It wouldn't be so hard if she'd stop popping her sleeping pills long enough to appreciate the effort."

"Is this a professional consultation?"

"Does it sound like one?"

"I'll take you at your word. For now." The line crackled as if submerging under dark waves, then just as mysteriously cleared again, re-establishing the old link between them. "How's my little Lizzy? Does she still look like Peter Pan?"

"I guess so." Yeah, he thought, she does, kind of. I hadn't noticed lately. "I don't get to spend enough time with them. This picture's got me by the balls."

"What else is new?"

Doug didn't say anything. He didn't know where to start.

"Sounds like you're really feeling the pressure. Don't push yourself so hard. You always did have a touch of the compulsive-neurotic about you."

"I can handle it."

"You don't say that with a whole lot of conviction."

"I shouldn't complain. It's what I've been working toward all these years. Only . . ."

"Only what?" True friend that he was, Gil waited for Doug to say it first.

"I was wondering. When are we going to take some

time off and bust loose for Ensenada one more time? It's been too long. We could catch some sport fishing, lie in the sun . . ."

"And get beat up in Hussong's, thrown in jail by the *federales*, all that good stuff, right?"

"No, man, I only mean . . . I don't know what I mean. But, damn it, something's missing. Don't you feel it?"

"Of course I feel it. We used to be wild dogs, Doug. We never kept up with the pack. We could run away and eat sweet grass and roll in clover whenever we wanted. There was no leash then. Sure, I know what you mean."

"So what happened to all that? Those years . . . we were trying to stand up for something. I thought we were. And now all of a sudden we're pushing middle age. Where did it go? Fifteen mother-fucking years, Gil. *Where*? Can you tell me that? How do you do it? Or is there something wrong with me?"

"To tell the truth, I don't know how I do it. Talking down one paranoid-schizophrenic after another all day long does tend to put a lid on things. You're better off, believe me. At least you get to sleep late."

"Who can sleep?"

"And make your own hours. The only demons you have to wrestle with are your own."

"They're the worst kind."

"I know," said Gil soberly. "Well, listen, Doug. What are you doing next weekend?"

"Uh, I was sort of planning on having a nervous breakdown. I think I deserve one."

"Pass it up for Lent. And come over here. We can get a boat at the marina, go out for half a day—your girls like fish, don't they? You'll bring home dinner, if that'll help you rationalize. I have a case of beer that's just—"

"Hold on."

"What's the matter with that? Hell, you can do it. We'll—"

"Don't say anything else."

Doug stuck a finger into his other ear and concentrated. There was a sizzling on the line, then a series of clicks. Was he being tapped? How was that possible?

Why? No, they were pulse-tones, coming from very close by. Like the other side of the wall.

He swung his legs down and started to reach for the light switch.

Then he understood. The phone—it was cordless. He was picking up another signal on the same frequency. And it was coming from somewhere else inside the house.

"Hey, buddy, what happened? You get struck by lightning? I can hear you breathing but you're fading fast . . . ."

The line was swallowed up in a swirl of white noise. He cupped his hand around the mouthpiece. "Gil, I'll have to talk to you later. Something's going on over here." He broke the connection and set the phone down. Then he picked up the gun and stuck it in his pocket.

At that moment he heard someone coming up the stairs.

He flattened against the wall as footsteps shuffled to a stop outside the workroom. Just there, on the other side of the plywood.

He held his breath and counted. One, two, three . . .

Pale fingers appeared around the edge.

He kicked the door open and jumped out of the shadows, crouched and ready. His hand closed around the pistol grip.

A streak of white, eyes as wide and bulging as hard-boiled eggs. He grabbed for a collar but found a throat. He yanked the figure toward him and feet went flying as a body collapsed into his arms.

Erin's face was blanched and spectral as a sheeted ghost's. He crushed her to him and stopped her mouth with his chest before she could cry out. She didn't fight back; for some reason there was no more fight left in her. He held her and rocked her, waiting for his heart to slow down. Finally he released her to arm's length.

"*What*—?"

"Please don't be mad at me," she said. Her face was a terrified mask, puffed and all but unrecognizable. He adjusted the lamp to get a better look.

"Sorry," he said. "Sweetie, I thought you were—"

"Who?"

"It doesn't matter. Christ, did I hurt you? Are you—?"

"I'm fine, fine! Fu-u-uck. You scared the living shit out of me, you know that?"

"What are you doing out of bed?"

"Something woke me up. The phone, that's right. Some dick. I couldn't get back to sleep. Then I heard you talking up here. Are you really pissed off? Are you working? I can go back to bed if you—"

"No, of course not. Come here." He cradled her in his arms and sat in the chair, carrying her into his lap. Her phone, he thought. It must have caused the interference he had picked up. "What did he want?"

"I don't know. I couldn't understand him." Her arms went around him and he felt her breath on his neck. Her lips were cool as desert flowers and there were goosebumps on the arms. Her hair fell like cobwebs across his face. He took one of her hands and blew on her fingers to warm her.

"I'd never let anything happen to you," he told her. "You know that, don't you?"

"I guess so."

She sounded so young and defenseless; he was wrenched with tenderness. She put her feet up on the desk, scattering his papers. He didn't care. He rubbed her long legs, stroked her back and sides through the T-shirt. But she wasn't getting any warmer.

"I get scared sometimes," she said.

"That's all right. So do I." Her complexion was still pale and bloodless. Like an alabaster statue, he thought. Poor, sweet baby . . . He hugged her as tight as he could, trying to give her some of his own warmth. It wasn't working.

She shifted positions as he kissed her at the hairline. His lip stuck to her flesh, which was lifeless, doughy. It was still firm, but it no longer felt healthy, resilient as it once had. As he pulled away a bit of her skin flaked loose and adhered to his lip. He picked it from his

tongue like a piece of tobacco, and was surprised to see
that a few of the fine hairs from her widow's peak had
also come off with the skin.

"What's happened to you?" he said, determined to
account for it. "Are you sick? Do you need to see a doctor?"

"I'm all right," she said. But when he smoothed her
hair back from her face, more dead skin rolled up under
his nails. "I'm just peeling. I must have been in the sun
too long."

"You haven't been in the sun at all."

"Oh," she said. "That must be why I'm so cold.
What's this?" She attempted to open his robe. It was
the revolver in his pocket. She traced the thick barrel
with her finger.

"Nothing." He took it from her and shoved it under
the papers. I must be crazy, he thought. I don't know
what I was thinking. "Just another bad trip, that's all."

She poked at the desktop, uncovering a drawing he
had made of the three symbols, the pentagram and the
other, simpler designs with three lines crossed inside the
circles.

"I don't know what this one is," she said, pointing to
the modified peace sign. "Angie's got one on her notebook. This other one—I was going to tell you but . . ."

"But what? It isn't a joke, you know."

"I know. Well, it is a joke with some people. It's supposed to be an A. For anarchy. It means—"

Down the stairs and out on the patio, Towser
growled.

He sat up, sliding her lumpen weight to his knees.

Then the kitchen door creaked on its hinges.

He killed the light.

She arched her back and hugged him tighter. "Why
did you do that?"

"Shh."

Trembling, she held him. "I need to get warm
again," she said into his cheekbone. "Help me . . ."

He set her feet down and rose, as a loose floorboard
moaned in the dining room.

"Don't make me go back to bed," she said, covering his ear with her mouth. "I want to stay with you all night. Please? I need . . ."

He gripped her elbow and whispered, "Didn't you hear that?"

"I heard what you said. But I—"

"Do what I tell you. Stand by the door. The phone is on the desk—here. If anything happens call the police. Don't wait. Do you understand? Dial the operator, tell her—"

At the foot of the stairs, another door opened.

He picked up the .38 and went out onto the landing.

The lamp was on in Erin's room, as she had left it a few minutes ago. A V-shaped crack of light spilled out across the dining room table, refracted by the glass fruit bowl like shadows coalescing in a crystal ball. He recognized the humped shape of her bed, an exaggerated projection of the edge of her stereo. Between the two silhouettes was another, very much taller shadow. This one was moving.

"*Erin,*" called a husky, breathy voice. "*Erin, where are you . . . ?*"

Doug held the revolver at shoulder level. It scratched the wall on the way down.

One, two, three . . .

"Don't move!"

He crouched in the bedroom doorway, the pistol straight-armed in front of him.

The figure stopped, a puppet on steel strings. In the lamp's glare Doug caught a glimpse of a camouflage shirt hanging out over a pair of faded highwater jeans, black tennis shoes, a neck as scrawny as a chicken's. The figure turned slowly, jerkily, stopping and starting, stopping and starting, like a film run at the wrong speed.

"What do you want here?"

It was a boy, Erin's age at most. He had long, thin white hair and lumpy skin. "I—I have to tell her," he said.

Doug came all the way into the room and nudged the

door partially closed. "No," he said, "you tell me."

The boy shook his head.

Doug thumbed back the hammer of the .38. "Now," he said.

"Or what?" The boy's face split in a crooked smile. "Are you going to kill me?" He began to laugh.

"Stay where you are." Doug backed out, shot a glance up the stairs. Erin was cowering on the first landing. The phone was in her hand.

"I'm calling," she said.

"Come down here."

"No." There was genuine fear in her voice.

"It's all right. He's not going to do anything now. Is this boy a friend of yours?"

It took her a long time. She clung to Doug's shoulder and looked around the door.

"*Buddy*?" she said. "What are you doing here?"

"You know him?"

"No. I mean, he goes to my school—he lives down the street."

"So this is the one."

"But I've never even talked to him. What is it, Buddy? That is your name, isn't it? Why have you been following me? What do you want? Why don't you just tell me?"

The boy refused to speak. He looked as if he wanted nothing more than to bolt for the nearest rock or hollow log.

Doug took the phone from her. The operator had already put a call through to the Sheriff's Department. Doug told them to send a car. Breaking and entering, caught in the act. By the time he finished he heard Lori's door popping open, Casey beginning to stir upstairs. How had he ever thought he could keep them from knowing? Foolish, foolish . . .

"The police will be here in a few minutes," he told the boy. "Don't make it any harder on yourself. Talk to me." Damn it, he had to know. He *had* to. "What is it you want from us?"

"I can only tell Erin."

She brushed past Doug. "Buddy, what is it? Why are you afraid?"

He dropped his chin to his chest, too shocked and embarrassed by the reality of the moment to meet her eyes. My God, thought Doug, he's got a king-sized crush on her, and he's lame in the head to boot. He's probably been trailing her for weeks, ever since we moved in. Too shy or retarded to come up and introduce himself, he's been haunting her, sending notes, trying to work up the courage to break the ice. But he doesn't know how. So he lurks in bushes, throws rocks, peeps in windows, steals pieces of the ground she walks on to save between the pages of a book; if she had a bicycle he'd probably sniff the seat. He's harmless—he's sure as hell no burglar or rapist. Doug lowered the gun. But he did not cancel the call.

Suddenly the boy fell to his knees at Erin's feet and held his head, as if a great pain had begun to pound there. The sight was pathetic. Doug had trouble watching. But not Erin. She laid a hand on his white hair, as though offering a benediction.

"You can tell me now," she said. "Whatever it is, I really want to know."

He bowed, racked with sobs. "The Darkside," he choked. "It's bad, so bad, you don't know! They know where you live! Move, go away before they come for you . . . !"

"What's the Darkside?" Doug asked them. "I don't understand that word. What does it mean?"

The boy would not say anything else.

She turned to her stepfather. "Nothing," she said strangely. Then she blinked and forced a silly, insincere smile. "I don't know what it means. Honest. It's stupid. It's a kids' game. It doesn't mean anything." But her eyes hid behind an icy glaze, as if someone had just told her that the world and everything in it was about to end.

five

Friday

I'm never going to get out of here alive, thought Doug Carson.

First the dry Santa Ana wind was washing through the sun roof, turning his hair into a brown flame in the jetstream, the radio was pumping out Herbie Hancock and Weather Report on KKGO, and the cars in his lane were zipping ahead like hellbent microwave ovens on wheels. Then, without warning, the Toyota Celica directly in front was riding its warning lights, locking brakes and laying rubber as a black shadow passed over its hood; the shadow enveloped Doug's car as well, the jazz music fizzling out in a storm of white noise, and he was lost in darkness.

Tires grabbed and he skidded to a stop behind a line of red-eyed taillights leading into the gloom. His hair stopped moving, sprung out into a fright wig, and then the first rivulet of sweat ran down from his scalp. Another second and the horns began, echoing insanely from the walls of the tunnel.

Doug had left the meeting in time to avoid the rush

hour, he thought. But this was his first venture onto the
Pasadena Freeway in years and he was wrong, dead
wrong.

He jabbed the dashboard and clicked on his lights. In
the spill from his low beams he saw the tiles of the
enclosed underpass curving ahead like the convolutions
of an inflamed intestine. The lighting fixtures in the ceiling were out of order, ossified tracks embedded in the
dank plaster overhead.

They should have put up a sign, he thought. Christ,
it's every man for himself from now on.

He rolled up his window and closed the sunroof as a
noxious wave of exhaust built up in the tunnel. He activated the air conditioner, shut down his headlights and
waited for the bottleneck to unplug. KKGO was blocked
out. So was most every other FM station except for
Spanish-language news, new-wave teenage rock and,
near the end of the dial, an evangelical Christian broadcast. He gave up and left it tuned to the preacher.

". . . *It's so easy to go from life to death or from
death to life! Isn't it hard* not *to go from one place to
another? We turn on the light switch, we turn it off. It's
no different with life and death* . . . ."

That was reassuring.

Around him engines revved up as a stream of automobiles lurched forward a few feet, then squealed to a
halt. The tunnel now glowed brighter; but it was not
daylight, only a segment of overhead neon tubing that
worked. The cars settled down again in a steady rumble,
the purr of impatient animals. He sat back, unhooked
his seat belt and used the time to review what had gone
down at the meeting this afternoon.

At the producer's home in Altadena, he had had his
first chance to view the fine cut of the film he was supposed to be scoring. He had seen a rough assemblage of
footage at the Goldwyn Studios a couple of months ago,
before the move, but now Murdoch had his own editing
table set up in his basement; Doug had sat hunched over
the Moviola until his kidneys ached, clattering through
reel after reel of one of the most ludicrous disasters he

had ever witnessed in his life.

Shot (non-union, of course) for a cannily undisclosed sum, *Is Anybody There*? began provocatively enough but soon degenerated into a confusing compendium of science fiction clichés and arty psychological pretension. The story, such as it was, made his head hurt; he refused to think about it now of all times. Suffice it to say that he had his work cut out for him. It was badly in need of pacing, emphasis, dramatic climax. He hoped that he was enough of a professional to get by on sheer technique. He pitied the poor editor who had been faced with the task of splicing together even this much of a feature from the limited coverage that the director, who was the producer's boyfriend, had provided.

How had Murdoch and company connived to obtain such a reputable actress as Susan Penhaligon for the lead? Undoubtedly the same way they had obtained his services: by offering a contract that was tied to a substantial upfront advance. The promised rewrite ended up being improvised on the set, to no avail. They didn't know it but they had paid his family's moving expenses to a Beverly Hills address. And now, with too much of the advance already spent, it was time for him to deliver.

Except that they were hedging on the terms. The portfolio containing his budget lay on the seat next to him, deflating with each passing second. It listed the usual bare-bones estimates for musicians, instrument rentals, copying, recording dates, mixing time, raw tape and all the rest that he had submitted with his original bid. Now Murdoch was haggling with him over every subtotal, including such standardized items as musicians' scale and hourly studio rates.

Fortunately he was able to furnish comparable breakdowns from several of his other films, and the budget he had given them for *Is Anybody There*? undercut *The Silvering* and *Halloween V* in every particular. He had managed to convince Murdoch that there was no fat left to be trimmed, and he probably would not have succeeded were it not the unadorned truth. He was

still left with the challenge of bringing in any kind of
score on such a ball-breaking sum, nearly a third of
which he had already spent without a single measure
recorded or even written yet.

It's amazing, he thought, how I do it. It really is. But
I've done it before. I can do it again. It's either that or
we all go under—Lori, Elizabeth, Erin, Casey, Towser,
the whole lot this time, straight down the tubes to the
place where the Devil throws his old razor blades, and *Is
Anybody There*? ends up getting scored by some starv-
ing music major from USC with a four-track tape
recorder and a Casio keyboard in his bathroom . . . .

". . . *Yes, it's the oldest fight of all—life against
death! The tree of the knowledge of good and evil is in
reality the tree of death! In Genesis 2 we have the seeds
of both trees, but in* Revelations *we see that death, the
last enemy, is cast into the lake of fire, but life abounds
in the New Jerusalem. Those who have been redeemed
will flow into the city of living water . . . .*"

At that, as if on signal, the traffic jam loosened long
enough to carry a few cars forward, taillights like
oxygen-depleted blood cells pushing free from the walls
of a hardened artery.

Increasingly nervous for no reason he could name,
Doug toed the accelerator and tapped the bumper of the
next car in line, eager to be on his way, leaving the
preacher's hellfire and brimstone behind in the darkness. The walls of the tunnel were pink with reflections,
then brighter a short distance ahead with the clear light
of day.

He stayed in gear, fumbling with the dial. The
preacher's voice detuned and a burst of music blipped
by. He centered the dial on it, then recognized it as the
desperate slamdance sound of the punk/new-wave station. He started to whip past it, but then he was out of
the tunnel and the late afternoon sun coruscated
through his windshield with the white fire of a nuclear
blast. He put up a hand to protect his eyes and flapped
the visor into place. The strident lyric held him by the
force of its apocalyptic vision. Is that what kids are into

now? he wondered. Then God help us. I never knew.

The track faded down and the DJ segued from Bad Religion into an even more nihilistic outpouring by Adolescent Fear, whoever or whatever they were, followed by a continuing farrago of bile entitled "Stress Rig" from a combo called Suicidal Inclinations, as near as he could make it out. It reminded him of something he had put off thinking about all week, and he tried to keep from following the thought back as far as he could, lured by the fascination of his own obsessions.

Doug's irises stopped down as he worked up through second and third gears. He was on his way home at last. He tried to take solace in that as he changed stations, but he couldn't clear his chest of a lingering nasty taste, like rotten eggs. By the time he reached the downtown interchange he remembered to tune back to KKGO. He found himself veering into the Santa Monica lanes out of habit, but once he got to the San Diego Freeway and the route that would take him to Sunset he almost passed it by, as if he had forgotten where he now lived.

Traffic moved up Beaumont Canyon at an impossibly sluggish pace. Cars bearing the names of swift and exotic animals—Impala, Lynx, Jaguar, Cougar and the like—surrounded Doug's sedan, trapping him in their uphill flight as though to some doomed roundup in the sky. From time to time a renegade Maverick, Mustang, Colt or some such would cut loose from the herd and charge ahead impatiently, only to be shouldered back into line by the boundaries of the trail. Mufflers grumbled sullenly in a steady processional of misery, broken by the occasional lowing of a complaining horn, but the mass of dusty bodies continued to press homeward at a regulated pace under the watchful eye of a blood-red sun. In the southbound lanes reckless workers from the Valley raced back to the Westside in their Dashers, Demons and Hornets in an untrammeled flow. Doug observed them enviously, gritted his teeth and wondered how much he had gained, after all, by moving to beautiful Beverly Hills.

He passed the secluded, unkempt housefront where the white-haired boy lived with his grandmother—had lived, before the Sheriff took him away. Was he back home by now? If not today then soon; the juvenile authorities could hold him for no more than seventy-two hours, unless charges were pressed—and Doug had allowed the week to slip by without doing anything about that. He felt sorriest for the old lady. Casey had walked down to talk to her about the boy and what had happened, but there was never any answer. Presumably his grandmother was willing to talk to the police. Without her cooperation Buddy would have no one to assume responsibility, and he would never get out.

By the time he reached the upper end of the canyon the Mercedes's temperature gauge had gone off the scale. His tires, softened by the hot pavement, barely dragged him up the steep driveway, the sidewalls wobbling half-melted on their rims. He cranked down his window and caught a whiff of the front end; the motor now exuded an odor that reminded him of burning hair. As he thumbed the remote garage door opener he dangled his left hand outside, idly tapping out a contrapuntal variation for *Is Anybody There*? on the chrome trim. The door lifted; he put down the control and gripped the wheel in both fists, and noticed that the fingertips of his left hand were imprinted with microscopic lacerations from the sooty pollution that had settled on the car's once-shiny exterior.

The car ticked, cooling. He unstuck from the upholstery and walked back down the driveway. The gardener had finally been by. With the mysterious circle hosed off and the shrubbery manicured the lot appeared eminently safe again, the boundary lines once more clearly delineated. It was hard to imagine a prowler, even the white-haired boy, approaching across the open expanse of the front yard; the sides of the house were protected by the same graded hill that secured access to the back yard. Only a desperate animal might dare to venture down the steep incline from the ridge; in any other case Towser would surely wake them all with his barking. Now, standing in the waning radiance of a late April afternoon, Doug felt reassured about the troubled events of the past few weeks. Thank God it was all behind them.

No, he told himself, it had all added up to nothing more than a series of pranks, a kind of initiation for the new family—and the new girl—on the block, made to seem much worse than it was by a bad case of the moving jitters. Either that or he would have to allow himself to regress and start believing in Liz's Space Spirits, the Lost Ones, whatever they were called, the latest recombinant Devil theory to account for everything that doesn't work out the way you want it to in life. And Casey kept him too rational to fall for any of that.

He closed the garage behind him, let himself through the gate and jiggled his key till it fit the back door. There were fresh scratches on the brass of the doorknob; it looked like he wasn't the only one having trouble finding the keyholes in the new locks.

Casey was waiting on the other side, determinedly cheerful for his sake. But in truth her face was markedly less drawn, the lines around her eyes softer and more natural. Her expression seemed genuinely relaxed as she greeted him; either that or she had discovered an amazing makeup. No, he decided, the change was real. She was finally settling in. He sighed with relief and caught her neck in the crook of his arm, nuzzling her.

"Hi," she said into his ear. Her nails skipped over the wet shirt on his back. "You feel like you just stepped out of a steambath. How did it go?"

Reluctantly he released her and swung over to the kitchen. "Oh, screwed, as usual, but I can live with it. At least they've got the print locked. They're supposed to send over a videotape Monday morning."

"The check's in the mail," she said, nodding. She'd heard it all before.

He plucked a cold one from the refrigerator door and rolled it across his forehead, as Lori came into the kitchen.

"Hi, Doug." She headed for the stove, where an especially pungent concoction was brewing.

"Hi, angel."

"Hi, Doug," said Elizabeth from the hall.

"Hi, baby."

"Hi, Lori," she added.

"Hi, yourself," said Lori. "I'm busy."

"Hi, Mom."

"Hello, darling."

"Hi, Mom," said Lori.

"Hello, Lori. My, that smells good. I should let you make the meals around here every night."

Erin came out of her room, her lips and eyes puffed from another of her naps, her hair tumbling around her head like the defiant coiffure of an underaged European sex kitten. "When do we eat? I told you I have to babysit tonight. Hi, Doug."

"Hi, sweetie."

"Hi, Erin!" said Elizabeth.

"*Chuh*," said Erin.

Lori giggled over her saucepan. "Hi, Erin! Hi, Doug! Hi, Lizzy! Hi, Mom! Hi, Towser! Hi . . ."

"That's enough," said Casey. "Doug's had a long day. This isn't the Brady Bunch, you know."

"The what?"

"I know," said Doug, "it's the Partridge Family, right?" He took a long pull from the bottle.

"Oh, Doug," said Lori, "you're *so* corny."

Casey took his arm and moved with him into the living room. He had planned to withdraw immediately to his workroom, but that could wait. This was a rare moment, one to remember: the day it all came together. It was as if they were putting on a show for him demonstrating domestic bliss, afraid that he might leave them as their biological father had. He decided to relax and enjoy the ego boost.

Before the children could join them he asked Casey, "How are you really? Any new crises?"

"Nothing serious. The tree service gave us an estimate."

"Expensive?"

"Mattie Stavers tells me it's less than they paid to have their oak topped. I guess we should be grateful."

He nodded, secretly pleased. That meant she was finally sending out lines of communication with the neighbors. The Staverses were a decent couple, as far as he could tell. Ted was a cinematographer and Mattie wrote gothic romances. That must be easy, he thought, with only one child.

He scanned her eyes for hidden messages. "Anything else I should know about?"

"I don't think so," she said, her eyes as clear and unclouded as water on the air. "Towser needs a bath, but it's still too hot. Lori wants to get her hair cut like Christina Crawford. Lizzy's got a map to make for school and—"

"What about you?"

"I've had my bath." She put her feet between his and kissed him for no reason. "You'd probably like a shower yourself. You taste like salt."

The girls drifted in and draped themselves over the furniture—it was all in place now, and as soon as the aura of recently-dried paint dissipated it would feel like a real home. They awaited his attention with exaggerated expectation, Lori from the easy chair, Erin from the leather sofa. Elizabeth pulled up the footstool. Casey touched the back of his neck.

"Can I get you anything before dinner?"

"Uh . . . hmm. Well, another beer wouldn't hurt."

Casey nodded agreeably and left the room. Again he felt their eyes on him, as though he were supposed to go into a song and dance. Surely they were putting him on. She must have prepped them on how to play their parts in a simulation of the perfect Sunday supplement family. It couldn't be true. Could it?

He drained his beer and took a seat next to Erin on the sofa. The setting sun broke through the spotlessly clean drapes of the bay window, centering Doug in a golden shaft of light. He raised his hand self-consciously to slick his hair down and Casey was suddenly there with another bottle, this one frosty from the freezer.

He cleared his throat. The natives shifted restlessly, drawing closer to catch his every word. He would not have been surprised to see Elizabeth unfurl a banner that read WELCOME HOME, BELOVED STEPFATHER.

"I—"

Casey slid in on his right side, plumping up the pillow.

"I was—"

Elizabeth dropped to her knees. Through the dining room doorway he saw Towser cease rolling his rubber pork chop across the patio and cock his head, listening from the other side of the glass.

He took a breath. "I was wondering. How—how is everybody? How was school?"

"Um, fine," said Lori.

"Okay," said Lizzy.

"Are you sure?"

"Yes," they said in unison, the first civil words they had spoken in each other's presence for months.

Doug turned to his wife. "Is this true?"

She shrugged, smirking. "Remember what they say about gift horses."

"I remember the one about Greeks bearing gifts."

"Don't knock it."

"We want to hear about *your* day," said Lori.

"Yes," said Casey, "why don't you tell us about the new movie?"

He took a swallow off the top of the second beer. It was so cold it numbed him. But it was a good kind of numb. They were all still in their places with bright shiny faces. There didn't seem to be any crew members lurking around the edges waiting to mark it and strike it. The shimmering spotlight of golden sun remained focused on him. God's in His Heaven, he thought. Children, I'm home.

"All right," he began. "The movie's called *The House of Women*."

"Oh, Doug," said Lori.

"You're right, I lied. It's called *Is Anybody There?*"

"Is it scary?"

"Well, I guess it's supposed to be. Hard to figure out what they intended." Nobody objected so he sat up and let himself get into it. "The basic idea is that one day everybody in the world disappears except for Susan Penhaligon . . ."

"Who's that?" said Elizabeth.

"She's on the cover of the new *People* magazine," said Lori. "Why do they disappear?"

"Don't interrupt," chided Casey.

"It doesn't matter—it's science fiction. Anyway, she sets out on foot, through town and country, looking for somebody—anybody—else . . ."

"What town?"

"What country?"

"I think it's supposed to be England, but it looks more like Sierra Madre."

They laughed politely.

"Anyhow, she keeps expecting somebody like Tom Baker to show up and rescue her . . ."

"Who?"

"Who?"

"You know, Dr. Who. Only no one ever does. At the end she winds up sitting on the floor of the Food Hall in Harrod's—that's a department store in London—having the feast of her life on caviar and champagne and wild pig, getting drunk at a big party for all her imaginary friends—she's gone nuts by now. She gets up on top of the candy counter and does a striptease, eating Sporting and Military Chocolate, when all of a sudden, *boom*! everyone in the world is back again! According to the movie they had been there all along, only Susan Penhaligon couldn't see them. Some sort of scientific accident made them invisible, get it? All except ol' Susan.

"She runs for cover in the lingerie department—she's half-naked, right?—and bumps smack into a guy who *does* look a lot like Tom Baker. They strike up a conversation. He doesn't believe a word she says, but he invites her for a drink. She's so happy to see him she accepts. She goes into the dressing room and changes. But just at the moment when she's all made up and ready to come out . . . guess what?''

"What?"

He was astounded at their innocence. "Now the guy who looks like Tom Baker can't see her. Neither can anyone else. As far as the rest of the world is concerned she doesn't exist anymore. The movie ends with her sitting there—she's transparent so *we* can see her, at least—crying to herself, trying hard to wake up. Only she can't. The End.''

Lizzy clapped her hands together half-heartedly.

"Well?" he asked.

The silence was deafening.

"You're right," he said. "My feelings exactly."

"Um, it's . . . kind of, well, far out, isn't it?" asked Lori. "Nothing personal."

"Why don't we ask Erin?" said Casey solicitously. "She's the farthest-out person around here."

All eyes turned to the leggy teenager.

"*Chuh*," said Erin, the moth within the moth-proof closet.

The resident metaphysician had spoken. "Would you care to expand on that?" asked Doug. "Not that I disagree. But I need all the help I can get. The material isn't exactly Academy Award caliber, if you know what I mean."

"It's dumb," said Erin. "The only people who go to a movie like that'll be the posers—people who get their hair cut by some guy with a French name. Why do you take jobs like that? When are you going to get back to *your* music? I think you should tell them to go fuck themselves."

"Erin," said Casey. Doug felt his wife's thigh tense next to his.

"Well, it's true. You're supposed to be an artist. Why do you dirty yourself with shit like that? You don't have to. *Do you.*"

Doug turned away from Casey and met Erin's eyes,

which were red and brimming over. "For now, I do," he said soberly.

"And why do you suppose he's doing it?" demanded Casey from behind a rigidly cosmetic but glacial smile. "Did it ever occur to you, young lady, that all this effort is so that you can get an education—"

"*Chuh.*"

"—and grow up in a decent environment? We're making sacrifices so that you, *you* and your sisters —look at me—can grow up happy and healthy. Do you know how lucky you are to have a man here who's willing to help you do that?"

"It's all right," Doug said. "It's not so bad. Really."

"Why do you listen to her?" Erin was trembling, livid. "I know how much you hate jobs like this. You think I don't remember how you used to stay up all night working on *Alien Lovers* and *The Syzygist*? How you used to mope around the apartment like you were dead? It aged you, Doug! If you don't watch out, she's going to turn you into a dried-up old man!"

"That's not true. Listen to me." He tried to encircle her shoulders but she pushed away.

"It *is* true! If you won't admit it to me at least stop lying to yourself!"

Casey rose, stepped calmly in front of Doug and struck her daughter across the side of the head.

"That's your answer, isn't it? Go on, hit me again! It doesn't prove anything!"

"I don't have to listen to any more of this," said Casey. She started to leave the room. "Are you coming with me, Doug?"

"In a minute." He touched Erin's arms, the fine honey-colored silk bleached there, her skin growing paler as he watched. "Listen to me," he said from an aching throat. "You've got it all wrong."

Casey slammed the dining room door. Lori ran after her.

He tried to pull Erin to him. "Sweetie, come here. I want you to go in the other room with me. I think you owe your mother an apology. Don't ruin it. Let's have a nice dinner together, the way she had it planned.''

"I'm not ruining anything. *She* is. I'm not hungry anymore. I don't care if I never eat another meal in this house. I hate it here, if you want to know the truth. If I split one of these days, you'll know whose fault it is.''

"Whose?''

"Whose idea was it to move here in the first place? Don't tell me it was yours! I'll go someplace where you'll never find me . . . .''

"You're not being fair.''

"Fair? Nobody's fair to me! I don't care anymore, don't you get it? About anything!''

She stomped to her room.

Doug sat there in the dying light, dazed. A moment later he heard the back door slam.

On the floor in front of him, Elizabeth was crying.

Erin running up the street: *I don't care if I ever go home again. I don't!*

She had been thinking for weeks about running away, had lain in twilight sleep dreaming melodramas of the road as she had read about it and seen it in films. She knew, of course, that the sixties were long gone, that the safety net of a support system to drop out into no longer existed; there was nowhere to go. No communes, no Diggers, no halfway houses for runaways, no underground. And still, behind it all, the treacherous but cunning afterimages from last Friday night lay in wait in her memory, the skull beneath the surface, ready to take her if all else failed.

The truth was that she was not quite desperate enough to go that far, even though there was precious little else to choose from. That whole sick scene, even as vaguely as she remembered her participation in it, bummed her out so much that it was no alternative at all. Still, Damon hadn't called; her only friend was already drifting away; she hated her school; she had no money; she was too young to do anything on her own; even Doug couldn't help her anymore. In short, everything sucked. And yet . . .

She tried to put away her dreams of the real world for another day. For now at least Mrs. Stavers would pay her something for her time, which was more than she could get anywhere else. It wasn't enough to make a difference, though. It was Friday night in a place she did not know, and she was alone.

Usually when she babysat the first thing she did after the parents left was scope out the kitchen to see how much she could dare to eat without getting caught, but tonight she had no appetite. But that was okay; six-year-old Richie Stavers was the trippiest little boy in the whole world. She had known that since the first time she locked eyes with him. He had been killing ants with a wet washcloth on the sidewalk a few doors from her house while she was out walking Towser, and he had looked up at her with that guileless face of his and begun talking about moon men and spider webs that reached all the way into space as if he had known her all his life. Most little boys made her watch television with them, *The A-Team* or *Magnum* or *T.H.U.G.S.*, the little girls *Nine is Too Many* or *Bees 'n Birds* or a *Bluesberry Cheesecake Special*. Richie, however, was adaptable to absolutely anything she suggested, from counting the number of faces they could find in the glow-in-the-dark stars on his bedroom ceiling to utter vegetable idleness. They demanded nothing of each other, and she felt infinitely more at home here with him than back at the house that was supposed to be hers.

Tonight was no exception. Mrs. Stavers was uncertain about what time she would be back but gave her permission to eat anything she could find in the kitchen. That was no temptation to Erin—even if she had been hungry it was all health food, unsalted peanut butter and sawdust bread and those miniature Saran-Wrapped baskets of bean sprouts that ruin everything.

Mom called once to be sure Erin was there but did not ask to speak to her, and then Mrs. Stavers left.

Richie was busy in his room setting up his terrarium; except for the running of water in the pipes and the low-key narration from a PBS Special about soldier ants that Richie had turned on for taping in the den, the house was empty and marvelous. She didn't need her books; she didn't know why she had brought them. There was no need to think about school now. She was wasting time and enjoying it with her feet up on the kitchen table, trying to decide whether to go through the drawers upstairs one more time, when the phone rang.

"Richie?" she called.

After two rings he still hadn't answered it.

It's probably Mom, she thought. I won't talk to her—I won't.

Four rings.

It could be Doug. But he doesn't know the number. Anyway, he's too chicken to stand up to her. She's got him faked out . . . .

Five rings.

What if it's Mrs. Stavers? She'll think I'm not doing my job.

"Hello?"

"Hello, who is this?"

She hated it when people did that. I didn't ring your phone and bother you, she thought. "Who are you calling?"

"Who do you think?"

"I'm sorry, this is the babysitter. If you'd care to leave a message—"

"I know who this is. We know where you are, what you do—we don't lose track of our own. I just wanted to tell you. *It won't be long now.*"

The line was breathing, as though the call were coming from a long way away, from beneath the ocean or from a cavern deep under the ground.

"Damon?" she said. It was hard to tell. She had hardly ever talked to him on the phone. "Is—is that you?"

"Is that *you*?"

She heard a mocking chuckle, though it could have been the soughing of a bad connection.

"Where are you? You sound like you're a million miles from here."

"It's close, Erin. Closer than you think."

It might have been Damon but she was not sure. Or he could have put up one of his friends to make a crank call. But why would he? What had she ever done to him? She had gone with him last Friday night, had let him know right off how much she liked him. But he hadn't wanted what she expected. What *had* he wanted? She pressed the receiver to her forehead, trying to remember.

"Listen," she said, "I'm sorry about that night, the way it worked out. I looked for you, I really did. I don't know what happened. But I got home all right. It wasn't what you think."

No answer.

"Do you want to come over?" She went on, taking the risk that he would laugh at her. But she had to know where she stood. "Nobody's here except for the little boy I'm babysitting. His father's out of town and his mother won't be back for hours." The telephone line echoed with a whispering that might have been his breath. "They wouldn't care. We could talk. Whatever." Still nothing. "Okay? I don't even want to go home, if you want to know. I don't know where I'm going to sleep tonight. Are—are you still there?"

"I'm here. You don't know where, but that's good, isn't it? That's the way it has to be for now. Until you join us."

Maybe it wasn't Damon. But she had made such a fool of herself already that she had to play it out.

"Later, I guess. But I can't go anywhere right now. I'm babysitting. I told you—"

"It isn't far. It's so close you can almost touch it. Can't you feel it already?"

"Feel what?"

"The Darkside, Erin. What else?"

And at that the part of the memory that she had been afraid all along to recall came flooding back, filling her veins with ice water.

It was not Damon.

"Wh-where?"

You'll know it when you feel it. A promise is a promise.

"Take a look around. It might be right behind you. Why don't you check the back yard in a few minutes? Until then . . . ."

"*Who is this? What do you want from me?*"

The line was dead.

Casey and Doug were having an argument. Or rather she was trying to have at him and he was refusing to cooperate. He sat there on the edge of the bed and allowed her to go on. After she had used up all her words the only thing he could do was doff his shoes, sit back against the headboard and utter in that intolerably innocent voice of his, so innocent it bordered on indifference:

"If you want to believe that, Case, go right ahead. I won't take the blame for what you think I think. But don't put words in my mouth. Why don't you stop flagellating yourself long enough to listen?"

Say it, she thought. At least Geoff would have fought her like a man . . . . She immediately hated herself for thinking that. But it was true. And all Doug could do was light another cigarette and try to worm his way out of it.

She said, "I know you resent me. You must. You couldn't have known what you were getting into before we were married. What it does to you, the time, the energy . . . . It isn't fair to you, us, or your work." It was enough to drive the girls' father away, she thought. "Admit it."

"You're starting to sound like a paranoid, Casey. That isn't like you."

"Saint Douglas! Oh, I can tell—you don't have to say anything."

She was ashamed but could not stop. Then the thought came: *Help me.* And that only made her more miserably disappointed in herself. She had thought she learned her lesson when Geoff left. It was folly to expect men to solve her problems for her, or even to remain happy living with so much responsibility. It wasn't in their nature.

And yet Doug was so much better at it than the girls'

father, it fit him so much more gracefully, that she had seduced herself into believing again. But the way he had been turning away from her, siding against her . . . the first telltale signs had already begun.

"Come over here," he said.

"That's your answer to everything, isn't it?" she said. "Well, it won't work this time. Not until we establish some ground rules for honesty in this house."

Downstairs, Erin's phone rang. There was no point in breaking her back to answer it. If her daughter wanted to run her own life, let her try. She'd see how hard it was.

She stopped folding clothes and let them drop onto the bed. She had no more heart for any of it.

"Listen. I know how good you are with the girls. I have no complaints about that. But there's more to it. You haven't been open with me. I hear you talking to them behind my back. If I'm driving you away, if I've driven everyone away, then you must tell me. I think I deserve that much."

"I said come over here. God damn it. And sit down. Now."

If he had raised his voice, thrown something, reached to hurt her, done anything but say approximately that and in that way she would have lashed out in a fight to the death. But he did not and so she waited to see what was coming next.

"We're not exactly kids anymore, Case. We're lucky. We got to work out all the bullshit with other people in other places before we got here. And this place, this house, what we've got and what we're making—that's what counts. For the first and last time. It's the payoff, the part that makes everything up to now worth it. I'm not going middle-aged crazy on you, if you haven't noticed."

"You can't promise that."

"*Listen to me.* We're going to grow old together from now on. The girls will be gone away from us faster than you ever imagined. Oh, they'll come to visit now and then—we'll still have that much of them, and they'll be by to take what they need. But all we'll really have is each other."

He said, "If you don't believe—if you don't *know* that that's what I want, then you've never believed a word I've said, ever."

He said, "I don't have any problems with you. Or Elizabeth or Lori or Erin. If I ever have any complaints you'll be the first to know—promise."

He said, "Because I love you. That's something I wouldn't know how to fake if I tried. Once, maybe, when I was young. But not now."

She sat carefully and covered her face from his eyes, and then made herself breathe again. "I should let you talk to the girls for me. I don't know where you get the words. Silver-tongued devil."

He cupped his broad hands around her head and brought her to him, erasing the lines from her temples, from between her eyes. At last she managed to imitate a laugh and cleared her nose. She shook her head, trying to see him clearly.

"I don't know why I can't talk to them anymore," she said. "Sometimes it's as if I'm fighting with someone I don't even know."

"If you mean Erin, try not to worry. Leave her be for now. It's hard for her, too."

"I know. But I can't just sit back. It's too soon to let go. She was my baby. I was twenty-six years old when she was born."

"She'll get there, too. It is too soon, you're right. But we have to practice, so we'll be ready when it's time." He tipped her face up before she could protest and kissed her deeply.

He was so warm. She buried her hands under his arms to heat her aching fingers. He smelled like himself and no one else, and she breathed him in and moved her hands up to the back of his neck so that he, dear, kind man that he was, would know how truly he belonged with her.

"The bedroom door's open," she said eventually. "The trouble with little girls is that you never hear their feet till they're right next to you.''

"Only two out of three this time," he said. "Better odds than we usually get." He drew her down next to him. The phone rang on the nightstand but he wouldn't let her up. Finally it stopped.

"Do you think I ought to call the Staverses again?"

"What time is it?"

"After eleven."

"It's not far, is it?"

"A few houses. But . . ."

"Nothing's going to happen to her. Let her come back under her own steam."

"I know. But what if she doesn't?"

"Where can she go?" He kissed her again. Outside a car braked farther up the block. He was right. The Staverses were home. It wouldn't be much longer. She held him so tight she was afraid she would break his spine, then rolled away and got up while it was still possible.

"Give me a minute," she said. "Or else we might find ourselves with four pairs of little feet to worry about."

While she was in the bathroom she heard the front doorbell. She opened the bathroom door in time to see Doug out on the deck, looking down. Through an odd trick of the light the leaves of the tree appeared to reflect a reddish hue, as if a fire had started in the street below.

"Doug . . . ?"

"I'll go."

"It is Erin? Did she forget her key?"

"No, no, I don't think so."

"Then what—?"

"It's probably nothing. Stay here."

He tramped downstairs.

She started for the deck, then changed her mind and followed after him. He was already to the front door. As she passed Erin's room her daughter's phone rang. On an impulse she answered it.

"Yes?"

"They're going to do it tonight! Go up in the hills. It's not so bad there, really. We'll find you and hide you. But you have to go right now . . . Erin?"

"Who is this?"

"Is this Erin?"

"No, it most certainly is not." The voice was talking gibberish, but the urgency of the tone brought her up short. "Who's calling?"

"Tell Erin . . . tell her they never forget. They can get to her through the tunnels. *The Darkside is here*!"

Click.

Blinking fast, Casey started for the living room. Doug was at the screen door. He was talking to a man in a uniform. Was it a fireman? Please, God . . .

She snatched the kitchen phone from the wall and dialed the Staverses number.

It was busy.

She slammed it down.

Across the living room, Doug turned from the door. "Casey, stay there," he called.

She was confused. The cacophony of bells, sirens, telephones . . . she couldn't hear herself think. She circled the bar, disoriented. Was Lori all right? And Elizabeth? Why hadn't Erin come home yet?

The wall phone rang again.

She snapped it up. "Yes? Would someone please tell me what is . . . ?"

"Uh, Miss-us Carson?"

"If you have something to say, say it! Where's Erin?"

"Missus Carson, can you come over right away? I think you better."

It was a child's voice. "Richie? Let me talk to your mother."

"My mother's not here."

"Where's Erin?"

"I called before. Lots and lots of times. But you wouldn't answer. The policeman called, too."

"*Where's my baby*?"

Part
II

The Lost Ones

six

The phone slipped out of Casey's hands. It struck the
bar and rebounded onto the floor, the impact ringing
the bell one last time with the clarity of a chime. The
coiled cord flopped after it like a children's soft spring
toy walking down a flight of stairs. The phone lay there
leaking words out of its fractured earpiece, but Casey
was no longer listening to the incomprehensible message.

Down the block, an auto burglar alarm began to wail.

She held herself erect and forced air in and out of her
lungs at a controlled rate as she turned to the living
room, though her heart seemed about to beat its way
out of her chest. She crossed the carpet as rigidly as a
sleepwalker. Doug was no longer there. She pushed
open the screen door with her white knuckles and came
out onto the front porch as the burglar alarm became
the rising and falling of a siren approaching at top speed
from the bottom of the canyon. As the black-and-white
sheared past and slowed to a stop a few doors to the
north she realized that she could no longer feel her feet
and ankles. Concerned that they might not support her,

she allowed her knees to bend and sat down briefly on the welcome mat, folding her legs shakily beneath her.

Another squad car was already parked in the other driveway. In the splash of the rotating light she saw Doug a few feet away, his features outlined in red so that the beads of sweat on his face resembled tears of blood. His eyes narrowed. He hurried forward, following the man in the uniform—it was a policeman, not a fireman. Casey strove to stand, only to find that she could no longer feel her legs.

"Doug," she asked, "is it all right?" Her throat had closed up in the night air and she was not sure about her words. "It is, isn't it?"

"I told you, stay where you are!" He was moving across the lawn. He jogged to the end of the driveway, then disappeared around the hedge. She knew that she must get up. It was not right for him to be the first one there. She shifted her legs and hammered her knees down to lock them and tried to stand.

Everything seemed to be happening in extreme slow motion. The flashing red lights no longer spun but fluttered around in weak circles. How many seconds or minutes would they take to complete the next cycle so that she could see? The sirens wound down to a low howl, then a drowning whimper. People on either side of the street were drifting out of their houses, curious somnambulists she had never seen before. What was wrong with them? She tottered along the path, slipped on the stones and fell to her knees in the wet grass.

Behind her Lori wandered out onto the porch, her nightgown flowing in lazy currents. "Mom . . . ?" she said sleepily.

"Get back inside!" Casey's words wavered as though her throat were choked with water. "See to your sister! She needs you." She had a fleeting image of Elizabeth waking, terrified. Who would comfort her?

"No, she doesn't. She's snoring. She's—"

"Don't argue with me. Lock the door. Don't let anyone in. And do not answer the phone."

"Um, what's all the . . . ?"

"Do as I say!"

Lori hesitated as pastel insects flew the beam of the porchlight, hovering above her head like falling petals. "Okay, okay! What did *I* do?" She tiptoed back inside and bolted the door.

Ahead, more sleepwalking strangers were crossing the street and converging on the other house, mayflies drawn by the rays of flashlights sewing the April night. Guttural voices boomed out of a two-way radio, too curt and accusing for her to understand. All feeling was gone now from her lower body, the numbness threatening to creep up her ribs and overtake her heart. She knew there wasn't much time. Swinging her legs forward and back in a spastic gait, she staggered across the empty yards between.

All the lights were on in the Stavers house. As she approached, more doors and windows were flung open to illuminate the darkness. Her husband came running back to her with his arms out in the manner of a referee.

"Casey, go back."

He was panting, his eyes swimming. Then he was holding her with oppressive force. Her arms, her face could still feel and his pulse drummed wildly through the bones of her skull. She permitted him to hold her upright for a moment. Then she inserted her arms under his and freed herself.

"Let me see to it," she said.

The neighbors moved aside but kept muttering. No doubt they were wondering why she had not been there all along. But she would show them. Erin was her daughter.

There were two uniformed men from the Beverly Hills Police Department in the house. Mattie kept such a nice home but Casey could see where their heavy shoes had turned up the throw rug in the foyer to leave black heel marks on the parquet floor. And the living room smelled distressingly of leather and gun metal. Erin's books were stacked neatly in the kitchen. That was good. It meant everything was all right, didn't it?

She swallowed, moistening her throat to be sure she

would be heard. "Excuse me," she said. "I'm Mrs. Carson. I'd like to see my daughter, please. Where is she?"

They stopped questioning the Stavers boy, straightened up and faced her as though confronting an intruder. One of them even hiked up his black belt and brushed his hand nervously over his holster, over the protruding rosewood grip. Richie looked up at her and said, "You're not mad at me, are you?"

"Where's Erin?" His expression was clear and direct, untroubled. "Will you take me to her, Richie?"

"Mrs. Carson . . ." The other officer touched her elbow, which she thought an inappropriately intimate gesture. "Ma'am, would you like to sit down?"

"No, I wouldn't. I'm here to see my daughter."

"I called you first," Richie explained. "I did. I looked out my bedroom window, and I saw her. But you weren't home. So, well—"

"The boy placed a call for emergency assistance." The first officer patted Richie on the head and came over to her. She felt surrounded. Did they think she was going to fall? She wouldn't give them the satisfaction. "Ma'am, if we can have a word with you . . ."

A car door slammed. Casey heard a woman's voice, and then Mattie Stavers appeared at the kitchen door.

"My boy!" cried Mattie, rushing in and swooping over Richie. She stroked the hair back from his forehead. "Are you all right, darling? Dear God, when I saw the police cars I thought—"

"I'm okay, Mama."

"But I left a number with the babysitter. She should have called if there was any trouble. Where—?" She acknowledged the others for the first time. Casey saw the accusation burning in her eyes. "Casey? Where is—?"

"Mattie, that's what I'm trying to find out. Only these rude gentlemen don't seem to want to let me."

"What is going on here?" Mattie Stavers whipped her head between the two policemen. "I demand that you tell me, or get out of my house at once."

Casey saw Douglas coming back up the driveway past the door, walking jerkily, like a marionette. His head was down so that he could not see where he was going. Was he drunk? No, of course not. She started for the door but again the policemen surrounded her.

"Get—your—hands—off—me!"

So many lights were on in the house that when she went outside she was momentarily blind.

"Doug?"

He extended a shaking hand. She saw past him to the pale coats of the ambulance attendants coming out of the gate to the back yard. They were rattling a gurney over the cracked cement. She paddled the air for balance, seeking Doug's hand. But he held too tightly; he intended to restrain her. She released herself from his grip and blocked their path.

"Stand aside, please."

"You get out of my way," Casey warned them.

"Is she the mother?"

"I'm sorry, ma'am. By the time we got here it was too late to . . ."

"Case, don't," Doug said. "Please, honey, come with me. I want to talk to you. Just a minute. Please."

She pulled the sheet down.

Erin was sleeping. There, she thought. That's better. Only they should know enough to leave her nose uncovered so that she can breathe. Her face was peaceful, her head back, lips slightly parted, the same way she had slept as a baby, her clothing clean and neat. Only an unhygienic smear of dirt marred her long white neck. Casey licked her own fingers and rubbed to remove it. But the stain was stubborn and didn't want to come off. It was under the skin, as well. But that couldn't be.

Mattie Stavers came out, saw what she was doing and screamed.

"Hush," Casey told her. Don't wake my Erin, she thought. She always needs her sleep. She looks so tired . . . . She frowned disapprovingly at Mattie.

Through the gate the back yard was perfectly ordered under the outdoor floodlights, everything in its place ex-

cept for a tatter of rope or cloth looped over the tree
branch next to Richie's swing. Was it a broken strap?
How unsafe, untidy. Not like Mattie at all. She licked
her hand again and returned to her duties. She shrugged
off Doug's arms and kept rubbing and would not stop
when the attendants attempted to raise the sheet again.

"Don't do that," she said. "Not yet. I have to take
care of my daughter. You understand. She needs me."

Mattie Stavers was sobbing.

"Would someone please do something for that poor
woman?" asked Casey. She was the one who needed
help. She would wake Erin. When the sobbing did not
stop Casey drew back her hand and slapped Mattie
across the face. It was for her own good. But it did not
stop her. That was because it wasn't very hard. Casey
knew because she hardly felt the blow herself. The chill
that had settled over Erin from being left outside too
long had traveled up Casey's arm to her shoulder and
neck. She tried to say something more but could not feel
her lips move. Then her jaw began to go numb and her
vision frosted over. Still she rubbed, working faster and
faster, hoping to finish before it was too late.

The drawer rolled out.

Oh sweetie, he thought, you really are in trouble,
aren't you? How am I going to get you out of this?

"Mr. Carson," said the attendant, "you don't have
to do this. She's been identified. Why don't you go
home and get some rest?"

"I don't think I can do that."

Reluctantly the attendant stood aside. "There's no
need to worry about making arrangements. Wait
until . . ."

"I don't think I can." Until you've all had a chance
to get your hands on her? he thought.

"We have to hold the body until the Coroner releases
it. If there's an inquest you'll be notified. You won't
have to talk to anyone else tonight. You can deal with it
all tomorrow, the next day . . ."

"I can't do that." Doug braced himself behind her

head and prepared to lift the sheet.

The attendant intercepted Doug's hand. "There's nothing to see. Except for the subdermal hematomas here and here—" His ridged and yellowed fingernail moved swiftly around the sides of her neck as though making an incision. "—All the injuries were internal, mainly the collapsed larynx, which cut off respiration. If it's any consolation to you she didn't feel any pain. Just a gradual loss of consciousness after her feet left the ground. Like falling asleep. Try to believe that." He attempted to replace the sheet.

Doug deflected his wrist, forcing the cover back down. "I can't. *Now will you leave us alone*?"

The attendant withdrew, his crepe soles cheeping over the tile floor. He removed his glasses and cleaned them on his white smock. "I know how you must feel. These teenage suicides are always the hardest. She's not even the first this week. Someone ought to do something about it. It's getting to be an epidemic. Such an unnecessary waste of resources."

"What?" What was he talking about? Did they really think she did this to herself? If that was what they had put down on their report they had it all wrong. "What do you mean by . . . ?"

But the heavy door was already closing on its rubber seals.

He held the sheet so tightly that it practically tore in his hands.

"Oh, sweetie . . ."

Her complexion was no longer blue but now close to normal, with only the slightest tinge of discoloration around the ears and nose. He lowered the tent of the sheet to see more clearly.

So pale, he thought. You should have spent more time outdoors. If you hadn't slept so much, if you'd gotten up at a reasonable hour, if someone had made you . . . .

He saw the tiny freckles spattered across her nose and cheeks, the fine peach fuzz embedded in the pores of her skin, along her jawline and in the cleft of her upper lip, like the sensitive cilia covering a leaf of the rarest and most delicate plant. He exhaled, emptying his lungs completely, and the all but invisible hairs drew droplets of moisture from his breath and condensed them there in the refrigerated air, freezing them into a mask of frost as he watched.

He leaned closer, cushioning the top of her head against his stomach.

You should have spent more time with me, he thought. Instead of empty strangers you met at school. They didn't love you, those people, do you realize that now? You should have listened to me, only to me. You should have been content with what you had for now, with the new house, with all I tried to give you. There was no need for anything more yet. We could have been so happy together. It was going to be fun, all the things we would have done, the games we would have played, the trips we would have taken, all the days and nights stretching ahead of us without end . . . .

Why didn't you listen to me? Why couldn't you do that much? Was it so hard? Were you so spoiled? Yes, you were, you were, but why didn't you let me teach you another way? I should have been stronger, I should have raised my voice, slugged you, locked you away in your room until it was safe for you to come out . . . .

He placed his hands alongside her head to turn her face up to his, to force her to listen for once, for the first and last time.

Her flesh was not yet cold, only slightly cool, as if waiting to be revived. He moved his hands from her ears so that she would hear, so that he would have all her attention. Her skin was still supple, ready to break into a grin of recognition at any time over one of their private jokes.

"Listen . . ."

There was so much he wanted to tell her. Where should he begin? With the story of his own life, how he had grown to be what he was, the good and the bad, so that she would understand before it happened to her and so avoid the mistakes? What details should he choose to make his points, to hold her interest?

"I want to tell you that you—you're like me. The same, it's all the same, don't you see? You only think you're different, that nothing happening to you has ever happened to another human being anywhere on earth before. But that's wrong, so wrong. You never thought I understood, but I do. What do you think I am, stupid? How could you think that? I have to tell you . . . I want to tell you to—to—"

A tear coursed along the side of his nose and splashed onto his hand, ran down and froze at once into a structure of pure white crystals on her eyelashes.

"Listen to me, you little bitch! Why do you act that way? Why did you have to go and get yourself in so much trouble? Your mother loves you, and your sisters . . . what are they going to do without you? Can you tell me that? Think, for once in your life, think what you're doing! Oh, God . . ."

He swooned over her, torn open by sobs.

"It wasn't your fault, it was me. *Me.* I was too weak to talk to you when she didn't know how. It's my fault, mine . . . ."

He lowered his lips to her forehead and left a kiss on the soft skin. His own head touched the point of her chin and her lips, cool on his face as he had always known they would be, made contact at last with the deep furrow on his brow. He clasped her under the chin and then caressed her neck, her shoulders, her arms to warm her so that she might move again long enough to embrace him fully this once in return. The sheet remained over her body and breasts, a body that was now lost to his and to all other eyes until the end of time. He had missed forever touching her, had never even diapered and powdered the sweet folds and dimples that he knew were there, had never had the right, and now it was too late; it would always be too late, now and evermore.

"I want to tell you that I love you, my dearest, my darling Erin, loved you before I knew you and will go on loving you. That can never change. I'll keep you here inside me always, always . . . . Don't leave! I won't let you! I'll stay up with you every night, as long as you like, I'll tell you everything I know, I'll make you warm again, I can do it, you'll see, only please, please don't go away from me so soon . . . !"

He heaved and shook, his mouth working uncontrollably in the tender hollows of her throat, which he knew was the tenderest thing he would ever touch, no matter how long he lived.

It was nearly dawn, but he was not ready to go home.

He drove the dark pipeline of the canyon three times from top to bottom before permitting himself to slow as he passed the house. Gil's car was parked in front and the porchlight was still on, a flimsy beacon in an otherwise inhospitable location. The surrounding homes were locked down and secured, withdrawn under the natural coloration of the terrain like the closed ranks of a wagon train regrouped in hostile territory. He knew that somewhere very close by, just over the ridge or in back of the wild groundcover, savage forces awaited the right moment to descend and obliterate all signs of life remaining in this doomed encampment. On the fourth pass he downshifted and pulled up the winding driveway. The rest of his family would be waiting for him; they whom he had so recklessly led into this wilderness needed his protection more than ever. But how could they trust him, now or ever again, to provide safe passage? He had failed them utterly and irrevocably, and the way to their redemption as well as his was now as tortuous and uncertain as an unmapped path through the long night of the human soul.

He cut the headlights and sat slumped over the wheel. There was no moon; the other houses lay blacked-out and shapeless as barrows under the overgrown oaks and sycamores. Behind it all the uneven sides of the canyon groundrise loomed like the walls of a parted sea, poised for the first faultline quake that would release them and shut off the sky, submerging everything that lay between. Shivering with dread, he keyed the garage door and watched it shutter closed against his taillights, leaving only a ghostly outline of his own head in the rearview mirror, a featureless mask floating adrift and unanchored in the darkness.

Should he leave the motor running, roll down the windows and breathe deeply so that he would never have to face them again? Surely they would be better off without him, without his destructive ambition. Casey's instincts for survival would see them through in much sturdier fashion. He had no right to risk another moment of their lives against his self-serving delusions of success. It had been murderous folly, the selfish fantasies of a man who had never come to terms with his own limited potential. All the notes of all the music he had ever written were not equal in value to one iota of living matter. If he could trade the lot, every vainglorious measure he had ever composed, for the sake of one precious instant more of life for Erin, beautiful Erin, or Casey or Lori or Elizabeth, he would do so now without hesitation. But he could not. It was too late. Not even his own life would count in trade. No, it would be a futile gesture without benefit to anyone; it was all he had, but it was not enough. And it was far too facile, so convenient and simplistic that it would be like every other decision he had ever made, so easy that it would be no decision at all.

He let himself through the gate. Towser grumbled and surrendered the back doormat, slinking away with his tail between his legs. *He knows*, Doug thought, and did not try to pet the dog.

The lamp was off. Gil was sacked out on the couch, still fully dressed, his briefcase on the end table. Within its open jaws jars of pills glowed in the cold nightlight from the kitchen like bottles of blue teeth. Feeling his cheek begin to twitch, he dragged his leaden feet up the stairs.

Casey was asleep on her back as though in suspended animation, with Lori's and Elizabeth's short forms at her sides. Except for the clutched handkerchief, his wife appeared to be at peace, the bedclothes taut, her abdomen rising and falling with a slow, healing rhythm. Whatever medication Gil had given her had done its merciful work—for now. Doug considered sitting up with her until the sedative wore off, but could not bring himself to approach the bed. The thought of her eyes opening later and finding him there in the unforgiving light of day terrified him.

He went back downstairs.

In the dining room, Gil stirred.

"Doug . . . ?" Gil's face looked like a used mattress. "What do you need, buddy?"

"Nothing."

Not with friends like you, he thought. Lester Bauman and his wife from next door had come down right after it happened, along with other people he hardly knew. Soon the house had swarmed with overly-solicitous neighbors offering to take the girls for the night, to stay with Casey, to assist in any way that would prove nothing had happened to affect their own happiness. Where were they now? Not that there was anything more for them to do; Doug was relieved to find them gone back to their snug lives. With Casey's relatives far away in Colorado, there was no one who ought to have been here except a doctor, and Gil more than filled that role. Of course the girls' real father would have to be told. Had Casey called him already? Not likely; she had all but turned to stone by the time he got her home.

The house retained the lingering aura of uninvited visitors. The atmosphere was stifling. And there were physical aftereffects: an overful ashtray, coffee cups, furniture subtly rearranged—details inconsequential by themselves, but which when taken altogether added up to evidence of intrusion, of violation. How would he ever restore the natural order? It seemed an insurmountable task.

"Casey's out cold," Gil told him. "I had to give her the strongest stuff I had. She needed it."

"I know."

"What about you? Can I give you a hand with anything?"

Doug stood before the sliding glass doors to the yard. The patio was etched in hyperreal bas relief under the first pitiless rays of a new morning. But there was nothing outside that was more foreign to him now than the interior of his own house.

"Yes," he said. He thought: Tell them that something wild is loose out there, something that wants to destroy us. Go with me to shake them out of their false sleep; ring doorbells, pound windows, sound an alarm that will shatter the deadly complacency of this canyon before it's too late for them, too. Make them understand. And then help me find it. "Tell them that they've got it wrong."

Gil got up from the sofa; in the plate glass Doug saw his lanky form unfolding to its full height and enlarging as he came toward the window. He placed a hand on Doug's shoulder, near the back of the neck, and left it there.

"Got what wrong?"

"They think she did it to herself." Doug swallowed a horrible laugh. "Can you believe that? That she put a strap around her own neck and hanged herself until she was dead. They wouldn't even search the hill. They don't want to know."

The hand closed. Doug hadn't realized how iron-hard his posture had become. He felt the ropes of muscle in his shoulder break apart painfully and begin to uncoil. His eyes watered.

"Wait for the autopsy," suggested Gil.

"What do you mean?" The thought of crenelated gloves opening her body cavities, defiling her made his stomach convulse. "There won't be one. As far as they're concerned the case is closed. I told you, they don't want to know."

Gil grunted and cleared his nose. "I can press for an inquest, if you like. Only it might not—that is . . ."

Doug pulled away. "You mean you might not find anything. You think she did it, too, don't you? You think she was flipped out on drugs, fucked up in the head . . . . You think she had nothing to live for. That she wanted to die. Well, let me tell you something. Let me tell you . . ." Like a boxer Doug raised his fists to cover his face.

"I don't think anything. Neither do you. We'll wait. And then we'll know."

Doug walked haltingly into the living room. The sky was washed out, robbing the canyon of protection. Everything was flat, grainy, without character. He observed the houses on the other side, each one set back a safe distance from the street in a fallacy of anonymity and isolation. In truth none was immune. He wondered which one would be next.

Gil came up behind him.

"You don't have to stay," Doug said.

"I told you, we'll wait."

"And I told you to go. Now. Please."

Gil sighed but did not argue. "I'll come by tomorrow. Get some down time, if you can. I left more pills in case you need them." He made for the front door.

"Gil?"

"Yeah."

"Did I say thanks?"

"For what?"

As soon as the car drove away, Doug went for the gun in the workroom. He swung the cylinder out to be sure it was loaded and came back down. He pushed every door and window shut as tightly as possible, checking and rechecking the locks till his fingers hurt. When he was finished he stopped in the middle of the rug and turned around and around, trying to decide what to do next.

Erin's room was unavoidable, the door under the stairs still cowled in shadow like the entrance to a vault.

The doorknob was clammy, the musty air inside laced with the residue of her soap and incense. He drew the blinds up but the room remained dark. The hill beyond the retaining wall appeared deceptively innocent, covered by an apparently random pattern of ivy and wildflowers and doglegged trees. But Doug knew better. There was a meaning to be read there in the calligraphy of the vines, a message encoded in the iconography of every boulder and hanging branch, if only he could learn to decipher it. Somewhere he would find a clue. If he didn't, who would?

He turned away and surveyed the contents of the room. But he could differentiate only broad masses indicating the artifacts she had left behind, the posters on the walls reduced to charcoal sketches, the layers of her record collection stacked like shingles between rough, porous cinder blocks. A single LP hung atop the spindle, waiting to be played one more time. He could not leave it that way, like a freeze-frame of a black frisbee in midflight. He pressed the power switch of the turntable he had bought for Erin. Her thirteenth birthday, he remembered.

The apparatus completed its last cycle as the changer released the record onto the platter with a thump.

He circled the room, touching the bristles of a hairbrush, the fur of a stuffed animal, a jewelry box, pencils and pens, a feathered headband, felt hats, the lace on top of the dresser, belts hanging like mummified serpents, their buckles cold against his skin. He sat on the edge of the bed, her bed, as the record began to play, then lay back. He stuffed the gun under the pillows and stretched out, seeing the gray dawn creeping into the dining room on the other side of the open doorway, and let out all the breath in his lungs.

The record spun on, scratching and hissing through its final revolutions. He did not recognize the album at first, but halfway through the side the driving instrumentals gave way to a song he thought he knew. Yes, it was a selection from *Quadrophenia* by The Who. He had bought a copy of the rock opera himself when he was much younger; the track, "Love Reign O'er Me," had been a favorite of his a long time ago. As the recorded sound of rain and wind threatened to overwhelm Roger Daltry's impassioned vocals, Doug's eyes closed, and he slept.

After what could not have been more than a minute or two, he was jarred by a shrill and insistent howling. Only after he forced himself to sit up did he identify the source as Erin's electric alarm clock, screaming from across the bedroom for him to get out of bed. The stiletto hands warned him that it was ten minutes to seven.

She forgot to turn it off, he thought. She would have reset it herself, if she had been here. It was Saturday and there was no school to worry about today.

He lay there, unable to move, as the alarm cried out.

seven

Saturday morning

When Doug awoke again he was gasping for breath.
He was being strangled.
He wrenched one hand free and tore at his throat. A
powerful cord was tight around his neck, binding his
windpipe. He struggled to open his eyes but his face was
jammed into the pillow. He scissored his legs, hooked
the edge of the bed and bucked onto his back.

There was no one else in the room.

Somehow, he could not imagine how, he had become
entangled in the sheets. He had done it to himself. That
was all. He unwrapped the twisted cloth and removed it
from his head. He lay there breathing heavily, his heart
hammering hard enough to send angina pains shooting
through his chest. When the pain subsided, he sat up.

Now there was a ringing in his ears. He looked to the
clock, but the alarm was no longer buzzing. It was the
doorbell, he realized. He crawled off the end of the bed
and sighted into the living room.

On the other side of the picture window an unfamiliar
car was docked at the curb.

Go to hell, whoever you are, he thought.

He sat on his haunches and stared back at the approximation of himself in the dresser mirror. He hardly knew the face. It was bloated, the eyes pouched, the hair spiked like some determinedly dissolute teenager's. He felt gritty, as if covered with spider webs. He moved his hands to brush them away. Long hairs the color of spun gold, Erin's, had attached themselves to his eyebrows and beard stubble. Delicately he picked them off and noticed that his hands smelled of her, the special bouquet that always remained in his skin after she had touched him. He wiped his face; his forearm smelled the same, like Erin. He climbed out of the bed and tucked in his shirt. Even his clothes reeked of her.

Somewhere music was playing, faint as the sounds made by ants caught in a microscopic war. He dragged himself into the dining room and his heel made contact with the loose board in the floor. As if in reply, a creak echoed from the top of the first landing. He turned to the stairs, startled, half-expecting to see himself standing there. But it was only Lori.

She cringed, watching him furtively from the corner of the stairwell, her chin down against her collarbone.

"I heard somebody at the door," she said weakly.

"Yes." He shrugged, surprised that his voice was audible. "I heard it, too."

"Who was it? What did they want? Were they trying to break in?"

Doug saw her round, lidless eyes, her cowering stance and went at once to the stairs. He caught her up in his arms and sat with her on his lap. Her fingers gripped the back of his neck tightly enough to make holes there. From the floor above came the mechanistic vamping of electronic pop music.

"Of course they weren't. It was probably one of the neighbors wanting to—wondering if we needed anything."

"Do we?"

He didn't answer that. Then, "Mom's not awake, is she?"

"No. Lizzy's up. She's watching TV."

"Oh." It was out of the question, of course. So was such a discussion at this time, under these circumstances. But what other way was there to handle it? "Are you hungry, angel?"

"No."

"Good. I mean, neither am I." He cocked an ear at the hallway overhead. "You'd better tell your sister to turn the music down." Never mind, he thought, I'll tell her. "Mom needs her rest. She'll be resting a lot for the next few days. You and Lizzy and I will have to start taking care of things for ourselves, like cooking the meals, doing the shopping. You might even have to stay home from school for a while. Would you like that?"

"There's no school next week. It's spring vacation."

He shifted her on his lap. She wasn't very heavy but his lower back hurt. He prepared to stand up. "I'd better see how Lizzy's doing."

Lori did not want to let go. "She's doing okay. We're all doing okay. We are, aren't we?"

It was difficult to say it, let alone believe it. He nodded. "We're all going to help each other."

"Daddy?"

"I'll just be a minute. I have to—"

"What really happened?"

He exhaled shakily. He didn't know how to answer, but he couldn't lie to her. "I don't know. But I'm going to find out."

"When?"

"Right away."

"I'll help."

"No. Mom needs you here."

"But I know a lot of things. I know about the Lost Ones. Plus I know who Erin's friends were. I can—"

"The Lost Ones? I thought that was one of Lizzy's television programs."

"That's what grownups always think. But it's real. They live in the hills. Sometimes at night you can see their fires. They live in cardboard boxes. When it rains they have to come down. All the kids know about it."

"Have you ever seen them?"

"Well, no. But my friend Mara, she—"

"Then it's nothing to worry about. Is it?"

"Well then, I can talk to Erin's friends from school. Their names are—I think there's one named Justice or something like that. I can find out. I can ask them questions, get clues—"

"I'm going to do that."

"But they might not talk to you. You're an adult. Excuse me, but you are. They'll think you're a cop or something, that you want to get them in trouble."

"Nobody's going to get in any trouble." Unless they deserve it, he thought. "I'll turn everything over to the police. They'll handle it."

"*Please*? Can't I do anything? She was my sister." She tilted her head and her lip began to tremble as her eyes filled up and overflowed. "What's the matter, do you think I'm a child? Well, I'm not a little kid anymore. I know a lot. I'm not dumb—I'm not!"

She shrank to the corner of the landing and wept into her knees. Outside the skylight windows life went on as before. Just now a young boy, it looked like the Stavers child, churned down the sidewalk on a skateboard. A woman's high-pitched voice called from up the block. Richie hefted his skateboard and started home, while inside the Carson house a conversation that mimicked normalcy was in progress. Which was more absurd? Doug came back to Lori and took her head in his hands, tried to raise her face from the tear-stained nightgown. But she would not look at him.

"Stay out of it," he told her. "That's the best thing you can do. I'll take care of everything. Whatever has to be done, I'll do it. I promise."

"Oh, sure. Like you promised Mom."

These last words pierced his heart. "Stay out of it, I said. Give me your word. Do you hear me?" She would not answer. He let go of her head—his hands were shaking—and left her there for now.

Casey was sleeping in a fetal position. Her lips were dry and cracked from breathing through her mouth and the veins stood out on her hands. Her respiration was deep and raspy. For now there was nothing anyone could do to make it any easier for her. He moved on to the family room.

Elizabeth was squatting Indian-style before the television set. This time there was no bowl of cereal; a pretentious, neo-expressionist rock video filled the screen. He knelt and kissed her. She didn't respond. Her elfin face was faded and unreadable, like a line drawing made through carbon paper.

"Is it too loud?" she said.

"Maybe just a little," he said gently. "But it's all right this time." It was good that she was doing something. Surely Casey would not be able to hear anything for a while. For Elizabeth's sake—or was it for his own? —he made an effort to think and exist moment by moment. "What happened to your friend this morning? You know, the duck. What's his name? Dippy, wasn't it?"

"Dappy's not on anymore."

"Sure he is. You've got it on the wrong channel. Here, let me show you."

She stopped his hand. "I want to see this."

"I didn't know you liked MTV. I thought that was for teenagers."

"Erin used to watch it. It was her favorite program."

He closed his eyelids heavily, took a deep breath, counted while the tremor passed.

"Besides," Lizzy said, "Dappy's only going to get canceled, anyway."

"No, he isn't." It seemed important. He punched the selector box. On channel 7, her channel, a tennis match was in progress, with commentary by Renee Richards. The Fresh 'N Female Sanitary Napkins Doubles Championship for Women, proclaimed the billboard behind the court. "See? It's a sports special. Old Dap'll be back next week. You'll see." Tenderly he arranged her glorious tresses over her shoulders.

"Will not. Don't tell me that. I know he won't. That Bluesberry Cheesecake is gonna take over his whole show. He won't ever be back. Not ever. Not in a million, zillion years.'' She set her lips in a pinched line and gazed stonily at the screen, determined not to cry. Then she punched back to MTV and sat there, not moving a muscle even when the song was over.

When the doorbell rang again Casey was still down. It rang two, three, several more times over the next hour; he could not ignore it forever. The house filled up with women he did not know. One by one they maneuvered to follow after him with apologetic, birdlike footsteps whenever he went up to check on his wife. Occasionally now she muttered incoherently to him as from a fever dream, but she stayed down. He removed her sleeping pills from the medicine chest and hid them along with those Gil had left. An unnecessary precaution, he rationalized. But he did it.

The women—Mrs. Bauman from next door, a hairsprayed maven from the Beaumont Canyon Association, a young woman named Judy from Beverly Hills Presbyterian, which they had never attended, several unblinking housewives who claimed to have met Casey at the Convenient Food Mart, the dry cleaners, the savings and loan, the PTA—seated themselves apprehensively on the outer limits of the sofa and chairs, their hands folded nervously away from the notions on the tables and shelves, as though worried that anything they might touch could not tolerate the handling and would break. Did he need the washing done? Would Lori and Elizabeth like to come home with them for lunch, a snack, to play with other children? How about dinner? There were casseroles ready in refrigerators, extra bags of groceries waiting in trunks of cars, offers of day care and even sleepovers in spare guest rooms. *If Mrs. Carson doesn't mind* . . . . He had the impression that nothing he could ask would be too much, and that only made him more uncomfortable.

Where had they come from? How had the news traveled so fast? Not until someone mentioned the newspaper did he understand that part of it; he opened the

morning edition and saw the story but could not read it
through. It was eerie. So soon. Was there a column inch
already reserved on the obituary page for his own name,
as well?

He had not guessed that such a tightly-knit community existed in the canyon, ready to pull together when a
crisis struck one of its own. As usual, he had misjudged
his resources. But he was not quite ready to accept their
help. Even the girls kept instinctively apart from so
much overweening attention, positioning themselves
safely under the stairs or loitering half-concealed behind
doors, prepared to take cover at the first raised voice.
Intellectually Doug knew that he should appreciate his
neighbors' willingness to help. In actual fact he wanted
them out of his house, and the sooner the better. He
paced between the hall and the bar and excused himself
as often as possible to sit alone in Erin's bathroom with
his head in his hands, feeling his joints knot up as he
wiped away the cold sweat of nausea with a wet towel.

The bell rang yet again, and then someone was tapping politely on the bathroom door.

"Yes."

"Um, Mrs. Bedrosian from the carpool is here. She
wants to know how Mom's doing."

Was Lori relaying a message or asking to know for
herself? He heard the *tsk*ing of voices gentle as doves'
and the whisking of nylon stockings. "I'll be right out."

He splashed cold water and toweled off. When he
came into the living room, the gaggle of high-strung
women had gathered around a large, somewhat butch
matron in a polyester pantsuit. She looked over their
heads, spotted him and started swinging her hips across
the carpet. She was coming for him. He had nowhere to
run.

"YOU POOR MAN!" Her voice, a foghorn funneled
through a whiskey throat, made the china rattle and set
up a distressing harmonic reverberation in the wine
glasses. From behind her waist peered an anorexic teenager besotted with Clearasil. "IT'S ALL SO SHOCK-
ING, ISN'T IT? IS THERE ANYTHING I CAN DO?"

"No."

"DO YOU NEED HELP WITH THE ARRANGE-
MENTS? MY BROTHER-IN-LAW'S COUSIN IS
PUBLIC RELATIONS DIRECTOR FOR THE DRY
LAWN CHAIN OF SLUMBER EMPORIUMS. I CAN
CALL . . ."

"No."

"ARE YOU SURE? IT'S NO TROUBLE. IF
YOU'D LIKE TO TALK IT OVER WITH YOUR
WIFE FIRST. . . . HOW IS CAREY HOLDING UP?"

"She's resting," said Mrs. Bauman, gingerly touching the amazon's elbow to restrain her. "But I'm told
she's taking it remarkably well. She's very brave. Perhaps later, when she's had time to—"

"WHAT A TRAGEDY! WHY, I WAS TELLING
MY SARA ON THE WAY OVER, WHAT A TER-
RIBLE, TERRIBLE THING THIS IS FOR US ALL!
SHARON WAS OUR FAVORITE. SHE WAS MY
GEM. THE CARPOOL WON'T BE THE SAME
WITHOUT HER. WHY, WE'LL HAVE TO FIND
SOMEONE NEW NOW! GOD KNOWS WHO WE'LL
GET THIS TIME. WE ALL MISS HER SO VERY,
VERY MUCH. WILL YOU TELL YOUR WIFE
THAT FOR ME, MR. CARSON?"

"No."

Doug retreated to the dining room and flexed his
arms against the door jamb to keep from charging her
headfirst. Just then he heard a labored thump-slide
from above.

"Mom!" said Lori.

Elizabeth clamored halfway up the stairs and flung
her arms around her mother's legs. "Mommy, Mommy
. . . !"

Casey came down slowly, holding the rail for support. In her other hand, clasped against her chest and
partially concealed by the green terry-cloth robe, was a
pair of scissors. It was the long, ten-inch German steel
model from her sewing basket, the one she never let the
children use because it was too sharp. The blades were
open wide. She was holding one side as if it were the
handle of a knife. Doug wanted to go to her but was

afraid that if he moved too fast he would cause her to cut herself.

"Come here, Lizzy," he said. "That's it, come to me. Casey, honey, what are you doing?"

"Something," she said. "Something happened. Did it?"

"Let me help you," he said. "Let's sit down. Why don't you let me take those?" He held out his hands, inches away from the flashing steel points.

"I can't," she said. "Something. I can't re . . . remem . . ."

"Um, would you all please leave?" said Lori. "My mother's not feeling well. She'll talk to you tomorrow. Just go home for now, all right?"

The large woman attempted to get through. Doug managed to keep her away, then backpedaled her forcefully through the living room. The other women peeled off, embarrassed. They sent Doug looks of quiet sympathy as they gathered up purses and car keys.

He heard a snipping sound.

"Mom," Lori was saying, "what are you *doing*?"

Doug cut back through the hall to the kitchen. He reached for the phone. Gil would know what to do. The receiver came away too easily from the wall. It slipped out of his hand and fell into the sink, smashing a plate. The cord had been severed.

"Case? What did you do that for?"

She evaded him, dodging and weaving over the carpet in a simulation of Brownian motion. "Don't stop me. I have to cut them," she explained. "Strangers. They call up and say things to me, things that aren't true. Lies, all lies. I don't want to hear any more of their lies."

Bobbing in the doorway, she noticed the departing guests. Her eyes strained to focus. Lori and Elizabeth had already backed off. They were standing to one side, hugging each other, their faces animated with terror.

"Who is that?" said Casey.

"No one, honey. They came by to help. Case, give me the scissors. Please."

"That one," said Casey, pointing the blades. "Who . . . ?"

"Right, that's Mrs. Bedrosian. You remember. Here, let me—"

"The other one." She indicated the daughter, who had her hands full helping her mother through the door. Casey squinted. "Erin? Is that Erin?"

Lori sobbed.

"Why, it is, isn't it? Nita?" In a moment of lucidity she recognized the woman. "Why are you taking my baby away?"

Oblivious to the situation, Mrs. Bedrosian stumped back in and addressed Casey in her normal manner. "CAREY, HOW ARE YOU? I WAS GOING TO CALL, BUT I THOUGHT I'D DROP BY INSTEAD. IT WAS ON THE WAY. YOU KNOW MY BIG GIRL, DON'T YOU? SHE'S MY PRIDE AND JOY. SAY HELLO, SARA."

"Hi," said Sara, bug-eyed.

Casey's brow wrinkled. "You're not Erin. I thought you were." She was trying to understand. "I saw the ring. What are you doing with my Erin's ring?"

Sara hid her hand behind her dress.

Casey waved the scissors.

Sara drew back with a yelp. "Erin gave it to me."

"No, she didn't," Casey said. "She wouldn't do that."

"She did!"

"Doug, this evil child has stolen something of Erin's. Help me get it back."

Casey slashed, missing by millimeters. Her other hand darted out and gripped Sara's wrist in a death-lock. She aimed and slashed again, ready to cut the girl's finger off if necessary.

Sara bawled loudly.

"WHO ARE YOU CALLING EVIL? IF YOU WANT TO KNOW THE TRUTH ABOUT THAT DAUGHTER OF YOURS . . . !"

A scuffle ensued. Sara's mother stuck out her chest in what passed for courage among the thick-witted, prepared to do battle with cold steel to defend her idiot daughter's honor. Doug crossed the room in three steps and got into it before any harm was done. He bent

Casey's arm back and the scissors and ring dropped into his hand. Too large to properly fit any finger of Sara's except her thumb, it had come loose at the first tug.

"Keep your old ring," said Sara. "I never liked it that much, anyway!"

Mrs. Bedrosian towered over Doug. Then, somewhere behind her massive forehead, a dim inkling of place and circumstance must have occurred to her. She stood there seething with frustration, huffing like a beached whale.

"Go," Doug told her. "Now."

She sputtered, turned on her heel—it was the first time Doug had actually seen someone do that—and propelled Sara out onto the porch.

"YOU'D BEST GET THAT WIFE OF YOURS TO A PSYCHIATRIST IF YOU ASK ME, MISTER! SHE —SHE'S NOT WELL!"

Doug slammed the door.

"It was Erin's," Casey panted. "It was, it was . . ." Her knees gave out and she sank into his arms.

Lori ran over and took the scissors from him.

Elizabeth observed from the dining room, fingers in mouth, as he lifted his wife. Casey's arms continued to flail but the blows were rubbery, ineffective. Before he could get her to the couch her backbone went straight in a hysterical contraction.

"No," she screamed, "no, no, no, no . . . !"

She beat him about the head and shoulders, struck the lamp, her feet kicking over the vase and collection of crystal. He used all his strength trying to calm her but could not. He released her onto the cushions and spread his body over hers. Until she passed out all that could have been seen by the cars passing outside the picture window was the endless flailing of her arms and legs as he attempted to turn her face while Lori and Elizabeth added their weight to his. "Listen to me, only to me, shh, listen to me," he said over and over as curtains, porcelain, glassware and every other fragile relic of their lives came crashing down, the fragments exploding and falling over the intractable knot of their bodies like rain.

eight

Tuesday

By the third morning Casey had cut the cord to every phone in the house.

All along Doug had not known whether or not she would go to the funeral. From Saturday to Sunday he had sat with her nonstop through hour after harrowing hour, talking, not talking, sleeping, not sleeping, touching, afraid to touch, comforting, silently agonizing, while he slowly bled to death inside and the upstairs became as cold and insular as the waiting room of a mortuary. They cried together, escaped into brief periods of trivial conversation that under normal circumstances would have been reassuring, fell exhausted into delirium, only to awaken side by side, hearts beating in tempo, convinced that their home and everything in it had begun to decompose while they were down, melting out from under them as they slept. On Sunday she said she wanted to go to church, but she could not get dressed and make it down the stairs in time. Finally the children could keep themselves apart from her no longer and moved in, tentatively at first, to take his place. On

Tuesday morning, while Mattie Stavers cooked breakfast and Gil waited for him in the car, Doug cut himself
shaving; the face in the mirror was so ravaged that he
could not begin to mend its disintegrating appearance.

The police lieutenant listened indulgently and then
told him to get in touch with an organization called
Parents Against Teenage Suicides. It was all so pat.
Doug knocked an ashtray onto the floor in disgust,
tipped over a wastebasket and almost came to blows
with the commanding officer before giving up on them
for good. At last and this late in life it occurred to him
that the true nature of their job was to placate the community they served with a program of swift cosmetic
pacification; anything more drastic might lead them far
enough beneath the surface to disrupt and destabilize
the wheels-within-wheels that allowed the well-oiled
machinery of such a privileged economy to flourish
without opposition. If examined too closely, cracks
might appear at the bottoms of the swimming pools and
low-rise office buildings wherein this sector conducted
its rarified commerce; like the skull grinning behind a
facelift, the bones of those already sacrificed to the
widening fault over which this enclave was so precariously balanced might begin to disgorge at the slightest
provocation, sending the whole tremulous construction
tumbling into the abyss. Embittered and sickened with
pure loathing, he accepted Erin's clothing and personal
effects and left the police station for the last time without looking back.

"Well?" asked Gil, as if he already knew the answer.

"Well what?" Doug rested his stiff neck against the
seat and tried to concentrate on the neutral fabric of the
headliner. I should have known, he thought, never to
expect more than a grunt from a pig.

On the way back they stopped by the white-haired
boy's house. Again there was no answer. The blinds
were drawn, the doors and windows sealed to the world.
The police weren't interested in questioning him. So it
was up to Doug.

"He's in there. He got out of Juvenile Hall five days

ago—I know that much. If the old lady didn't bring him back here, where did he go?"

"Maybe he ran away," said Gil. "Does it matter?"

"Of course it matters. He didn't break in, try to get to Erin for no reason. He wanted to tell her something. He couldn't make her listen any other way. I should have paid more attention. He was trying to warn her."

"About what? I don't see the connection."

"You weren't there."

At home, Mattie had the tea service out, and Lester Bauman and his wife were there to drive anyone who wanted to ride with them. Lester looked worried; he had tried repeatedly to call, but when no one answered all morning—no one could, with the lines cut—he backed his El Dorado down the driveway and came to the door. Lori remembered her grandmother's funeral and got out her dark blue party dress and black patent leather shoes; Elizabeth followed the example with her very best clothes, which she ironed herself. With the puffed sleeves and ribbon in her hair she looked like a distraught Alice about to descend into the rabbit hole.

Somehow Casey reached down into herself for a last reserve of strength she had not known she possessed. The same reserve that would have enabled her to run back into a burning house or lift the wheels of an automobile provided the presence of mind for this last impossible act. She came down unassisted with her chin high under the veil and went out to the Mercedes without a word.

The trip there and the period in and around the grounds waiting for it to begin and then for it to be over seemed to be spent in another dimension outside the usual boundaries of space and time. Certain details registered on the mind so as never to be forgotten: the wreath from Erin's school with the pasted-on letters like silver merit stars already peeling from the black ribbon, the unexpected clash of colors in the flowers strewn about the bier, and over everything the sickly-sweet perfume of tuberose. The ceremony itself had the artificiality of a backlot diorama, a contrived composite of special effects complete with extras and the Carsons matted awkwardly into the shot by some unseen but all-powerful second-unit director.

Doug fingered Erin's ring, the star sapphire retrieved from Sara Bedrosian, like a pebble in his pocket as he filed past the casket. He wished that he had something, a special ring of his own, perhaps, to leave with her, but now he would never have the chance. He tried not to think of it as he followed Casey back to the pew and turned around, hoping to spot any of her classmates. They might be able to help.

He did see one teenager, a long-maned boy, by the side exit. If he could get to him as soon as the services ended, learn his name, ask a few crucial questions later . . . yes, he would have to do it on the way out. He'd approach him in exactly the right way, lay an easy hand on his shoulder so as not to frighten him off. Introduce himself without accusation, then try to coax from him the vital piece of information that would give everything meaning. Either that or he would have to go through Erin's personal phone book (had she kept one?), dial each number, explain who he was and what he wanted to know before they could hang up. But how could he get the answers he needed if he did not know what questions to ask? Was she into drugs? Who had she been seeing the last few weeks? *This is Erin's father. Well, not her real father, more like a very close friend. More than that, really . . . . Listen, I'm not interested in busting you. If you'll just tell me . . .* But tell him what? *What*?

Casey refused his arm but Lori and Elizabeth crowded him on either side, nearly tripping him with their small rounded shoes. When he put his arms over their shoulders to steady them they pushed into him as if to hide under his coat. He said something to them then, it must have been something inconsequential and ineffectual as usual because they would not answer or even look at him. Yet they did not leave his side. On the steps outside they lagged behind. Then Elizabeth broke and ran ahead, as Lori placed her hand in his and squeezed with all of her might.

Where was Elizabeth going? Casey stopped in her
tracks with her legs apart, as though braced for an
earthquake. He could not see her face.

"Honey, are you . . . ?"

A man was walking up the steps toward them. He had
Elizabeth. He held her under the legs and her arms were
around his neck. Doug felt a stab of pain in his kidneys
as his back steeled in a primitive defensive stance.

The man came up and blocked the steps as the teenager left for the parking lot. Doug was powerless to stop
the boy. He wanted to take Elizabeth back and hurry
ahead. She was within arm's reach but she was not
going to let go of the other man. Doug flushed as adren-
aline charged his blood.

"Casey," said the man.

His wife slipped her hand into Doug's and would not
speak.

"Daddy," Elizabeth wept into the man's neck,
"you're here, you're here . . . ."

The words devastated Doug. His chest began to give
way as though in the grip of an unstoppable force. His
skin prickled.

Lori pressed herself between Doug and Casey and
said, her eyes never leaving the ground, "Why did you
have to come? Nobody cares, if you didn't know. I
don't care, Mom doesn't care. Erin didn't care. Why
don't you go back across the country to your new house
and your girlfriend? Why don't you do that?"

He was a compact, stocky man, with the shine of hy-
pertension on his receding forehead and the drawn vertical lines that appear on the faces of middle-aged men
who subject themselves to strenuous jogging schedules.
The tendons bulged on his neck as he shifted Elizabeth
to free one arm.

"Lori, that's not true! I called him and he came,
didn't he? He came! Daddy came . . . ."

"Oh, yeah? Well, where was he when we wanted him
to be here? We don't need him anymore, ever!"

The girls' father reached out but Lori ducked her
head. *If he makes a move to hurt her,* thought Doug, *I'll
kill him where he stands.*

"Hello, Lori," said the man.

Geoff, Doug thought. So this is the famous Geoff.

"And this must be Douglas, isn't it?" His voice was gravelly, his smile case-hardened and gleaming.

Casey pulled hard on Doug's fingers. She wanted to get away.

But Doug stood his ground. Like it or not, there was a bond between them. It would have been easier to deny that it existed, but it was there, brought home by the tragedy. He extracted his right hand from Lori's grip, meeting the man's eyes without flinching.

"I just wanted to say one thing," said the man.

Doug succeeded at last in overcoming his old angers. There was no point to any of it now. The list of grudges and debts lifted from him like a great burden winging away into the eggshell sky. As it left him there was nothing to take its place. He felt open, clean and empty, light as a feather and no longer chained to the resentments he had lived with for so long. He held out his hand.

"Thanks," said the man, "for taking such good care of my children." He nodded toward the chapel. "Especially Erin. You cock sucker."

He bared his perfect, bone-white teeth at Doug from behind a crooked smile, his eyes burning like Greek fire.

When they got home Lori waited around while Doug and Dr. McClay settled Mom and Lizzy upstairs. That took what was left of the afternoon. Lori changed out of her dress and lay down in her bathrobe. When Doug finally came in she told him she was really tired. She even yawned a couple of times. He kissed her and closed the door and left her there in the gathering dusk. It was easy.

As soon as she heard him walk away, she got moving. First she closed the latch. Then she arranged her pillows under the quilt, hung up her robe and went through her dresser drawers to find something that would work.

After several false starts she decided on her K-Swiss tennis shoes, her tightest jeans and her Heaven sweatshirt with the cut-off neck. But when she finished changing and posed before the full-length mirror, she knew that the outfit would never do. Even though the legs of the jeans had been taken in as severly as Erin's, the effect was all wrong.

She'd never pass; she still looked like a kid, not a teenager. On the verge of despair, she rushed to her bathroom and began applying makeup, thickening her lashes and shading the lids, lining her eyes till they were ridiculously wide and almond-shaped, nearly Egyptian. She parted her bangs in the middle, combed her hair back, piled it high on her head, drew it into a ponytail, on the side, on both sides. Nothing was right. As a last resort she grabbed her manicure scissors and started cutting. She bobbed it below her ears, but that only made her look like a little Dutch girl. She kept cutting, making it shorter and shorter to keep it even, then hacked it off in chunks until she saw what she had done. Her eyes burned as the mascara started to run.

No, she thought, *I won't cry—I won't! This is no time to be a baby!*

She mussed it into a wild mop and left it that way. It was too late to change her mind. She reapplied eye liner until her face was like a clown's. She gathered up her long hair from the sink as tenderly as if it were the last vestiges of her sacrificed childhood and hid it in the bottom of the wastebasket. No matter how it grew back she would never look the same again.

She went to the closet one more time. Two insoluble problems remained: her figure and her height. She put on one of Erin's old flannel shirts and buckled a belt just above her waist. Cinched in, with the overshirt buttoned halfway and fanned out like that, well, it was the best she could do. There was nothing she could do about her height except to change her tennies for her white pumps, the ones with the stepped heels; they didn't add much, but every inch counted.

She heard voices in the kitchen, talking about Mom and the University Medical Center, where the doctor worked. That was good; if they took her there and didn't get back till late that would give Lori plenty of

time to do what she had to do and get home before they
noticed she was gone. Even if she was sure they'd notice
she'd have to do it. There was no way she was going to
be let out of the house anytime soon. Mom and Mattie
Stavers and Mrs. Bauman would see to that. They were
right to worry, but they had it all wrong. Lori wasn't
afraid. As long as she stayed clear of the hills she
wouldn't have to think about the Lost Ones. Unless it
rained, and it wasn't going to. Of course it hadn't
rained last Friday night when Erin went to babysit—but
that was something she was going to find out about, one
way or another, before the night was over.

As she was climbing out the window she had a flash
of inspiration. She shimmied back in, found her white
jacket, uncapped her Carter's Marks-A-Lot and drew a
big circle on the back. She made an A inside, crossed it
all the way to the sides of the circle, then retraced the
design until it was so dark you could read it from a
block away. It would be a kind of advertisement, she
hoped.

She dropped from the sill to the front yard, scooted
under the picture window and down through the daisies
and ivy to where the sidewalk started again on the other
side of the hedge to the next yard. Once she was out of
sight she crossed the street so that she would be facing
the oncoming traffic and began the long trek down
Beaumont. She ran a few blocks, then walked the rest of
the way after her mouth got dry. It was two-and-a-half
miles to Sunset but it was all downhill and she made it in
thirty minutes.

She caught the RTD #2 Westbound in front of the
hotel and rode the short distance past UCLA and into
the Village, getting off at Westwood and Le Conte. She
stashed two quarters for the return trip in her back
pocket along with the dog-eared schedule from Erin's
room. The last bus left from the corner in front of Flor-
sheim Shoes at 11:38. She prayed that would be long
enough. She zipped her sports wallet with the rest of her
money in the side pocket of her jacket and headed
toward Weyburn.

The sky was turning from mauve to cobalt blue and signs were coming on everywhere, transforming Westwood Boulevard into a giant neon boardwalk. At the end of the block firefly bulbs winked at her from the trees outside the Hungry Tiger. Overhead streetlights buzzed as though about to short-circuit, luring pillars of lonely moths to drub against the fixtures until the air was dusted with powder from their torn wings. The streets were filling up fast with restless teens decked out in full competition regalia; it was Easter vacation week and no time for anyone to be content with adventures conducted by proxy over Princess telephones.

The traffic was already so bad that she took her life in her hands even crossing with the signal. Droves of Trans-Ams, Camaros and metallic van conversions rallied at the starting line of the crosswalk, revving up for a fast break. In no hurry to challenge the overloaded intersection, a white-gloved lady cop dallied in the doorway of the Bi-Rite Drug Store, nibbling from a roll of Certs. Lori made it safely to the curb in front of Croissants USA, and felt her nose lifting to the aroma of warm chocolate chips wafting up the block from Mrs. Field's Cookies. She had forgotten to eat anything since breakfast. She ignored the pangs and hurried on.

She swam against the milling crowds, anxious to recognize a familiar face. But the fixed, all-purpose grins became indistinguishable one from another as soon as she approached. It was hours until curfew and overeager fifth- and sixth-graders shared the sidewalks with parading teenagers out to score fast food and phone numbers, all the while intent on disposing of the spending money they had wheedled out of their parents in as short a time as possible. At the Postermat she saw the twins, Cathy and Kathy, from Mrs. South's class, but they were too busy trying on Shuttle Shoes to notice her. Which was just as well; she would rather not be seen by anybody who might tell.

The bodies became dense and impassable; someone stepped on her toe and an unguarded cigarette ash brushed the sleeve of her jacket, knocking loose a

shower of orange sparks. Ahead, a line had formed
around the block from the Bruin Theater, where
Camping Out starring Stephen Nichols and Jon Cryer
was playing. On the other side of the street a crush of
older college kids waited for a sneak preview of the new
Stephen King film, *It*, spreading off the curbs between
parked cars as lustrous as hard candy. There was no way
to get through. Lori turned left on Broxton, working
her way back to the main drag.

The Regent was showing something called *El Diablo*
starring a couple of old actors she had never heard of.
There was no line outside, only a straggle of middle-
aged wine-and-cheese types adjusting their eyeglass
leashes in the lobby. Taco Bell and Winchell's Donuts
had been taken over by derelicts and shopping cart
ladies. (Where do they go when everything is closed? she
wondered.) AAHS was asquirm with Japanese tourists
buying up scented erasers and cute T-shirts by the
armload. Rastafarian panhandlers and beach bums with
matted hair and sunburned noses frightened people
away from the entrance to Wherehouse Records, while
the patio next door bustled with Iranians in silk body
shirts hawking earrings and gold-filled neck chains. The
street was temporarily closed to automobiles to prevent
party cruisers from completely overrunning the Village
and blocking the high-priced restaurants and clothing
shops from plying their upscale trade, but there was no
way to stem the foot traffic. No one took any notice of
Lori in her chopped hair and anarchy jacket; when they
lowered their eyes long enough to see her at all as she
scampered by under their linked arms, she registered as
only one more disaffected microbopper on her way to
Burger King for a hastily shared clove cigarette with her
new best friends. So far she had succeeded in moving in-
conspicuously through it all, but unfortunately so had
every other underaged pedestrian. She would never find
any of Erin's friends; the natives here looked impossibly
alike, an army of gene-splices forced from the same in-
bred culture.

She broke from the sidewalk and crossed the Glendale

Federal square, where a hungry legion of blissed-out
fakirs beat gourds and tambourines in a hypnotic frenzy
of recruitment, and dashed toward the McDonald's at
Westwood and Kinross. That was where Erin used to
hang out after school or on Saturday afternoons
whenever she came up with a good enough story to convince Mom to let her stay out for a few hours. Lori was
dangerously close to giving up. Where else was there to
look?

She ordered a large fries and a medium orange drink
and picked one of the front tables so she could watch
the street. The usual coterie of junior high posers
manned the tables around her, swapping rumors of
parties as they eyed the sidewalk with a cultivated
boredom. Two guys with crewcuts and a girl with
double-pierced ears loitered by the parking meter in
front, trying to con a UCLA exchange student into buying them a six-pack from the 7-Eleven two doors down;
when the student finally stopped smiling and begged
off, they sat down outside by the door with their heads
against the glass and waited for another sucker. Lori
decided that she had never seen them before, but she
couldn't be sure.

She dipped her French fries and checked off each face
in the passing horde, but it was no use. It was a dumb
idea in the first place, she told herself. She'd never spot
any of Erin's friends, not even if she managed to avoid
the curfew sweep and sat here all night. She stopped
chewing in midbite and stared at the tabletop, miserable
with failure. How could she have thought she would
find out anything this way? Even if she did see someone
from her sister's crowd there was no reason to believe
they would talk to her. Age was all that mattered here;
they didn't trust anyone under twelve or over sixteen,
and then not unless you were dressed exactly right. They
looked for details that were the badges of their kind.
There was no way Lori could hope to get it right. *Dumb,
dumb!*

"Look at me."

Lori dropped down in her seat so fast that her orange

drink tipped over. Fortunately the lid was still on. The voice was so close she felt puffs of breath like bullets whizzing by her cheek. She looked up guiltily, as if Mrs. South had materialized over her shoulder to catch her doodling instead of doing her homework.

"Wh-what?"

"My God, you are, aren't you? I knew it."

Lori faced the huge green eyes of a sallow teenaged girl with short, tortured hair peeking out from under a black leather cap. "Um, do I know you?"

"It's that nose. I'd know it anywhere. Yeah . . ."

There was something about her. Yes, it was that girl, the one Erin had liked so much—it was! She had come to the house once and Lori remembered. Despite the hair she was sure now. Her heart soared. She stammered to come up with a name. It tingled on the tip of her tongue.

"What's wrong with my nose?" she asked. She felt a big grin stretching her face. "Are you—is your name Angel?"

"Close. Shit, I knew it. I saw you when you came in. It must run in the family. Let's see, you're Lizzy, right?"

"Lori." She let the insult pass and climbed higher in her seat. "And your name's . . ." What was it? ". . . An-Angie. You know my sister, don't you?" Knew, she corrected herself. It was hard to remember; it didn't seem real yet.

"Erin? Shit, she was the only friend I had in that whole school. The place'll be a fucking graveyard without her. That's why I'm never going back."

The questions Lori had practiced came bubbling to the surface now. But where to start? The first ones, about Erin's friends and the boys she dated and where she went when she sneaked out at night, stuck in her throat and made it sore. "I know" was all she could say.

Angie ran her hand up the back of Lori's neck, fluffing the short hairs. The hand was cold. "I like your hair," she said absently. She took off her cap and arranged it jauntily on Lori's head. "Here. Knock yourself out. You look great—really. Anyway, I gotta jam. There's nobody here but a bunch of zombies. Except you, of course." She did not laugh. "See you sometime, okay? Don't take any shit off anybody." She started for the door and the sidewalk, where a grungy-looking old lady in a moth-eaten sweater was handing out religious pamphlets.

"No!" It wasn't fair. Lori hadn't had a chance to ask her anything. "I mean, you can't go yet."

Angie came back over to the table. She must be high, Lori thought. She was so slow and her eyes were like black holes. Angie blinked lethargically at the tray, at the picture of Ronald McDonald in the cockpit of his own space shuttle, at the ripped open plastic packets oozing ketchup thick as cold blood, trying to zero in on Lori's face amid the distracting circus decor. "You miss your big sister, don't you?"

"What kind of a question is that?"

"Sure you do." Angie nodded knowingly. Her jaws were sunken and her neck was so thin it could hardly support her head. "A lot?"

"What do you think?"

Angie looked right through Lori. "If she could see you like this, all worried, pushed out of shape . . ." She touched Lori under the chin the way the school nurse did when deciding whether to send someone home. "You know, if she could, she'd probably tell you not to let yourself get so bummed out."

"What good is that supposed to do me?" said Lori, her voice too shrill. "Why don't you just ask her for me the next time you see her?" She jumped up from the table, scattering French fries like amputated yellow fingers daubed with red.

"Why don't you ask her yourself?"

"Why don't you shut up?"

Angie reached out dodderingly. "Hey, Lizzy, mellow out. I'm only trying to—"

"Don't touch me! How do you know what Erin would say? Was she *your* sister? *Was she*?"

"Listen, I'm only trying to help you." Angie came to some sort of decision and bumped the door, trying to get it open for both of them. "Come on."

"Where are we going?"

"To see Erin, where do you think?"

The evening had gone cool all of a sudden. Sorority girls in shorts pumped along the sidewalk on legs puckered like the surfaces of golf balls. A campus patrol car passed, the whirling red bubble machine on top highlighting Angie's hair in a flaming aureole. Lori trotted to catch her. When she came up even she swung one fist and hit Angie in the back as hard as she could. The skinny teenager almost caved in under the blow.

"All right," said Lori, "I get it, it's a sick joke, okay? Only it's not very funny. *You're* not very funny! I was going to ask you to help. I thought maybe you'd want to find out what happened to Erin, too. But I was wrong. I don't know why she chose you for a friend. What do you care? You didn't even go to her funeral."

"I didn't have to. I knew where she was."

Lori drew back her fist again, aiming at the cadaverous face. "Why don't you make another joke about it? Go on, I'd like to see you try!"

Angie barely dodged the next blow and used her height to catch Lori from behind before the kicking started. People were watching. Angie dragged her out of the way.

"Listen, you little shit," she whispered in Lori's ear, "don't you know when somebody's trying to do you a favor? Now do you want to see your sister or not?"

Lori twisted one arm free and clawed at the girl's bony wrist. "Fuck you!" she snarled. "Fuck fuck fuck fuck *fuck* you!"

"Well then, fuck you, too, kid," said Angie, and let her go.

Lori was breathing so hard she thought she was going to have an asthma attack. As she stood there trembling, staring daggers at the teenager's back, the lady in the moth-eaten sweater pressed a pamphlet into her hand. Lori glanced at it as she caught her breath.

"*. . . Go ye into all the world, & preach the Gospel to every living creature.*" —Mk. 16:15

"*. . . To comfort all who mourn . . .*" —Isa. 61:2

"*. . . Seek ye first the kingdom of GOD, & His righteousness . . .*" —Mt. 6:33

What was that supposed to be about? She looked up. The old lady was gone. Angie was free-floating across the intersection at Lindbrook. At that pace she would never make it before the light changed. Lori let the pamphlet go on the breeze and followed after.

She couldn't think of anything else to do.

Angie's route led south of Wilshire and out of the Village, up a sidestreet beyond the Metro Theater, then south again to the parking lot of All-American Burgers, where a carload of homeboys from Pacoima were hustling four blond cheerleaders in a Volkswagen convertible, then east toward the simple residences near St. Paul the Apostle School. A few more blocks and she turned west again. She wove a crooked trail past quiet houses where cellophane-wrapped lampshades glowed yellow as jack-o'-lanterns and blue television faces lisped behind closed drapes. The sky bloomed with the lights of the Village, projecting a ruddy dome across the horizon and tinting the golden statue high atop the Mormom Temple with tongues of rusty fire, as though from the reflection of a burning oasis in the electrified wilderness below. Angie limped to the corner, tarrying under the lamppost to regain her sense of direction; or was it only to make sure Lori had time to catch up? As she followed, Lori had the unsettling sensation that she herself was being trailed by someone who did not want to be seen. Could it be the old woman in the tattered sweater? A fragment of ripped paper blew along the gutter, catching around Lori's ankles. She took too long kicking free. When she looked up again, Angie had disappeared.

Lori heard worn shoes shuffling over the pavement, echoing between the Spanish-style bungalows around the corner ahead. Or was the sound coming from somewhere at her back? She folded her collar over her neck and urged herself forward, as if to a secret rendez-vous of unspeakable significance.

As she circled back toward the boulevard the sound of moving cars was strangely reassuring. This stretch of Westwood was much quieter than the Village, a dead-space between the frenetic bustle of Wilshire and the railroad tracks that marked the Santa Monica Boul-evard alternate. The storefront travel agencies, second-hand bookstores, beauty parlors and ethnic bakeries had closed up shop for the night, with only a few bars and drive-thru food stops remaining open for the neigh-borhood trade. Not even the used record shop would be doing business at this hour. Lori approached, keeping to the lawns and driveways, and heard a crunching in the gravel of the alley across the street.

There was Angie, her bleached, uneven skullcap of hair beckoning a way past shadowed garages and the back windows of shuttered shops. A few yards down she slipped between a battered line of Dempster Dumpsters and emerged into the narrow parking area behind a row of loading docks. Lori could not figure out where she was going. Then she saw neon lettering over one rear en-trance, and a congestion of parked cars that filled every available inch of the rest of the alley. As Lori crossed and squeezed through the densely-packed fenders and bumpers, she was able to read the illuminated script, a blue circle with two words inside:

CLUB ZERO.

The lines in the circle, behind the words, looked like this:

Angie went to the rear door and opened it. There was a burst of muffled music. Then the door closed, the sign arcing over the afterimage of her head like a halo of static electricity.

Lori sideslipped between the buildings to the street. The other side, the front, gave the impression of one

more closed shop. The windows were papered with
flyers for local bands, some of the names of which Lori
would be embarrassed to say out loud. She cupped her
hands and tried to see through the cracks but it was too
dark inside. Yet she knew the club was open. Angie had
gone in through the door in back. Lori had seen that,
hadn't she?

She returned to the parking lot. Now there were
voices as one more car entered the alley, tires spitting
rocks.

"That's it . . ."

"W'll all ri-i-ight!"

The car parked illegally and two guys with zippered
clothes and long hair on one side of their heads got out.
They made straight for the door under the circle. The
music pulsed loudly when they went in; then the alley
was quiet again. Before it closed all the way this time,
Lori caught the doorknob.

Inside, the two guys were showing their IDs to a pair
of hands behind a ticket table. The atmosphere was
smoky and thick with glowworm lights. Lori couldn't
hear what they were saying. The music formed a solid
barrier between her ears and the moving bodies; it was a
record Erin had, "For Your Love" by The Yardbirds.
She could only see the hands pointing a flashlight at
open wallets, palms-up gestures of explanation. The
hands took the wallets aside to show them to someone
else. *The time to hesitate is through*, said the Doors song
of Erin's. Lori pulled the cap over her ears, puffed up
her courage and eased the door open a few more inches,
wide enough for her to slide through.

She cut hard to the left till her shoulder bumped a
wall, then dropped down to a low crouch in the corner.
She couldn't see anything but a misty outline of her
knees and feet. She elevated one hand very slowly and
raised the brim of the cap. She still couldn't see
anything. She was below the end of a table. She flexed
her legs and rose a few degrees.

The lamps along the walls were so faint she thought
they must be about to burn out. Then she realized that

they were supposed to be that way. They were the purple kind you saw over fish tanks in pet stores, the ones that put out a soft, blurry, underwater light that made your teeth and fingernails a funny color, and they were shining over posters printed in that droopy, distorted style that was impossible to read. Psychedelic, Erin called it. Between Lori and the black-light posters bodies swayed and melted into each other as a pair of enormous speakers boomed out of the low ceiling, stirring up the smoke-filled air.

Now she saw other tables, and a waitress with a flower painted on her face. And, among the leather pants, motorcycle boots, spiked hair and mohawks, there were a few moccasins, fringed vests, headbands and shirts with huge teardrop designs. That was it. Lori recognized the hippie part. It would be the reason why Erin was here—but of course she couldn't be. If Erin *had* come here . . . It was like the sixties all mixed in with the way kids were now. But in spite of the posters and imitation flower-child costumes it didn't look like the sixties were winning. The next song was "Heart Full of Soul." Lori recognized that one as well.

She backed along the wall and came to rest under one of the purple neon reflectors. She stuffed her hands under her jacket and kept her head down, and noticed with horror that her white jacket was now phosphorescent. She turned her face to the wall, picked at a poster and moved deeper into the shadows, stepping over a young man who was balancing a Coke bottle on his knee.

He smiled, his teeth an impossible blue-white, like piano keys in moonlight, and said something to her.

"Wh-what?" Lori plugged one ear with her finger and tried to hear. His was the first real smile she had seen all night. She leaned closer.

"I said, I like your jacket. It's rad." He kept looking at her as though he expected her to say something more.

"Oh," she said. "Thanks."

"Can you find your way there?"

"Um, I don't know. I was—that is, my sister, she—"

"It's right out that door." He pointed to the side of the bar. It was hard to see. The smoke was like fog now and the bodies were moving more restlessly.

"Oh."

What was she supposed to do now? If there was another room, a private place where Erin's friends went . . . She took a step closer to the door. Then she saw that it had something spray-painted on it: a circle with lines inside that formed an A. Just like her jacket. The music pummeled her eardrums. She couldn't think.

The young man grabbed her ankle, sliding a finger up her pants leg. His hand was clammy.

"You need any help?" he said.

"I—I don't think so," she said. She pulled away and out onto the floor. Now she felt like an animal in the open, waiting to be nabbed. If she could just—

A circle of bodies surrounded her, dancing to the driving beat. She was swept into the center, spun about, knocked from one pair of arms to another as huge sweating faces loomed over her. Their eyes were too large with sandbagged, amphibious lids, their noses flattened and disproportionate, their mouths wide and bottomless with broad, greasy tongues lapping shiny lips. She wanted to scream. She was afraid to scream. Their flat feet rapped the boards like cut-out wooden puppet legs, shaking closer. The misty lights spun in a carousel around her. The blades of the ceiling fan drooped nearer to her head. The air turned to steam, filling her lungs with water so that she could not breathe. Then hands were on her, pushing and pulling. She did not know what they wanted. The posters revolved, Day-Glow mazes coming to life, inks lifting off the paper, two-dimensional figures reaching out, smothering her . . .

The next thing she knew she was looking down—or was it up? If she could touch the surface and break through . . . Then she was lifted and carried away. Ripples like waves ebbed overhead. The door next to the bar opened. Cool air flowed over her.

"Ho' up." The bartender interceded, his face stern as

a principal's. "Where did she come from?"

"I'm taking her down."

The bartender breathed on her, his face ballooning as if through a magnifying glass. "This one's only a kid. How did she get in here?"

"She knows what she's doing. Don't worry, I'll pay for her."

A pale stalk of an arm crossed Lori's chest, stopping the boy with perfect teeth from carrying her any farther. "Not this one," said Angie. "I'll take care of her myself."

"Well, one way or the other, get her out," said the bartender. "I could lose my license letting school kids in here."

Angie attempted to take her into her own arms. "Can you stand up?"

"Out, I told you," said the bartender.

"That's what I was trying to do," said the young man.

"Why don't you shut the fuck up?" said Angie. "I'll take care of it."

"Out!"

"How many times have I paid to come in here?" said Angie. "*And* to go down? How many new customers have I brought you? Do you mind if she uses the goddam bathroom first? Is that all right with you? She's my—my sister, for God's sake. Okay, flyface?"

"Five minutes, tops." The bartender, Lori noticed, was really a woman, sort of. "I never saw her."

"Come on, Lizzy," said Angie.

Lori, she thought. "I feel sick. Want to go—"

"This way." Angie draped a boneless arm over her shoulders and led her to a hallway on the other side of the room. It was just as dark here but there was not as much noise and the air was better. "It's down there at the end. Put some water on your face. Then I'm going to show you what you came here to see. I'll meet you right here with a nice cold Coke first. Okay?"

"Do they have orange?"

"You got it, kid."

Angie left her in the hall.

Don't call me kid, Lori thought. She stumbled along the hall, feeling for a door. She bumped into something hard and cold. Metal segments skidded across her knuckles like a writhing snake, catching her wrist. She shook it off—it was the coiled cord of a pay phone.

Angie was gone. The main room was a luminous sliver from here, the music a rumble that swelled the walls.

Lori opened the side pocket of her jacket. It was already unzipped. Her wallet—

Gone!

She must have lost it back there on the floor with all the stomping feet, or on the streets.

Now what do I do? she thought.

She felt for the wall phone, found the coin return. The receptacle was empty. She hit the plunger. Nothing. Then she remembered. There were two quarters bus fare in her back pocket. Yes!

She dropped in the first one and dialed her own number. It rang and rang but there was no answer. But how could there be? There was no phone at home that worked. She got the Baumans' number from Information but no one was there. No one was home at the Staverses', either. This time the quarter didn't come back.

There had to be a way.

She dialed the operator. She could think of only one other person who might help her. It was the only chance she had.

She told the operator a story about how she was really his daughter but she had lost his number and something terrible was about to happen, please, it was a matter of life and death, even worse than that. The operator wouldn't give out the number but connected her to Personnel. They wouldn't give her the number either but when Lori started gasping into the mouthpiece like she couldn't breathe—it was only partly an act—they dialed it for her.

A miracle happened then. He answered.

She babbled enough of it so he'd understand and told him what to do, where she was and where to meet her, he had to come, she had no one else to call and no more money, right now, yes, all right in half an hour, she'd get out somehow and be there, crawl out the bathroom window if she had to, only—

A cold hand closed over hers.

Angie had a soft drink in her other hand, wrapped in a clear plastic bag. She handed these to Lori and took the phone from her, breaking the connection.

"Ready?"

nine

Tuesday night

Gil spread the contents of the plastic bag over the table:

A pack of Krakatoa Cigarettes.

A gold wristwatch with a black band.

Two tardy slips.

A progress report.

A crumpled one dollar bill, some change.

A Bazooka bubble gum wrapper.

An unused bus transfer.

A book of matches from the Rabbit-In-Red Record Store.

A folded sheet of three-hole notebook paper.

A button, a box of Tic Tacs, a tube of ChapStick.

"Is this everything?"

"That's what they handed me." Doug turned up the lamp in the dining room so they could see more clearly.

Gil sifted through the pieces of Erin's personal effects, laying them out jigsaw-style. He made sure the bag was empty. "I don't see it."

"That's the problem." Doug poured two shots of Orendain tequila.

"Something's missing."

"Yeah. A motive." Doug tossed down the shot and sucked air, drying his teeth. An excuse for what happened, he thought, a reason that would permit him to lay her to rest at last. He took up the watch. It had stopped at 9:20. It didn't fit his wrist. He tucked it into his pocket. He handled the notebook paper, unfolded its white wings.

"I mean the belt."

The paper fluttered, opened. Inside was a crude but stylized study hall cartoon. An emaciated man, his skull bashed in, crucified from a scaffold of unknown materials. The drawing was signed *Henry*. That's me, thought Doug. Henry, how did you know? There were two telephone numbers scrawled across the bottom. He had already checked them out. Neither of her classmates knew anything, or if they did they weren't talking. "What?"

"You said there was a belt."

"Drink your tequila."

"I'd like to look at it."

"There was a blouse, pants. Shoes. She wasn't wearing a belt. The clothes came back in a separate bag."

"Where is it?" said Gil. "The strap that—"

Doug poured again. "What difference does it make?"

Gil pushed back and looked at him calmly, almost cruelly, his hands flat on the tabletop.

"Okay," said Doug. If we're going to do this right, he thought. Even though the thought of that particular piece of evidence made him sick to his stomach. "But there's nothing to see."

He got up. The night was black against the glass, the reflections of the lamp and furniture like a mirror image of another, more idealized room suspended in the darkness outside. It looked warm and inviting. He went away from it, came back carrying a flat parcel of clothing folded inside a larger plastic bag. He set it down and drank again.

Gil opened it and took out the strap on top. A length of black leather, edged in chrome studs, with two buckles. Gil held it up, then dropped his hand with the dead sound of meat hitting a counter and let the strap lay there on the table. He raised his other hand to the side of his face. "Oh Christ," he said.

"What's the matter?"

"Why didn't you tell me?"

"That—*thing* wasn't hers. I told you, she wasn't wearing a belt. That means it belonged to—to whoever did it. There's no name on it, for God's sake."

"Have you looked at it?"

"Why don't you line up everybody in this town and ask them to try it on," said Doug impatiently, "till you find the waist it fits?" He couldn't look at the leather piece. It made him want to strangle someone himself, some anonymous person out there moving freely even now. Anyone.

"I don't have to." Gil finally finished his drink, spilling a few drops down his beard. The fumes left his eyes glassy. "You think this would fit anyone's waist, even a child's?"

"I don't know whose it is. That's the point. Neither do the police. And they're not going to take the time to find out."

"Take another look." Gil held out the strap but Doug wouldn't touch it. "These things don't fit that way. That's not what they're made for."

He hooked it together to demonstrate. The tongue went through the buckle and the holes locked, closing into a small loop at the end. There was a second buckle halfway down the strap. It closed into another loop no more than a few inches wide, this one in the middle. Two buckles.

"Let me see that."

Doug snatched it from him, his eyes opening at last. Whatever it was, it was not a belt in the conventional sense. It was not a belt at all.

"What is this?"

"It's what I was afraid of," said Gil. "I didn't want to say. Oh, Christ. You're sure this is the one that was on the tree, with the other end around her—?"

"Answer the question."

"I had to see it for myself. I could have been wrong."
Gil glanced at the stairway and lowered his voice. "Is
Casey asleep?"

"Say it!"

"I wish to God I didn't have to get you into
this . . . ."

"I'm already in it." Doug bore down on him, cheek
twitching, eyes sharp as scalpels.

"All right." Gil refastened the short hasp through
one set of holes, pulled. The studs held. He pulled
harder. The studs slipped down the strap one by one,
ratchet-like. The loop opened. "The notches are what
makes it work. They're cut shallow to hold the weight
for a short time. They're adjustable. When it gets heavy
enough, after one, two minutes, whatever notch you set
it to, it slips through and releases automatically."

"When what gets heavy enough?"

Gil closed his hand firmly over Doug's. "It's not supposed to hold the neck very long. Just long enough to
cause unconsciousness."

"You're out of your mind!"

"I've seen these rigs before. You can get them
through the mail, in s&m shops. It's a big industry. And
it's getting bigger every day. Only nobody likes to talk
about it."

If Doug could have tipped the table over and scattered it all to hell and gone so that he would not have to
think any further, he would have. But he had to know.

"I have to deal with a lot of parents after there's been
a death in the family. Most are going through the usual
stages of denial, and I try to help them come to terms
with their grief. But occasionally there's something
more than grief involved, something they're too
ashamed to talk about with anyone else. It's been that
way a lot lately.

"I did some research. There are thousands of teenage
deaths every year that belong in a special category. It's
this country's best-kept secret. Local police shine it
on—sticky p.r. for the community. The same with life

insurance companies. There are four or five possible categories for medical examiners to check off. None of them is correct. And most people have never even heard of 'autoerotic asphyxia.' So the cover-up is easy.''

"That's enough." Doug stood. He grasped the strap by the plated end, as if it were a poisonous rattler. "You mean to tell me you think Erin *did* kill herself? Is that what you're telling me?"

"Not exactly. That's not what this rig is for, killing yourself. At least it's not supposed to be. It's for—"

"She wouldn't. She would not, understand? Don't you think I knew her, knew my own—?"

"You're right. She didn't mean for it to happen. They never do. If they're serious they use a rope, a cord, an ordinary belt. Or gas. Or pills. Or they jump off something high. No, it was an accident, technically. 'Death by misadventure' is the usual phrase. You told me yourself there was no note. There's almost always a note."

"Unless it's murder."

"I don't think so. Not this time. Not this way."

Doug brought the silver head of the buckle down, narrowly missing Gil, trying to dash its brains out. "She wouldn't give up. She never quit, no matter what. She was a fighter. She was strong, tough—"

"And that's what took her over the edge. Struggling when she realized she'd gone too far this time. The carotid artery is extremely sensitive. It feeds the brain. Turn the wrong way once, just for a second, and it's too late to go back. Something happens, the rig jams . . .''

Autoerotic, he thought. The word made him nauseous. "You mean she did it for some kind of sick, dirty thrill? Well, *you're* sick if you think that! You think her life was that empty, that she didn't have friends, normal activities to keep her . . . ?"

Doug heard his own words in his ears, tolling a message that could not be denied. He remembered. The boredom. The absence of friends. The withdrawal, the escape into sleep, so much sleep. Because I brought her to this huge, empty house cut off from everything familiar. Because she had no one to talk to. I was always busy. She already had one mark on her neck, a bruise that might have been caused by—

Doug turned away and drove his forehead against the patio door. The thick glass fractured but did not shatter. He saw tortured, asymmetrical lines radiating out from the crack in front of his face, like the rays of a collapsing sun or the tilted, off-center web of a spider drunk on the blood of the insane. Outside, distant yellow eyes rose up at the top of the ridge. They were gathering above the house, growing in number and preparing to descend the hillside, closing the circle.

There was a sound from the stairwell.

"Hello, is anyone down there? Oh, Dr. McClay. I thought I heard voices. I didn't realize you were still here. Can I get either of you anything?"

Doug hid his face from Mrs. Bauman. "No, thank you, Mary. Is my wife sleeping?"

"She is. The best medicine for her right now. Oh, did you cut yourself?"

Doug returned to the table and lowered his head, his back to her. "An accident, that's all. Nothing serious. Thank you for staying." He waited for her to leave them.

She kept a respectful distance. "Certainly. It's the least a neighbor can do. I offered to make your little one something to eat, but she won't leave her mother's side, the darling."

In the disjointed window reflection Doug saw her unoccupied hands itching to rearrange the house and his life. Does she see the glass? It was an accident. What's so hard to accept about that? An accident.

He stared at Gil, seated so smugly with his hands folded on the tabletop. "I'll bet you could hardly wait to join the establishment," Doug said to him under his breath. "You doctors are all alike, ready to spread the latest load of king-size elephant shit. What are you trying to do to me?"

"Mrs. Bauman," said Gil, his eyes never leaving Doug's, "may I ask you a question?"

"Leave her out of it."

"Why, of course, doctor. Is there something I can . . . ?"

"How long have you lived in this area?"

"Well, let me see. It's been nineteen years now. Lester owned the house before that, but he kept it rented out. When we moved in . . ."

"I'll bet you know everyone in the canyon, don't you?"

"I suppose so. I was treasurer of the Hillside Association for four years. We've seen them come and go."

"What do you think you're doing?" said Doug between his teeth.

"And you've seen a lot of children grow up, I suppose?"

"Oh, lord, yes. I couldn't begin to count."

"Don't do this . . . ."

"Mrs. Bauman, this is a painful subject, I know. But I've been compiling some statistics for the University Medical School. There have been a number of other fatal accidents involving young people, haven't there, since you've lived here?"

Mrs. Bauman hesitated. Doug heard her dry skin rubbing as her hands washed each other in the stillness.

"It's so sad," she said in a compressed, modulated tone. "There never seems to be any reason for it. I say that to my husband every time. The way young people live these days . . . Excuse me, I don't mean Erin. She was such a perfect girl, so quiet, not like some I've seen. But there are so many opportunities for mishaps in today's world. I see that now. It's almost a blessing that Lester and I didn't have children of our own. Sometimes I wonder if we're any of us as safe as we think we are. It can strike anywhere, at any time. There was Ricky Mayer, the Wister boy, Laurie Strode, the Martin child, so many other tragic incidents . . . ."

Her voice faltered.

"Oh dear, but I've said too much. This is no time for me to be going on about such things, is it?"

"Thank you, Mrs. Bauman," said Gil. "You've

helped me. I'll talk to you more about it another time."

Doug held himself in check. "Yes," he said. "Thank you."

"You'll let me know if you need me? Lester, too. Any legal matters that—"

"We'll let you know."

"Good night, then. I'll say a prayer for Casey." She closed her purse and prepared to leave.

"What's that supposed to prove?" Doug asked Gil.

Before Gil could answer, there was a pounding in the living room. Was Mrs. Bauman having trouble with the door? That one had never stuck before. If she couldn't get it open he'd have to . . . but now the pounding was louder, like thunder. The dog was going crazy.

He heard Mrs. Bauman working the bolt.

"Oh! Mr. Carson, I think someone's trying to break in! What should I do?"

Doug sprang from his chair. He didn't have the gun. This time he wouldn't need it. He threw the deadbolt back and flung the door wide, ready to tear through the screen to get his hands on whoever it was.

"Is your name Carson?" A man in white Levi's and a denim shirt stood there. "You have a daughter, right?"

Doug started out onto the porch. "What did you say?"

"About yea-high, straight hair, big blue eyes?"

Doug raised his fist.

"Name of Lori, right? I'm sure this is the house. I met her here a week ago. In there."

Was he pointing at Erin's bedroom?

Doug grabbed him by the shirt and slammed him against the house. He wanted to—but Gil was there to hold him back.

"Wait a minute. Let's hear what he has to say."

"You go to hell," Doug said over his shoulder.

"I thought you should know," said the man. He drew his fingers through his hair, which had come loose in the altercation. It hung to his shoulders. "She was trying to get through to you. Only the line's not working. I think she needs help."

"You're nuts," Doug told him. "Lori!" he yelled.
"Come out here!"

Mrs. Bauman went back to the hall, reappeared a moment later.

"Why, the child's in bed," she said. "What . . . ?"

Before the man could say anything else, Doug had an
unspeakable premonition. He left him there and ran to
Lori's room.

"Angel, are you all—?"

He shook the blanket. But all his hands found there
were pillows. Loose hair was everywhere. And then he
was on an elevator that was dropping at something near
the speed of sound.

"Don't hit me, man," said the guy on the porch.
"That's not gonna do anybody any good. But I think
you'd better come with me. If I heard her right, your
little girl's gone off and gotten herself into some real
deep shit, know what I mean?"

They told Mrs. Bauman to stay with Casey and
Elizabeth, and then they were roaring down the canyon,
the soft plastic windows of the long-haired man's Jeep
flapping around them with the sound of leathery wings.

Lori had remembered his name, Shannon, and that he
worked for the phone company, had cried and begged
the supervisor for his number when she couldn't get
through to her own house.

"The way I got it, she was in that neo-sixties hangout
near Westwood. It was hard to hear with the music, but
I got that much. She said her big sister used to go there.
They can't wait to grow up, can they?"

"Christ," said Gil.

"It used to be a punk spot, but when that got old . . . .
It's called the Club Zero now. Anyway, by the sound of
it she was scared out of her gourd. Somebody must have
tried to hassle her."

"How did she get in the door?" said Doug. "She's
not even eleven years old yet, for God's sake!"

"Can't say I'm surprised. Those places are run by
sleazeballs who'd hustle the Pope if he had a sawbuck in

his pocket. They must have seen her piggybank. I told
her to get out. She was going to meet me at McDonald's
for a ride back. Only she never showed."

"Doesn't this crate go any faster?" Gil's face
bounced in the rearview mirror, shaking apart, about to
lose its veneer of composure.

"Relax, we're almost there. I cruised the Club but I
didn't see anyone outside. Then I thought she might
have found somebody else to take her home. But I
wanted to be sure. Either way, I knew you'd want to
know . . . ."

They took Sunset to Hilgard, cut right on Kinross,
then left again. The front of the Westwood Marquis was
ajumble with zippy, androgynous New York types of in-
determinate ethnicity seeking shelter from the first
drops of a spring rain, while the Village itself began to
steam, preparing to melt down under the press of
overheated teenagers and late-night party animals. The
Jeep gripped the pavement with oversized treads and
bounded across Wilshire in high gear. Shannon handled
the shift like a tympani stick as he pounded up Warner
Avenue, his long hair waving in a black jetstream. There
were shadows behind garbage cans and unsorted trash
accumulating under signposts and in the opening
mouths of thirsty storm drains, but no person standing
alone or moving through the drizzle on foot. They made
a gyroscopic turn and a minute later the sidewalls were
shearing off as the wheels slammed against the curb.

Doug dropped the sidepanel and saw that they had
come to a stop in the middle of a particularly desolate
stretch of the boulevard, with few lights showing except
for a used car dealership on the other side and, a few
hundred yards to the south, an intersection moving with
automobiles wet and flushed under the sodium vapors
as a fistful of nightcrawlers. Next to the Jeep was a
small, dingy storefront wrinkled with posters and hand-
bills. An arrow indicated that the entrance was in back.

The driver zipped up the window panel on his side. A
blue bus on its last run of the night swept past, wavery
as a prowling shark on the other side of a soft

aquarium. Shannon tapped the dashboard. He had a
cellular phone mounted there.

"You want to bring the cops in on this yet?"

Doug finished closing the window. "If it comes to
that." He touched the pistol stock under his jacket and
pulled on the door handle. "Let's go."

They hit the alley single-file, stepping around empty
fifths of cheap wine and a half-pint flask of Southern
Comfort set out like milk bottles on the back porch. At
the side of the long building a couple of teenage boys
completed a transaction involving a baggie and some
large bills. When they saw the three men they lit up men-
tholated cigarettes and started practicing smoke rings.
The smoke drifted up to the moist blue neon sign, where
three straight lines were arcing and snapping inside a circle. Late-model cars were packed like sausages behind
the building, their hoods speckled with insects drenched
and trapped by the sudden shower.

Doug opened the door.

It was not a nightclub, not even a bar. It was nothing
more than an old store, converted under a new lease to
fit the times. A few tables and folding chairs had been
set up, leaving the center of the floor clear, with a
counter at one end serving as a dispensary for soft
drinks. It was a contemporary version of an old-
fashioned soda shop, except that instead of football
pennants on the walls there were commercial posters
mounted under purple Gro-Lux lights to commemorate
various rock and roll martyrs whose popularity defied
death and the trivializing passage of years. In place of a
juke box, a young man in dark glasses and tight black
clothing manned a turntable in the corner. At this moment the patrons, a motley crew of pop romantics and
societal rejects, were not dancing but mostly lounging at
the tables or along the walls as the dj took a leisurely
break. It was too dark to be absolutely certain, but Lori
did not seem to be among them.

"Four dollars cover," said a bald-headed bouncer
from behind a card table. "Apiece."

"What's your age limit?" asked Doug.

"Forget your ID?"

Gil dropped a twenty on the table.

"I got to get change," said the doorman.

His hands disappeared from under the lamp without opening the cash box. He went back to the soft drink bar and conferred with the owner, a muscular woman with an assassin's eyes. She reached down and a red light bulb came on over the counter. At that signal two more baldies appeared out of the shadows, one at the fire door and the other at the entrance to a hall.

"Oh, great," said Gil, "they think we're heat."

"If they don't have anything to hide, what does it matter?"

The bouncer returned and handed them the change. He seemed slightly relieved to see Shannon's long hair and work shirt. But only slightly. They were allowed to pass. Once inside, they regrouped under a likeness of John Lennon, Christlike behind baby moon specs.

"There are several ways to play this," said Gil. "One, if she was here, somebody must have seen her. We can ask around. Two, she's still in the building, though I don't see where. Three, she's already home and we're stuck here with no way of knowing . . . ."

"I'm not leaving till I find out exactly what went down. Did you see that sign outside? It all connects with Erin. There's something going on here that doesn't scan. Kids don't come to an empty room and pay four bucks to lay around sucking on Cokes."

"They might. Remember that place we used to go to on Fairfax in '67, *The Psychedelic Experience*? All we did was sit on Samsonite chairs and wait for people to walk under the black light so their shirts would light up."

Doug remembered. But this wasn't 1967. This place might be a camp on the sixties, but bent, with a black edge of meanness and impending violence showing through. If the sixties had come back, it was with a vengeance.

"I'm going to take a look around."

Doug headed over the dance floor, feeling eyes at his

back that wanted to pin him squirming to the wall, as
the dj lowered the needle and the opening bars of a
record boomed out. It was Hendrix, "Purple Haze."

A guy with motorcycle boots and a cossack shirt
pulled his girl to her feet for a dance. She had ironed
surfer-girl hair, fringed moccasins and a Sex Pistols
T-shirt. The combination was disconcerting. Doug
couldn't talk to them if he wanted to; or rather he could
talk but they wouldn't hear him. Before he could get
across the floor several more gyrating bodies filled the
spaces around him. A colored track light beamed out
into a multifaceted globe hanging from the ceiling, and
hundreds of bright squares cascaded around him like
autumn leaves caught in a waterspout.

The room became airless, stifling, rife with half-seen
but vaguely aggressive movements, recalling other situa-
tions in years past that had turned ugly and threatening
without warning—the time the party at the Ardmore
Temple had been raided, the Century City march
against LBJ, Hussong's Cantina and the fight that had
started there. He waved behind his back to Gil and
Shannon and hoped that they were watching, would
understand. Gil would remember: one man to the front
entrance, one to the back to clear the way if necessary.
That had gotten them out of Ensenada in one piece after
the knife was pulled there.

He got through to the counter. He used a finger to get
the muscular woman's attention.

"Did you see a little girl? She got here a couple of
hours ago. She—"

The woman shook her head. "I don't hear a word
you're saying," she said. "The music."

"I said—" He elbowed across the counter and posi-
tioned himself tight enough to spit in her ear. "I said,
there was a little girl, a child here tonight. She came in
to use the phone. I was wondering if you saw her."

"No children. Only sixteen and over. I don't allow no
children in here. This is a clean place."

"That's cute," he said.

"I don't hear you, mister."

"And I said cut the bullshit. I knew another little girl who came in here. She was all of fourteen. Did you hear what happened to her?"

The big baldy from the fire door left his post and assumed a position at her right hand. His eyes were flat and hard, hammered aluminum without depth or character.

So this is the way it's going to be, thought Doug.

He turned back to the room and the bodies dancing in a vortex of color, and saw that Gil had moved along the wall to take the big guy's place at the fire door. Across the floor at the entrance, Shannon nodded.

There was still the hallway to be checked out.

On the way there Doug passed the disc jockey. He paused by the turntable. He tried to strike up a conversation but it didn't work. The young man was wearing earplugs, his ferret eyes safe behind graduated dark glasses. Doug moved on.

"Rest room this way?"

The third baldy let him pass. The hall was dark as a coal mine. A wrapped silver loop swayed from the wall. That would be the telephone, the one she used. At the end strings of silverfish light shone under a pair of doors. He knocked on the one marked WOMEN. No answer. The music clapped like distant cannon fire. He knocked again.

"Anybody in there?"

He tried the door. He saw the white walls, the sink, the open cubicles. No window. He left the hall.

"Going home already?" said the third bouncer.

Doug had to turn sideways to get past him.

"Have a nice night," said the bald-headed man. "You come back and see us again real soon, hear?"

The music faded out on an extended chord. The dj was about to cue up another record, earplugs still in place.

Doug reached to uncork one of the ears. As he did so the needle touched down. It hissed around a worn lead-in groove.

He looked over at Shannon and the doorman, at Gil

and the second bouncer at the fire door, at the third
baldy who had left the hall and was coming this way, his
head down to keep from scraping the glitter ceiling.

Three on three, he thought. So be it.

He leaned over and knocked the dj's arm aside. The
stylus went haywire and screeched across the vinyl.

"Hey, man . . . !"

Then Gil turned on the lights.

Instantly the room went into shock. A waitress in a
miniskirt and white boots capsized her tray. The dancers
lost the beat and stopped shuffling over the hardwood
floor.

The place was even smaller and dirtier than he had
thought. There wasn't much to it: stark walls with
seams showing and a few pieces of stick furnishings,
just enough to accommodate the night's cattle call. The
kids rubbed their eyes, looking pale and scrawny as
children playing dress-up in clothes that were too big for
them.

"Can I have your attention for a minute?" he began.

The tall one from the hall clamped a hand around his
arm.

"I'm looking for a girl."

"Who isn't?" someone said, and laughed.

"A little girl. Her name is Lori Carson. Try to
remember. She's about four-foot-ten, big blue eyes,
straight hair—"

The other bouncer came over to grab him by the other
arm. Doug felt his feet start to leave the floor.

He did not resist as he prayed for someone, anyone to
speak up. Seconds passed; no one did. The bouncers
were surprised when he went limp and let himself
become dead weight in their hands. But his passive
resistance was only a strategy. He used the time to get a
fix on the layout. Shannon about to leave the entrance.
Gil leaning his buttocks into the fire door to get it open.

Two kids dozing against the wall got up and started to
leave. As he followed their progress with his eyes, Doug
spotted a wallet on the floor. It was a nylon trifold from
Le Sport Sac, with a Duran Duran button on the Velcro

strip. No doubt about it. It was Lori's.

"Free drinks for everyone," said the owner. "We don't close for another hour. Come on, lots of time to dance!"

Doug made ready. He would hang down between them and turn his feet under so they would have to drag him. That would slow them down long enough for him to drop back and stand, grab for the wallet. Before they could turn he would be at the fire door. At the same time he would yell for Shannon to get the Jeep. He knew what to say on the car phone. In a few minutes badges would be all over the place. Then maybe someone would talk.

Behind him, the door rattled. Not so hard, Doug thought. Gil knew better than that.

"Not now," said the muscular woman.

"What's goin' on, Viv? I saw the light. I was comin' up to—"

"Later, I told you. For now you stay down there." She touched the wall switch and the overhead lights went off again.

Doug twisted around far enough to see that someone had come in from the fire door. Gil moved aside and gave the boy room to stand. His clothes were without color, a loose, flowing top over white pants. He looked like a deranged messiah come up out of his bomb shelter to preach the gospel of Armageddon. He would have had a white beard, as well, were he old enough to shave.

"I just came up to spread the word," he said, smiling manically, flashing his teeth under the black light. They shone like white phosphor, even more ghostly than his garment. "Gee, there's plenty of room, if anyone else wants to come . . ."

"You know that's not the way. I told you, you can do what you want, but not up here."

The dj spun another record, "Stairway to Heaven," as the two bouncers gripped Doug under the arms and dragged him. They had him to the fire door and were about to escort him out.

"Hurry up!" said the woman.

Doug balked. "I don't know that I'm ready to go just yet."

"Doug," said Gil, "we can talk about it outside. Do you understand? *Outside*. Right now I think we should—"

"You heard the man," said one of the baldies. "Why don't you listen to your friend?"

"I'd kind of like it to be my idea," Doug said.

"Wait," said the teenage messiah. "There's no need for violence."

He moved closer. His eyes were bleached out, clear as glass, virtually transparent.

The bouncers let go and allowed him to lead Doug.

"This way, okay?"

They were outside in a narrow walkway between the buildings. The air was cooler with a heavy mist falling around them like ashes.

Behind them Shannon was saying, "We're going outside with our friend." But the baldies blocked the door, refusing to let anyone follow.

"I'll take care of him," said the boy.

"Not so fast," Doug said. "I came here to get some answers."

"About what?"

"What happened to the little girl?"

The young man smirked toothily. "W'll, don't worry," he said. "She's feelin' great, for sure. She's never been so happy!"

"I don't believe you."

The young man smirked again and spread his arms like a white messiah. Then he began to shrink, becoming a foot, two feet shorter, as if he were dissolving out of his garment. Then Doug saw that the boy had stepped into an outside stairwell leading below the surface of the alley, possibly the entrance to a basement or subterranean storeroom.

The white messiah held out his hand in the mist.

"Come with me," he said. "I'll take you there."

ten

Like this, then: down the steps to another, last door, hollow-core steel painted gray, as inconspicuous as any basement or utility entrance in the city, the kind that may have signs reading *No Admittance* or *Authorized Personnel Only* or *Danger High Voltage* or *Dept. of Water & Power* but most often are left plain to avoid attracting attention. There were doors like it in every parking lot in Westwood, behind restaurants and office buildings and shopping complexes and no one ever asked what they were for or where they led. Once Doug had taken Elizabeth to see *Close Encounters of the Third Kind—The Special Edition* and then afterward to the International Food Mall behind the theater; she was four years old and suffered from chronic incontinence at the most inopportune times, such as the exact moment of Richard Dreyfuss's ascent into the mother ship or after standing in line for ten minutes at Fatburger's without placing an order. He had no choice but to lead her by the hand through the big door marked REST-ROOMS. There were service closets and storage areas and power control rooms there, too, each door like every other and all of them unmarked; so that they had ended

up downstairs, below street level, facing one last door
that turned out to be the connection to an underground
garage. At least he assumed it to be a garage with its
cement pillars staggered ahead into infinity. Not this
way, he told her, and he carried her upstairs again and
back along the same route until they heard the clatter of
dishes and smelled hamburgers and falafel and pizza
and just before they came upon the big dining area with
the chairs and tables again there it was, WOMEN, plain as
the nose on his face, which he had been too close to see,
as well. But all the time he was waiting for her to come
out he wondered about the peculiar sub-basement that
could not have been a parking lot with no lights and
only the gray spaces leading into darkness; and he
wondered whether he had lifted her so quickly back up
the stairs because of the way she was whining and pressing her legs together or because of the shudder he had
felt pass between his shoulders when he discovered the
door no one ever tried that had been left unlocked in
permanent invitation. What if it had closed behind
them? A few weeks later he descended once more into
the bowels of the food mall in an attempt to settle the
question, but he was unable to find the exact location.
Since that time he believed he had succeeded in putting
it out of his mind. But now here he was again, entering
another gray door that opened into the same endless
darkness, about to find out once and for all what lay
beyond. Was what he heard now the same distant scuttling that had reverberated between other poured concrete pillars that black summer afternoon a mile from
here? It was, it was; he could not forget that sound. But
this time he no longer had the luxury of turning back.

"W'll hey, follow me, awright? Don't be scared."

Kiss my ass, thought Doug. "If I'm not back
here—with my daughter—in five minutes," he said,
"my friends are going to holler cop so loud you'll be out
of business till hell freezes over. Got that?"

"Oh, for sure. No prob. Lori's down here. She's r'lly
great, too. Watch your step, okay?"

Lori. So he knew her name. What else did he know

about her? Doug wanted to slap that self-satisfied face senseless, then mount him on the front end of the Jeep and use those teeth of his to tear the streets open, lay it all bare.

"You first," he said.

The boy shrugged and went ahead. Doug considered leaving the door wedged open so the others could see and follow. But it had already shut.

A cigarette lighter flicked on, illuminating the white sleeve of the boy's shirt, the bony wrist, then what lay before them.

The underground room expanded to accommodate the handheld flame, which soon became a huge yellow ball of light rolling back the darkness. There were reinforced concrete posts to support the low ceiling, piled blocks and unfinished subsections to suggest detours leading away on every side like the bifurcations of a sewer system. Doug heard a rushing overhead. When he looked up a downdraft of cool air struck his face. Far above, a car swished by at street level. So they were beneath the boulevard. The sounds of tires and the city collected in the ventilation duct, a sonic periscope that was now the only connection to the outside world. The boy held his Bic away from his satin shirt, like a candle-bearing monk on a procession through private catacombs.

Reluctantly Doug moved away from the shaft of fresh air. Were they in a stockroom? No, it was much too vast for that. Part of the storm drains, then, some sort of flood control system? But the sections were squared off, not rounded, not like pipes. "What is this place?"

"Isn't it great? Somebody built it way back in the old days—in the fifties, can you handle that? Some kind of Civil Defense thingie. It starts at the Federal Building, goes on for miles, all the way to the ocean. Only they never used it. Now nobody even knows it's here. It's cool, no sweat. This way."

"How much farther?"

"It's close, man. Closer than you think . . . ."

In the flickering light Doug picked out dark puddles

of condensation bleeding out of the pillars, crumpled refuse, a rusted shopping cart, a sleek rat feeding on formless remains, all grasping claws and ingrown teeth, its yellow eyes unblinking as their footsteps passed like the dripping of water from the ceiling. A long pile of soggy newspapers lay under the next post. As they approached, the pile moved.

"Who's 'at?" the newspapers peeled away and an old woman sat up. She grappled behind the pillar and came up with a baseball bat. "Keep away from me! I tol' you I ain't got nothin' you want, honey. Jes' keep to yo'self fo' the rest o' the night, hear?"

"Hey, what's happening?" said the boy. "Ready to come over to the Darkside yet, Minnie?"

She burrowed under the papers, found her upper plate and inserted it into her pink mouth, used the bat as a cane to stand. Her shawl was unraveling and her skin showed through, dull and crusted with white blotches like crushed limestone. "Never mind. Ain't but one Jesus an' he tol' me I was goin' t' make it. 'Lay not up your store in worldly goods', he say to me. He didn't say nothin' 'bout no white devil come to torment me. I been doin' jes' fine hewin' t' my own path of righteousness, thank you!"

"Hey, great. But, like, one day you'll be ready for the true peace, right? And when that day comes you'll know where to look, won't you? Till then, well, hang loose, okay?"

"You tellin' me t' move on, sonny? You know I can't go topside tonight. Weather man says it's gonna rain!"

"Hey, no biggie. My house has many rooms . . . ."

They went on, following a line of elongated splotches, and came out into a long, cavelike extension. Was that moonlight ahead? No, the ceiling was unbroken except for the ventilation ducts every thirty or forty feet, and the color of the light was all wrong. Warm and mushy, like the inside of a carved pumpkin.

There was a hint of movement, a subtle shifting and the pillars appeared to rearrange. Yellow eyes flashed in and out, clinging close to the stony supports. The boy strode ahead, his white bucks making splashing sounds that rolled ahead in a tide of time-delayed echoes. He stopped, lowered his Bic. The yellow eyes formed a tight group. They were candles, held chest-high in hands as white as the undersides of snow crabs.

"Lori?" called Doug.

The boy gave the railroader's high-sign and the candle bearers came closer. They were a mixed bunch, most in their teens; some were clearly not from around here. There was long hair and short, punk, new wave, imitation hippie, nerd, fat, skinny, black, white, Asian, Chicano. Here was a bookish ectomorph with taped glasses and a forest of pencils in his pocket protector; there a Rocky Horror groupie with wristband and dog collar; there a future homemaker with heavy rouge triangulating her cheekbones. They all had the same pale skin. Doug checked each face. He didn't see her.

He squared off in front of the white messiah. "What are you trying to pull?"

A bare-chested boy with braided hair separated from the pack. "White Feather," he said. He tried to give Doug the brotherhood handshake, missed, turned his hand the other way, missed again. "My friends call me Whitey. This here's my bud, Running Bear." A small, furry, Fearless Frank type flipped Doug a limp peace sign. Doug ignored him and shouted back over their heads at the leader.

"I asked you a question!"

"Hi," said a girl in a patchwork dress and water buffalo sandals. "My name's Rainbow. What's yours?"

He grabbed her arm, which was scored with cigarette burns. "The little girl," he said. "I want the little girl."

The messiah was busy embracing his subtteraneean flock one by one, long rocking hugs such as Doug had witnessed once at a touchie-feelie marathon that his ex-wife had badgered him into attending shortly before their marriage broke up. It hadn't taken then, either. He thought, *I don't want to have to do this . . . .*

He drew the gun.

"I came here for the child," he said.

He thought, that's all I ask. And I'll leave you. You can go on playing Drop-Out University down here till you go blind. Only let me have her. What can it matter to you?

They stopped and stared at him, at the gun. He jerked the barrel, using it as a prod through the crowd, back to the boy in white.

"Did you hear me?"

The boy smiled tolerantly. "Hey," he said, "where'd you get *that*?"

"Ooh!" someone else said, "look at it! Is it real?"

"Is it easy to shoot? What kind of bullets . . . ?"

"My dad's got one like that!"

They were all smiling now, their eyes focused on the blue steel like children crowding around a new toy. They were not afraid.

"Wow, that's pretty heavy!"

"Yes," said Doug. He crooked his thumb over the hammer. *Click*. "And it's real."

"No lie," said the boy. And he raised his hands in the moist air and began to applaud.

"Can I try it?" someone said.

Doug leveled the gun at the boy's chest. "The girl."

"Hey, why not?" He ceased applauding. "Who'd like to show our new friend the way?" He nodded knowingly at Doug. "You've been trying to find it for a long time, haven't you, man?"

"I'm not your friend."

"After you've been there you will be. You'll see. It'll be a shitload of trouble off your back, take my word for it." He laughed dreamily. "Man, I wish I was you. It's so beautiful."

"For sure," said a boy with perfect teeth.

"Greg?"

"Yeah?"

"Do me a favor? Take care of things while I give this dude what he wants, okay?"

"You got it."

Doug kept the gun up.

"Come on. It isn't far. It's real easy, long as you got somebody to show you the way . . . ." The boy in white grinned, his teeth lighting up the shadows like a Cheshire cat.

They lit out across the empty expanses. In the distance, Doug heard the group laugh. They're tripped out, he thought, one some kind of mindfuck game that's being laid on them with a shovel. *Darkside*. He had heard that word again. What is it, a cult, some kind of New Age mole-man sect that believes they've found the One True Way? He was glad to leave them behind for now. They made his feet sweat, like a gang of Jesus freaks who pretend to talk to you but end up using your own words against you to reinforce the delusion. They shrank away in a yellow spot of light; he passed another row of pillars and the circle extinguished. The darkness pressed in.

"Over here." The boy in white had forgotten to bring a candle. He didn't seem to need his lighter from here.

Doug's eyes adjusted somewhat. Faint bands of fugitive light penetrated the underground from the ventilation shafts, rippling over the colorless interior. The boy made a turn and the darkness closed around them. Doug jabbed the gun into the boy's back and held it there.

"This part isn't a game," he said. "Try anything stupid and I'll blow you away."

The boy laughed dopily. "That'd be pretty rad, all right. Not here, though, okay?"

Doug pushed into him and laid a forearm around the chin in a cross-face, keyed one of the boy's arms up in a chicken-wing. "*Where*?"

They bumped from wall to wall along a narrow walkway. A rough, raw cement opening skidded by, then another. Overhead, a truck passed thickly. The pilings groaned. Or was there a hoarse voice within one of the rooms?

The boy bucked to the side, stepping out of the tunnel and into a grotto-like orifice.

There was a fire in the sideroom. No, it was another candle, many candles set out on a platform of sticks and scrap wood, dozens of wax stumps burning and dripping over one another in melted-out icicles of color. It

was a small stone cubicle, one of many, all of them dank
and windowless as the annexes of a blockhouse. In the
guttering glow he saw an assortment of discarded furniture and sprung cushions, a burst mattress, tattered
posters strung up between lengths of clothesline and
other unidentifiable hanging objects. Planks, a ladder, a
broken fragment of mirror leaned against the wall. Scattered mounds of mildewed thrift shop clothes, all of it
disarranged in a nightmare parody of a middle-class
teenager's bedroom. A battered easy chair with three
legs, stuffing exposed like rolls of fat exploding out of
the seams. Styrofoam cups. McDonald's wrappers. In
one corner a pile of filthy pillows supporting rolls of
dirty clothes and polyethylene bags. He let the boy go
momentarily.

"Lori, are you in here?"

A patter of rats' feet passed overhead. He braced and
ducked defensively. The pattering spread over the entire
ceiling, then drummed throughout the whole of the
underground complex. A long peal of thunder broke
through the corridors from above; outside, the streets
hissed with wet tires and then the muffled pistol shots of
shoes running.

"Heck, it's startin' to rain. There isn't much time. In
a few minutes it won't be so private anymore with all
Minnie's friends comin' down here, you know?" said
the boy into his ear, and looped the clothesline around
Doug's neck. "So we better do it *now*!"

Doug felt his body arch as a knee was placed in his
back, bending him in half. He clawed at the rope but it
was already burning through the skin of his throat.

"Don't fight it, man. I did, too, the first time. I
didn't understand. It's easy. I try to tell them that. But
sometimes they won't listen. So I have to show them. A
promise is a promise, I tell them. And I promise them a
lot. Go with it. Don't fuck yourself up . . . ."

Doug contracted, hoping to flip the boy forward onto
the mattress, but the knee was set. He tried to slip down
and out but the cord caught at his ears, sawing them
away from his head.

"I really don't want to hurt you, okay?" said the
boy.

The ends of the cord crossed in back, forming a gar-
rote. Then with his free hand the boy drove Doug forward onto his knees.

"What do you want to be like that for? Take a look.
She's happy now. She's got the peace. You can have it,
too. Don't dog it . . . ."

Doug was shoved to the mattress. The rolls of dirty
clothes there had shape, form. He grabbed hold with
one hand, anchoring for an advantage. The top layer
fell away, revealing a white jacket, next to it another
long form, the upper portion of this one covered by a
plastic bag. His fingers found a small, cold hand.

"Don't mess up her trip, man! She's on the Darkside
now. But she'll be back, you'll see!"

Doug wrestled his right arm up. The gun was huge in
front of his eyes. The boy took control of the wrist,
turning the barrel around. Doug sighted down it as
the bead centered.

"Not that way, guy! It's *too* rad, see? Drop it!"

Doug dropped his head and jammed the trigger back.
There was another peal of thunder as a bolt of lightning
flashed in the room, limning a perfect oval face inside
one of the plastic bags. It was a face he knew despite
the concentration camp hair. Lori's face, the eyes open,
the mouth round, the plastic sucked halfway down the
throat. Next to it another face, larger, older, with wet,
bleached hair curled against the plastic. The flash subsided and there was only the dim fluttering of the
candles.

"Close, brother! Too close. Drop it before you hurt
someone. It's not supposed to be for keeps. Come on,
do you want to get there or not?"

Doug's head swelled, the blood pressure about to
burst his eyeballs as his lungs heaved for air. The room
swam. He kicked out and the construction of planks
collapsed. Candles scattered, spattering the walls with
red wax. His pulse beat in his ears like an army of foot-
soldiers stalking him through mud and slime, tramping

closer, shaking the walls . . .

Someone was at the door.

Above his pounding heart he heard a loud *thwack*, the sound of a melon breaking. The noose loosened and the boy hit the floor next to him, as Buddy Kasabian raised his foot and made ready to kick the head again.

Doug rolled onto the mattress and flung himself over Lori, ripped the plastic film from her face. She was blue. He pinched her nose and covered her gelid mouth with his own, breathing in, out. His head reeled from lack of oxygen. He turned aside, gulped air, covered her again and tried to blow his own life into her. Her chest swelled, went flat.

Buddy tore the bag from the other face. It was a bloodlessly pale teenage girl with one dangling earring.

"Angie? Aw, not you, too . . . ."

"Help me!" panted Doug.

Beneath him Lori's frail body twitched, then was still again.

Now there was a great thundering in the hallways beyond, the scuttling of feet running out all around, coming closer.

Doug sat up and hugged her to him. The jolt loosed a cough. He enveloped her with his arms as her chest rose, fell weakly. "Don't die, angel," he said, squeezing her head, covering her cold face with kisses, "please, no . . ."

He shook her, then slapped her a stinging blow across the cheek. Her skin flushed where his fingers had struck her, first white, then bright red. He put his ear to her mouth. Nothing. She fell back, her eyelids rolling up.

"For the love of God," Doug choked, "help me get her out of here!"

"There's one chance," said Buddy. "It's not much, but my friends . . . come on."

They lifted Lori. The other girl on the mattress was a stony, sepulchral white.

"Forget it. It's too late for her. She didn't make it back. She never really wanted to . . . ."

Doug ran blind, carrying Lori, barely keeping up as the rain erupted into a full storm outside. The air shafts dashed by overhead like a line of tracers. They ran the line. Above the drum roll of feet Doug heard a door opening, a heavy, dragging thump-slide on the cement. Directly in front of them, an arrow of lightning zig-zagged out of a widening doorway.

A rumpled silhouette with ropy hair shambled down to block the steps.

"Get out of my way," said Doug.

"Stan' back!" The silhouette raised a stick with nails in one end. "This is my spot! I'm sleepin' here!"

"Not that way!" called Buddy.

Doug ran ahead, feeling Lori cold and lifeless in his arms. He kicked a shopping bag in the shadows, stumbled over an elephantine ankle and almost lost his footing. Now more derelicts from the city streets were entering through doorways behind dark parking lots and abandoned buildings, settling in for the long night. Doug began to see spots before his eyes, bouncing over the pillars, undulating across the floor. He glanced back. One of the spots, the beam of a distant flashlight, caught him in the eyes. He saw the veins of his own retinas superimposed like a red cage around him.

"*There they are!*" someone shouted.

"Almost there," said Buddy. "I brought my own people with me. They call 'em the Lost Ones . . . ."

Voices, boots pounding the concrete.

"*Halt!*"

Doug turned and fired. In the muzzle flash he saw shadows without legs coming out of corners, mountains of rubbish that moved, shopping carts in the grip of arthritic hands, reptilian eyes without faces sharing the cavern with nests of rats. More flashlights stabbing like icepicks. He hoisted Lori higher and ran on. An oil slick shaped like the map of an unknown continent lapped his shoes. His feet went out from under him. He tried to get up, fell. The flashlights cut closer.

Buddy came back for Lori, took her from him. Doug saw her passed from hand to pale hand as arms emerged from the walls, carrying her away. He could not follow.

"*There! Get him!*"

He crawled around and fired the .38, again, again.

With each shot the piston legs strobed and froze. He aimed higher, guessing where they would be next, and pulled off his last shot. A grunt and something splattered and went down. Then he rolled over reflexively to cover Lori who was no longer there. As his arms closed over his own body and the memory of her, he barely had time to start praying before they were upon him.

Part
III

The Darkside

eleven

So this is what it's like, he thought.

Doug Carson hung suspended beneath a white sun. His body was dead. It must have been; when he moved his muscles his arms and legs did not respond. He tried to open his eyes but the light pressed hot fingers into the sockets and held his lids shut.

Eventually a shadow passed over, blocking out the sun, and his senses began to reassemble.

He heard chimes like bow bells in fog. The skin that encased his body came alive again, containing him and giving him shape, pricking him with needles of pain. His tongue tasted blood and plastic. The acrid smell of antiseptic sliced up his nostrils, watering his eyes, dissolving the membranes that sealed them. He became aware of the table below, the coarse paper sheeting. He made an effort to sit up.

He was strapped down.

He thought, I have things to do, important things.

"Lori . . ."

"Shh."

"Where?"

203

"She's alive. And so are you."

Was it Gil?

"Don't talk. The cops are outside. I can hold them off as long as you're down. That last shot of yours, well, no need to go into that now."

"Tell me."

"You hit someone. We'll talk about it later."

"Who?"

"Shannon. You took out Shannon."

No, he thought.

Gil was silent.

"Shit," said Doug.

"Anyway, the cops did a number on you before I caught up. Just like old times. All they could see was a guy running, a gun blazing. Nobody knew it was you."

Doug slipped a swollen hand out from under the straps and shielded his eyes.

Gil's face swam into focus, behind it the scrubbed, reflective walls and instrument cabinets of an examination room. He touched his head. It was bandaged and taped.

"What about Lori? We did it, didn't we? We did that much. We got her out. Tell me that you—"

"Not me. The boy, Buddy. He had friends, other kids, a whole bunch of them. That tunnel system runs under all of Westwood and then some, including UCLA and the Med Center. They had her up to Emergency before we figured that out, before we got you here."

Doug unfastened the top strap.

"Whoa, not so fast. I signed you in, but I'm *persona non grata* around this part of the hospital. They wouldn't even let me clean your abrasions. What do you need, Doug? I can get you something for the pain."

"I need to see Lori."

"She's stable and holding, but it will be awhile before—"

"Where?"

Doug was already at the door. He saw two cops huddling in the corridor, making neat little marks in their notebooks to sum up what had happened. He started out anyway.

"Not that way." Gil saw that there was no stopping him, snorted and gave up. "All right. Only take it easy, will you?" He steered Doug to a connecting door on the other side of the room. "I can tell them Kelly had you moved upstairs for X-rays. That'll give us a little time."

They moved through an adjacent office, out again into the next hall where chimes continued to signal like padded doorbells above the clanging of wheeled carts and the whir of unseen machinery.

Intensive Care was around the corner.

The chicken-wire glass inset in the door was the size and shape of a television screen. As they approached the window, only i.v. bottles and tubes and monitoring equipment were visible at first, strung overhead to resemble the off-screen booms and technical apparatus of a broadcast studio. Doug centered his face before the grid, panning down to take in the end of a bed, a chair, the back of a woman's head. The arm extending across the bed was so still and colorless that it might have been a fold in the sheet. A beeping came through the window, synchronized to the faint blips on a wall screen.

"Everything's being done for her that can be done. She's strong, healthy . . ."

Before Gil could stop him, Doug opened the door and went in.

Doug opened the door and came in.

Casey ignored him. She remained seated in the straight-backed chair, massaging her daughter's wrist, trying to stimulate the pulse there. She had no time to talk to him. She had too much to think through.

How could it have come to this? *How*?

First she had been in the bedroom with Elizabeth sleeping against her back like a spoon and her husband's voice an almost reassuring drone through the floor as though the house were purring, tempting her to sleep without her medication; then the door from the TV room to the bathroom was opening, the faucet running, and Mary Bauman was coming in with a glass of water and more pills. She took the pills into her mouth, accepted the glass but did not swallow or speak; she had to keep track of Elizabeth's breathing. Some time earlier in the evening she had dared to rest her eyes for a moment; when she opened them again her little girl was deathly quiet, as if her tiny lungs had forgotten how to keep pace. Only when Casey rolled over and clutched the child to her breast did she feel the heart take hold again. So this time Casey held the pills between her teeth and lips, lay back down without a word and pretended to sleep. When Mary went out she spat them into her handkerchief. She was thankful that Mary was only reading in the other room so that there were no distracting television voices. Elizabeth hacked at a build-up of phlegm in her throat and continued dreaming, as Casey resumed her watch.

If she had only listened closely enough none of this would have happened . . . .

She had noted the rise and fall of her husband's voice; she knew Lori was sleeping in her own room tonight but even with Doug downstairs she had no feeling of safety. Had he remembered to lock the doors and windows? At one point his voice took on an angry coloration. Did that mean anything was wrong? Then there was the sound of impact, as if he had dropped something in his clumsy way or accidentally kicked the patio door. Mary must have heard it, too, because she immediately left the TV room and went downstairs. Then the voices were calm again. If it was minor Mary could take care of it. But a few minutes later there was that terrible pounding down in front, shoes running on the carpet, shouting, a car driving away. If she had been able to hear her husband's words clearly enough she would have understood what was happening. What reason could he possibly have that would justify leaving Lori, leaving them all alone?

Mary wouldn't let her out of bed but instead made up a story that was almost plausible about a traffic accident down the canyon. If Mary had been able to control her tone Casey might have accepted it; it would have been so much more convenient since there was no way she could rationalize leaving her youngest child, and she was not capable of carrying Elizabeth downstairs with her to be certain. She was so groggy from the accumulation of drugs in her system that she had not the strength to fight her way out of the bedroom in any case. If she had ignored the advice of Doug's doctor friend, had refused the medication all along . . .

What had happened?

That was the latest part of the mystery. How could she hope to learn even that much from the squibs and lines of the oscilloscope above Lori's bed, from the nerve-wracking hum of the heart-lung machine, the cryptic dials and readouts and scribbled charts? They were in a language she did not understand.

Tell me, she thought, leaning closer. But someone had covered Lori's mouth with a plastic mask so that she could not answer . . . .

Casey had waited for Doug to return and explain himself. After a while, with the house so peaceful again and tears of rain beginning to purl over the roof and cleanse the windows, she had come close to accepting Mary's story. But then there was the rumbling in the hills, shaking the trees as if the earth itself were opening. The dog, all the dogs in all the back yards of the canyon had gone wild with barking as the bushes on the ridge trembled under a mighty outpouring, as animals scrambled out to escape—what? a mudslide? Casey fought Mary off long enough to see some of it from the skylight. Then Elizabeth was mewling in her sleep and Casey was holding her again, waiting for it to pass. But she had seen enough to know that some of the animals were almost human.

Then the sirens and the police car stopping in front, more pounding and she would not have been able to answer in time had Mary not gone down for her. Casey needed to get Elizabeth and Lori out and away from danger. But the police had not come for that reason. They had not even put on the flashing light this time; the sirens she heard came from the fire trucks up on Mulholland Drive. Why had they come, then?

Lori was not in her room.

But they knew where she was, they would take Casey to her . . . .

As they went away with her and Mary and Elizabeth in the back seat she saw Mrs. Kasabian, whose son belonged in an institution, outside on her front porch at last, waving her arms at the hills, crying out *Buddy, come home! Come home to me now!* as the coyotes set to yipping and a living darkness moved down from the crest like a swarming from out of an anthill.

And now she was in a strange hospital room and for some reason Lori was here, her own precious Lori, who was even now slipping away from her and there was nothing she could do to stop it and no one was able to tell her why. She had tried, but she could not make sense of their words. She needed someone to explain it to her.

Doug came up behind her and touched her back.

"Case," he said.

Casey only sat that much straighter.

He saw Elizabeth asleep on her lap then, came around to take the child. Casey would not let go. She rocked Elizabeth with one arm, left her other hand on Lori's chill wrist, massaging the fine purple scrimshaw veins. She did not know if it did any good. But she would not give up.

The pulse was weak, only a slight pressure under the skin as if a worm were moving slowly, so slowly. Casey increased the rhythm. Lori's hand grew colder, the peaks and valleys on the screen lengthening across an ice-green plain, like a printout of a lie detector attached to the dying earth.

He gave up trying to take Elizabeth from her and added his strength to her hand. But he was not strong enough to make any difference.

"Case," he said again. "Case, I . . ."

He began to cry.

Poor, weak man, she thought, nearly as weak as I was ever to have trusted him with Erin and Lori. I won't say anything, not a word and he'll go away and leave me here where I should have been all along before he seduced me away from them . . . .

She went on massaging until her fingers ached. But she would not let him or anyone else take Elizabeth from her, nor would she leave Lori's side. She wanted to be with her, to go down all the way with her, to comfort her so that she would not be so alone. She's such a little girl, Casey thought. She must be terrified where she is, just as Erin was, so terribly young. She needs me to be there with her, to keep her warm and help her find her way back. It would be too much to expect her to do it by herself.

Behind her, Doug quietly left the room.

Doug left the room.

"I won't try to bullshit you," said Gil as they walked away. "It was as close as they come. She was severely oxygen depleted when they brought her in. But she's young, resilient. With time . . ."

"A coma?"

"The higher brain centers have shut down while her tissues replenish. If there's no organic brain damage . . ."

"Is there?"

"We won't know that until the brain scan comes back. As long as her vital signs hold . . ."

"You mean she may not come out of it."

"She's a tough kid."

"So was Erin."

In the examination room Doug sat down and wept, not caring whether Gil or anyone else saw him this way. When he was finished he sank into his chair with his feet out in front of him and his hands hanging uselessly at his sides, like some devolved throwback to an earlier, lower life form.

"So it wasn't one of your sex cults, after all," he said finally. "They were taking kids down there and offing them, as plain as that, as part of some kind of ceremony, a blood sacrifice to . . . I don't know what. Purify their souls."

Gil left the lights off so that no one would know they

were there, so that they would have a few more minutes. Beyond the Levelor blinds the hazy red letters of the outdoor admissions sign burned warmly in the night. Part of the word was cut off by the edge of the building. EMERGE, it read.

"Not exactly," said Gil in the gentlest voice he had ever used, as though some things were not meant to be spoken of in such surroundings, would disturb the carefully controlled reality that had taken millennia to achieve and which now barely held them both from sliding back into the primordial ooze. "A suicide cult, but with a twist. Your friend Buddy laid it all out. I listened for a while. He opened up to the nurses first, then the cops. I think he'd wanted to spill it for a long time but didn't think anybody'd believe. He was probably right. If he'd come to me with the story . . .

"Anyway, they're sweeping the place clean right now. When they're finished they ought to hold a press conference on national TV and save some more lives. ·It's not just here, by the sound of it—it's everywhere. Are you sure you want to hear this?"

Doug thought, There is nothing between me and the darkness now. If there's something more that might help Lori . . .

"What do you mean, not exactly?"

"The way I get it, they were selling the ultimate trip, the Big D."

Gil went to the window, continued speaking with his back to Doug.

"The s&m crowd I told you about, they use the same neck rigs, plastic bags, anything that cuts off the normal intake of air long enough to cause a blackout. *But.* Suppose you want to take it one step further, to the limit, beyond that? Interrupt oxygen exchange and it doesn't take long for the pulse, the metabolic processes to stop, and clinical death occurs. As long as you revive before somatic death sets in—within about six minutes—then you're one of the lucky ones. You were medically dead, but you made it back. You survived the biggest thrill ride of them all."

"You mean they do it *voluntarily*? Why would anyone want to die like that, least of all kids?"

"You've hit it. They're kids. They don't have a firm idea of death in the first place. When they did it they convinced themselves that they were seeing 'the other side,' the which than which there is no whicher. They always came back with a story to tell. When they came back. The ones who did were out to spread the word."

When Doug found his voice again he said, "They were into more than spreading the word. They weren't just evangelists. There was nothing voluntary about it. Their leader put a noose around my neck. He would have strung me up if Buddy hadn't been there."

"They thought they were doing you a favor." Gil hunched his shoulders, a gesture that was a combination of a shrug and a shudder. "They knew you couldn't accept it till you'd passed through the fire. Buddy says they'd find some stoned-out kids, promise them the big one, heavier than any drug on the market. They'd make a pact to do it. Once you'd promised, the cult never forgot. They were True Believers."

So that's what happened to Erin, Doug thought. She went to the Club and somebody—the one in the white clothes?—conned her into trying it. She didn't know what she was agreeing to. It didn't take the first time, or she saw what it was about and got away before it was finished; that was why she already had one bruise on her neck. But she still didn't realize how deeply she had been sucked in. *A promise is a promise*. And they came after her before she could trust me enough to tell me about it. If she even remembered. She didn't know what she'd set into motion.

But Buddy knew. He and the others like him, the kids who left the cult, they knew. They were caught between two worlds. They didn't belong to either anymore. Not unlike those who were damned for other reasons, the derelicts, the walking mad out on the streets, in the dark places below the streets, the only ones who would accept them after the death-tripping had left its mark.

"How did they get to Erin again?" Doug asked. "She

never went back. She couldn't have. She was babysitting that night."

"If what we saw down there is any indication, that so-called Underground of theirs reaches a hell of a long way. Maybe even right into your own back yard."

And Lori? She said she knew something about it. She must have found out what they were into, went out on her own to do what I should have done. But she didn't know all of it. She didn't know what she was playing around with. But she tried. She tried because she loved Erin, and wanted to help. And then someone got ahold of her and tried to "help" her, too, the other one, the other girl, the one who was there with her. The one who didn't make it . . . .

"Why wasn't booze enough?" said Doug. "Or pot, acid, *anything* else? PCP, for God's sake? Why did they have to go that far?"

"Those were the old ways, the ways of their parents. Our ways."

Doug started to shake. "If you could have heard them. Those poor, deluded, wasted kids. They talked about it like it was some kind of nirvana. But Buddy was the only one who told the truth. He said, 'You don't know how bad it is!' If it really was, why would anyone want a replay?"

"That's the part that keeps witchdoctors like me in business," said Gil. "Why do people shoot smack, drive ninety miles an hour, smoke cigarettes for that matter, when they know it'll probably kill them? Some jump off the Golden Gate Bridge and change their minds halfway down. Others try to burn before they hit. Eros and Thanatos, Dionysus and Apollo. I learned all the words. But in the end they're only words. Descriptions, not explanations."

Gil pulled the cord, opening the blinds fully to the activity in the parking lot.

"The only other explanation," he went on, "is that they really were seeing another place, a better place than this one. If you can accept an idea as crazy as that . . . ."

Outside, a van caromed up to the rear doors.

AMBULANCE, it said across the front in mirror-image.

"Of course if I really thought that I'd be no different from the True Believers, would I? The Eternal Hereafter, the White Light . . . . Sometimes I wonder if I dropped one too many tabs myself back in the old days."

Doug felt the bandages binding his skin like burial wrappings. "Get me out of this," he said. "I don't need it anymore."

Gil turned from the window. "Listen, I want you to lay up tonight. We'll get you a room. There's nothing you can do for Lori. I can give you something to sleep. Casey, too. I'll let you know if there's any change."

"Not on your life." Doug pulled at the sweat-soaked bandages. "Give me something to cut with."

Gil put on the desk light. He was looking at his friend without surprise, as if he would have been disappointed to hear anything else. For a moment they held each other's eyes, making a connection that passed between them back through years too deep and too sharp for words.

He poked through a drawer and came up with a tray of tools. As he took the scalpel in hand, a child began crying in another part of the wing. The sound cut Doug to the quick.

"Can't someone do something for that baby?"

"Someone will, don't worry." He started toward Doug with the blade.

The crying continued.

"Who?" said Doug.

"Christ, you're not responsible for the whole world. The first thing I had to learn in here is that I can't personally save the human race. I do what I can. That's got to be enough. If it isn't . . ."

The crying was closer now.

"For the love of God," said Doug.

"Let it go."

"I can't." He cut loose the gauze himself and left it behind on the chair.

Suddenly the timbre of the crying hit home. The catch

in the throat, the tremulous wail . . .

He yanked the door open.

At the end of the hall, a small girl was dashing frantically between the waiting room and the coffee machine. She saw him, bent her knees, slapped her tiny hands on her legs and tilted her head as her face deflated into a squashed mask. She opened her mouth wider than it had ever opened before and let a hair-raising shriek out of the darkness in her throat.

"Dad-*dy*!" Elizabeth screamed at him as though he had betrayed her in a manner too grave to forgive. "Where were you? I didn't *see* you!"

A young nurse left her station and ran over, her ribbed soles squeaking over the dangerously polished floor. Doug got there first. He dropped down and grasped Elizabeth's arms.

"Baby, what is it?"

"It's Mommy! She's locked in and she won't come out!"

"Show me."

"Just a minute, sir. Is this child . . . ?"

He shoved the nurse off and carried Elizabeth around the corner, running with her on his shoulders.

What did she mean? Intensive Care was not locked.

"No," cried Elizabeth, "there!"

The door marked WOMEN. Doug set Elizabeth on her feet, then started pushing. It wouldn't open.

It was wedged shut from the other side.

Two more nurses and an intern rushed over to restrain him. He needed them to help but they did not seem to understand. Predictably the police were nowhere to be seen, now that they were needed.

Gil finally got there. "I'm Dr. McClay. This man is my patient. What's going on here?"

"It's Casey," Doug told him.

They rammed the door with their shoulders. It opened partway. Doug raised his foot and kicked from the hip. A waste can and a chair went flying.

At first he could see only the blood on the broken mirror, then the lower half of her body, as though she had been cut off at the waist. She was slumped forward over the basin, a shard of glass still buried in one wrist.

He understood at once why she had done it.

As more staff forced their way in and called for a stretcher, he thought of Lori, lost and alone, fighting for her life. As the starched uniforms turned red around him, he understood that Casey would do anything to bring her daughter back. Anything. As Mary Bauman appeared and held Elizabeth away from the operating room, he knew that Casey was with Lori even now, somewhere in the borderland between life and death.

Now Lori had an ally. Mother and daughter were together again as one.

". . . a lot of blood," someone was saying.

"Her temperature's dropping."

Bottles were inverted, fibrillator plates applied to her chest.

"Again."

"Still nothing."

"Again!"

She's got two, three minutes more, thought Doug. If they give up before then she and Lori are both lost.

He rushed out, past Elizabeth and Mrs. Bauman.

"Daddy, don't leave me! Where are you going? I want Mommy!"

"I'm going to get her," he said.

Or die trying, he thought.

"Doug, listen—" said Gil when he caught up back at the examination room.

"Don't try to stop me. Not you." Doug tore through the cabinets for something, anything. A piece of rubber tubing, a scalpel? Yes, either would do.

But they might take too long.

There. The respirator, a plastic mask with elastic bands to make it airtight. He cranked open the valve and oxygen hissed out. He spun the valve the other way and it stopped.

"What are you doing?"

"I'm going over."

"Where? The other side? Doug, it's an illusion!

There *is* no other side. It's physiological. Listen to me!
The muscles go slack and the pupils dilate—there's your
so-called white light. Then the optic nerve bundles close
down, narrowing to a kind of tunnel vision. The so-
called out-of-body experience that everyone talks about,
the sensation of floating, that happens while you're losing consciousness from lack of oxygen to the—''

"There's one way to be sure. I don't have a choice.
Get someone to stay with Lori. Her mother can't hold
on to her from this side anymore.'' Doug reached into
his pocket, took out the gold watch with the black band,
Erin's watch, wound it and flung it across the table.
"How long can you give me?''

"Doug, I can't do this. I'm a doctor.''

Doug fastened the mask over his head, started to
lower it over his mouth and nose. He tested the valve
again to be sure the air supply was all the way off.
"You're not doing a damn thing. I'm doing it to myself.
Now are you going to help me or not?''

Gil uncapped a syringe and advanced on him, squirt-
ing a few drops as he crossed the room.

"I can't let you,'' he said. "I'm going to give you a
sedative. Don't fight it. After you've slept it off—''

He went for Doug's back. Doug saw it coming and
grabbed the hand, forced it around so that it was pointing the other way and leaned his weight back into it. He
felt the plunger close under Gil's thumb until it was
empty. Gil grunted, fell back and did not try to stop him
again.

"If you're a doctor, do your job! Start worrying
about saving lives. Time me—I want the full six minutes. Pray that it's long enough. And that I'm not too
late.''

Doug lowered himself into the swivel chair, closed his
eyes, dropped his head to his chest, and waited to die.

God give me the strength, he thought, *to do this one
thing*.

He held his eyelids down and exhaled deeply into the
empty tube, waiting to slip into unconsciousness. When
the battle started he refused to fight. He kept his eyes

shut and willed himself down, as his muscles relaxed, his temperature dropped, his kidneys swelled and his brain prepared to liquefy. He did not see the convulsions under his ribs, the white knuckles gripping the sides of the chair, did not see the room begin to spin as he lost contact with his body, nor the intersecting planes and angles of the walls and furniture that would have blocked his view of the doctor's already unconscious form slumped on the floor where he had fallen after the struggle, the point of the discharged hypodermic needle embedded in the flesh of his own arm.

twelve

When he raised his head again, he knew that nothing
had changed.

No . . .

Nerves ragged, pushed beyond despair and beaten, he
ceased struggling.

His eyes stirred and opened without expectation.

It couldn't matter now.

It was too late. It always had been.

And from this point on it always would be.

He saw the contents of the room as they had been before: window, desk, cabinets, examination table, tray,
chair, oxygen tank—the windows louvered by knife-
edged blinds, the desk half-covered by a green blotter
the shape and color of a fresh grave, the cabinets glassed
like grandfather clocks with visible mechanisms of tem-
pered steel, the examination table with sanitized sheeting torn to expose the blackness beneath, the gleaming
porcelain tray outfitted with sharpened and sterilized
tools, his chair as unaltered as a launch pad after an
aborted countdown, the oxygen tank still pressurized,
ready to ignite and propel him beyond this world. Obvi-

ously he had failed to turn off the air supply completely. The umbilical tube that fed his mask was lined with jeweled drops of condensed respiration. He removed the mask, seeing for a split second into its segmented interior: a translucent cave dripping with stalactites of moisture like the nodules of a silently screaming throat. He sat gazing down at his hands, at the white half-moons rising on his thumbs, with the calmness that comes only from the realization of utter defeat.

There was no one else in the room. The black-and-gold wristwatch still lay on the desk. Gil had not picked it up. He reached for the splayed band, retrieved it and stood. The watch wasn't even working right; impossibly, the minute hand had moved only two notches—to 9:22—since he set it down.

There was nothing more he could do here.

As he backed across the floor the room seemed to retract, shrinking before him in size and importance. Whatever happened to Casey and to Lori was in greater hands than his. The outcome never had been up to him. Only his inflated, all-suffering ego had made him believe otherwise.

He let himself out.

After so long in relative darkness, the brightness of the hallway scorched around the edges of the door with an almost physical pressure, forcing it open further; he had to put up a hand to ward off the blinding glare. At the same time a clash of sounds from the corridor pummeled his ears, the hospital's background noises boosted to an unbearable level. It was a din made up of half-tones signaling the arrival of elevators, the pumping shut of retractable doors, the beeping of telephones, the trackless rolling of life-saving machines, fragments of laughter, the squeaking footsteps and rustlings and swishings and snatches of conversation blending into a rushing chorus that was the sound of life itself. It was almost too much to bear. He felt his nerves stripped bare; he cupped his hands to his ears and locked his eyes shut until he was ready to let it in again.

When he opened his ears the overload had subsided to

a tolerable level. Ahead of him the flaring reduced down
and converged to a single point at the end of the corridor, a cold sun beyond the glass doors of the waiting
area. The polished walls hinted at unseen movement,
a constant shifting of light and darkness just outside
the range of vision. Where was Gil? *I'll let you know if
there's any change.*

They should know something by now.

He moved along the corridor to the visitors' room.

There was no one at the nurses' station. A cupful of
pencils, clipboard charts hanging from one wall, an
Easter gift plant wrapped in metallic foil and tied with a
bow. A multi-line telephone with call lights blinking. No
one to take the calls. They're on a break, he thought.
How convenient for them.

The waiting room was empty as well. The molded
chairs and lowboy couches were conspicuously unoccupied; plastic-bound magazines lay strewn over the
tables—*Humpty Dumpty, Venture, Time, Sunset, Re-
tirement Living, Geo.* He heard voices nearby but saw
no sign of life. Even Mary Bauman had gone home.
That must mean that the crisis was over. Perhaps everyone had gathered in another part of the wing. Were
Buddy and his friends holding forth for the police even
now? Or were they in the midst of that press conference,
with reporters and news cameras? He rubbed out a spot
on the doors to the parking lot, but a heavy mist had
fallen outside, thick and dark as oil smoke. He couldn't
even see himself in the glass.

He turned left toward Intensive Care. The layers of
voices remained close by. It was an acoustic trick; it
seemed to be coming from behind as well as in front of
him now. Was there an intercom system in the ceiling?
He came to the reinforced glass inset and looked in on
Lori.

Gil had let him down. There was no one attending to
his daughter. The straight-backed chair was empty. He
scanned the room. Only high-tech equipment juryrigged
over the bed, tubes and wires still connected to monitoring devices, the screen on the wall . . .

Which was now reading out in an even green line.

The bed was empty.

Lori had been moved. That meant she was past danger. She had come out of the coma, yes, and been transferred somewhere else.

He continued down the hall, drawn by the invisible chorus of voices. They seemed to be speaking to him from every doorway he passed but they remained hidden, eluding him around each new turn in the white walls. The women's restroom door was still sprung on its hinges. How long would it take them to get a crew up here to repair it? He did not glance inside.

This time there was no one to prevent him from entering the operating theater. He looked around for a nurse or doctor who could tell him about Casey's condition, but this branch of the wing was understaffed, as well. Where were they all? Something of great importance must have been taking place in another location. And wherever they were, they had Lizzy with them, unless she had gone home with Mary. He was sure they would treat her well. He consoled himself with that thought.

The operating room, too, was as barren and sterile as an autoclave.

Where was his wife?

The massed voices drew him around another turn.

At the central receiving and reception lobby, he went to the counter, passed its entire length, seeing manila folders, a computer terminal, registration forms, pens, steno chairs, drawers, a massive wall of files, but no human being on duty. The lobby shone with the circular brush strokes of an electric floor polisher, distorting the overhead fluorescents in its spun surface. By the doors, wheelchairs leaned collapsed against one wall, their canvas backs folded into loops like barber strops. A telephone buzzed near his left hand.

He put the receiver to his ear, and heard ocean waves.

"Hello?" he said. "Is anybody there?"

The waves ebbed, and someone began whimpering into the mouthpiece.

"*Who is this*?" he demanded.

The weeping stopped. Then a voice said, "Who is this?"

Thank God, he thought. "Listen, I'm at the front desk. Can you help me? I'm trying to find my wife and my little girl. They're both patients here. Only there doesn't seem to be anyone on duty. My name is—"

"We know who you are."

He hung his arm over the counter and punched the other lighted buttons. Nothing. He came back to the original line. "Are you calling from inside the hospital?" he said. "If you are, please send someone over here to—"

"Is that where you think you are?" The voice began to laugh.

"Let me talk to someone who—"

"We know where you are," said the voice.

"Where?"

"It's close. Closer than you think. Why don't you take a look around?"

The line clicked off.

He heard the chorus of voices again, continuous as a Muzak tape loop. But it was not a tape; they were real voices, he was sure. He went to the front doors. The fog outside rolled up to the ramp, curling against the glass like ectoplasm, blotting out the parking lot and everything beyond.

The voices . . .

They seemed to be coming from another part of the lobby. He had two ninety-degree turns to choose from, both antisepticized corridors stretching away to distant vanishing points. The only other opening was a private doorway behind the counter, access for authorized personnel to the inner workings of the complex.

He let himself behind the counter and went through.

This time the burnished floor ended at a short flight of steps protected by a pipe handrail. He followed it down, and came to a service door. When he tried it, it opened.

Inside there were several more doors to choose from. They might lead to storage facilities, supply rooms, the central heating and air conditioning controls for the hospital, or . . .

Only one of the knobs turned in his hand.

He slapped the walls for a light switch.

"Hi," said a boy's voice.

A cigarette lighter flicked on.

The boy's hair was a platinum flame against the blackness. Doug sighed with relief.

"Buddy! Thank God. What are you doing down here?"

Buddy didn't say anything.

"I'm trying to find out where they moved Lori. Do you know? And my wife. I don't even know where to—"

Buddy nodded and extinguished the lighter. "Follow me."

The chorus of voices buzzed louder, as if they were approaching a nest of bees. Presently bits of shadow took form around them, rough indications of familiar concrete cylinders staggered across a vast subterranean plain, illuminated faintly by shafts of wan light from above. This time there were no tires passing overhead.

"This was the way you got her out," said Doug, "and up to the hospital. Thank you for that. I owe you a lot. You saved my daughter's life."

"Don't thank me. Thank them."

The buzzing choir ceased. The pillars changed shape and moved. Eyes separated from the concrete and came cautiously forward.

"Come on out," said Buddy. "This here's a friend of mine. He's okay!"

They sidled out and into the tunnel, bright eyes and dull, tall and short, each face framed by the same shocks of prematurely whitened hair, as if they had seen too much and been frightened by what they saw and run away, but not before it had left its indelible mark. They were Buddy's friends, the real drop-outs, who now belonged nowhere. Their smiles were quick and fleeting, their poses defensive, like young deer surprised in moonlight. They had been talking among themselves, muttering to each other below ground in a restless undercurrent. Doug wondered what they talked about.

They came closer as he passed, used pale hands to touch his clothes, his pigmented skin and hair, as if he were a visitor from another land. He returned the gesture, clasping their hands warmly, mumbling his thanks to each one in turn. Their numinous eyes turned away shyly.

Each one seemed more familiar than the last, until Doug felt that he was meeting old friends whose names he could not quite remember, friends he thought he had lost long ago. Behind him the curious, unsettled choir of their voices resumed, talking endlessly. Was that because there was no one else who would listen? His heart swelled with emotion.

"I can't believe they got you all," said Doug. "Why didn't you leave as soon as you saw what it was like, tell someone, blow their cover before the horror went any further?"

"It wasn't horror," Buddy told him. "That came later. At first it was like people always said. I read this book once. It said all the same stuff. The big light, the heavy-duty feelings, like nothing you ever did in your life mattered, no matter how bad. That's why it holds you. Trouble is, you like it so much you start doin' it over and over again, to yourself. But that's a whole 'nother thing . . . ."

Then it wasn't a bad trip, after all, thought Doug, is that what he's saying? That would explain the bliss kids, the first ones he had met below the Club, Rainbow and White Feather and the others. Did that mean the boy in white wasn't selling a lie? That it really was instant satori?

"You told Erin that it was bad. I heard you. What did you mean? If it was so beautiful—is *that* what you're telling me?—then why did you finally break away, you and your friends here?"

"Because there's always a catch. They don't tell you that up front. There ain't no free ride. Everything's got a price. And this one ain't worth paying. What I lost I ain't ever gettin' back, follow? Hey, we're almost there. That what you're lookin' for?''

He pointed his chin ahead, to a blue-white sphere hanging above the cement. How far had they walked? Doug had hardly been aware of his legs working, his feet making contact, yet he had the sense that he had come a very long way. As he drew closer he saw that the sphere was nothing less than the moon itself, and before it the silhouette of a bearded man, holding out a hand to help him up.

"Gil! What are you doing here? I'm sorry about that stunt back there. It was pointless. I know that now."

"Forget it," said Gil, leading him up a short flight of stairs to an opening. "I have. Here."

He accepted Gil's hand and ascended into the great healing balm of light from the oversized moon above the horizon; it was as if it was rising just for him, its cool radiance purging him with loving grace.

"Where are we? I was looking for Casey and Lori and . . .''

"There," said Gil, a beatific smile on his lips. "Don't you recognize this place?" He waved his arm to include the hillside onto which they had emerged. "It's all there. Everything you wanted."

"What?" He looked down from the ridge, past the cat's-eye swimming pools, the wet, cleansed brush and shrubbery leading to the back yard of a house on Beaumont Canyon, his house, built by the music inside him. "Where . . . ?"

"They're waiting. I had them brought back here. There's nothing more I can do for them. I thought you'd want them home where they belong."

If Gil said it was all right, then it was all right. "Thank you, man. From the bottom of my heart. I owe you more than I can ever—"

"For nothing," said Gil.

His eyes burning, the moon blurring, Doug slipped down from the mouth of the tunnel. The descent was remarkably easy. He left the plateau and glided through scrub and giant ivy as if on wings. That which had provided an entranceway for the evil that took Erin from him had now been flushed clean; soon it would be sealed as it always should have been and the Lost Ones would have to seek another haven, or would find salvation in a way that would enable them to share what they had learned with others. For now there was still time for it to provide one last passage, an access. He was coming home. And he was bringing Buddy with him. That did not seem like such a bad idea. It was a start.

The fog lifted and he saw the back yards of his neighbors, the Baumans' heated pool a rippling opal, colored Malibu floodlights tinting the Spanish-style roofs, fashionable dogs enthroned in upholstered doghouses, a swing set rusting behind the Staverses'. Of all the homes on the block only his was unlighted, a dark gap between the landscaped plots; he identified it by a process of elimination. He skidded down to the retaining wall, followed Buddy's example and walked the wet stones as if they were eggs and miraculously did not fall. Towser, jadded old sophisticate that he was, did not bother to raise his snout. The back door was open.

The dining room was as blacked-out as a coal mine; not even the nightlight over the kitchen range had been left on. But he knew the house by now. He turned to the left, trailed his fingers along the tiled surfaces, recognizing only the occasional lambent edge of an appliance or the ghostly furniture back in the other room, the cushions and chairs arranged like a jury of mute witnesses. A single gas pilot flame pulsated below the rangetop, a tiny waning eye as blue as a luminous cataract.

He heard the suctioning of Buddy's sneakers behind him on the linoleum. The boy had not gone home to his own house down the street; he was a stranger to it, had been for a long time. But that situation would change. For now he could stay here, if he wanted to.

"I'm going to look in on the child first," Doug said. "Wait here."

He followed the wall left again into the short hall to Lori's room. The door was not latched. He nudged it open.

The white mound of the bed was clear in the moon-light through the curtains. He sat on the mattress and stroked the contours of the quilt, expecting to find the wisps of angel hair at her temples. He eased the bed-clothes down to uncover her face.

An arrangement of pillows tumbled out.

She was not there.

It was like the time before, when she had left a decoy in her place. Then where—?

He jumped up, groping for the lamp. The table rocked and the lamp fell.

Now he would never find the light. But that was all right; the three of them, Casey, Lori and Elizabeth, were probably resting together upstairs with Mary Bau-man or a registered nurse close at hand. Still . . .

He went to Lori's closet, felt for the chain to the bare bulb. He had trouble finding it. A hangerful of Lori's clothes hung from the ceiling. He pushed past it and pulled the cord. The light came on like a flashgun.

It was not a bunch of clothes.

It was Lori. She hung there from a strap around her neck. The strap was attached to a hook in the plaster. She swung back and forth, back and forth, her arms engorged, her face blue.

This time she was beyond his or anyone else's help.

He let out an animal cry and hugged her to him. Too large for her body weight, the rig slipped its notches at last and opened, releasing her into his arms.

"Let me take her," said Buddy.

"No." She was cold as ice, a rigor-mortised doll. He lifted her out through the hall, through the living room to the stairs. He went up with her in his arms, Buddy a shadow presence at his heels, past the skylight and the smudge of sodium lights out on the street, to the big bedroom.

The covers were thrown back from Casey's side of the bed, revealing only dark splotches which spread up the headboard like the shadows of leaves. In the room he heard a breathing that was not his own.

Beneath the deck windows, someone was sitting on

the ottoman. He saw the black outline of a head rocking forward and back, forward and back.

"Casey?"

"Don't come any closer." She straightened, the needle-point of her scissors catching a stray beam of light, then sank back into the shadows and resumed rocking.

She began humming.

Still carrying Lori's stiff form, he found the lamp on the nightstand. When it went on he turned the shade up and aimed it.

Casey sat there under the windows in her robe, rocking Elizabeth on her lap. The robe had been green once, just as the bandages on her wrists had once been pure white. Now she was covered with dirt from head to toe. He staggered toward her, Lori frozen in his arms, and saw that the dirt was brown in places, red in others. Elizabeth's naked body was also smeared with the blood, as was the ottoman, the walls. It had run out of the second mouth below her chin until there was no more. Casey had done this. With the scissors.

His legs turned to jelly. Lori's hardened body went sprawling.

"Put her here, Douglas." She held out her arms. "Now it's almost complete. We can be together always. Here."

"Buddy!" He crawled over Lori, grabbed Casey's arms to keep her at bay. "Take the little one, quickly!"

"Get away!" Casey snarled. "You can't stop me. It was your fault. Yours! It's over!"

"I won't," he told her, grappling with her arms which were now ramrod-strong. "I won't give you up. Do you understand me?"

"Even now?" she said. "Do you see what I've done?"

"I love you."

She stabbed him in the shoulder, in the chest, in the neck, in the side. "Do you love me now? Now? Get away from me, you bastard. Leave us! It's too late. There's nothing else!"

"I will not," he said. Her blows struck and penetrated his flesh but he could not, would not feel it. "Do *you* understand? *I will not!*"

"God damn you to hell! God damn us all to—"

He hit her across the jaw with his fist. The scissors dropped. Then her eyes rolled up and she folded over. He caught her under the armpits before she reached the floor.

"Call for an ambulance!" he said.

"Can't," said Buddy. "The phone's cut. Come with me. We'll do it the same way as before . . . ."

Somehow they got the three of them downstairs, one child each and Casey between them. From the patio every other yard was now dark. It was too late to rouse help.

"Hey!" Buddy called up the hill. "Down here!"

No one came. Doug saw a gauntlet of eyes, the burning yellow slits that were coyotes or wolves, high atop the ridge. At the scent of fresh blood they began to descend.

Doug slung Casey over his shoulder and cradled Lori in his arms as the boy took Elizabeth and climbed ahead. The path was steep but clear to the first plateau. From the top of the ridge the canyon was a black and formless sea; as they stepped over, every light in the San Fernando Valley disappeared as if concealed by a magician's black cloth. Now the predators were closing in on all sides, growling and snapping hungrily.

Doug couldn't get over the lip. Trees broke behind him.

"Don't look back," said Buddy. He found a gnarled stick, thumbed the lighter. The flint struck and the branch ignited with a whoosh. "Now! Go!"

The tunnel tapered and constricted around them, bands of light undulating over the close, slimy sides. Doug ran as best he could. The weight did not seem to slow him down. A short distance in, the recessed shadows in the walls sprouted limbs. The boy gave Elizabeth over to them. Doug saw her carried away, as if she had never really been there. He still had Casey and Lori.

"Give it up." The boy held the torch away and

melded into the shadows. "It's easier that way."

Doug would not give up his burden, not even now. He pushed ahead through the torchlight. He had never before felt so strong, so tireless. Not even his wounds bothered him. As he brushed past, knocking loose a shower of sparks, he saw that the boy was no longer wearing a camouflage shirt and highwater pants; now his clothes were bleached-out, white.

"Who are you?"

"W'll hey, what's the difference? We have you now, anyway, right? What else is there?"

Doug reached with his one empty hand as if to take the torch. Instead he seized the boy's neck below the ivory smile. He gripped the throat and rammed him into the wall. The torch dropped and flames licked up the edges of the flowing white garment.

"It doesn't matter," said the boy. "Don't you get it? Nothing matters!"

Doug let go. "The hell with you."

The boy roared with laughter. Through the fire, Doug saw him applauding.

"You'll never get out now, never. Nothing's changed. Nothing ever changes. You've always been here. You always will be here. With me!"

The flames licked higher. The torch rolled and smoldered, about to go out. Doug picked it up.

"Go for it!" yelled the boy. And laughed madly.

Doug left him behind. He ran with renewed energy, like a mighty engine, hardly aware of the exertion. The tunnel widened to the familiar pillars and sweating concrete. There was a massive heating intake duct that led up into the foundations of the hospital.

Gil was waiting on the stone steps.

"This way!" he yelled. "Here, let me—"

"They stay together," said Doug. He shifted Casey's weight on his shoulder, hiked Lori higher and headed up. "There isn't much time. I've got to get them—"

As he shouldered past, Doug saw that it wasn't really Gil. He had been tricked again. It was Shannon, with his hair tucked back and an artificial beard.

But Shannon was dead.

The man's clothes burst open, his body transforming into a thing with crooked paws instead of arms, the beard on his face growing out to become a great coat of fetid hair. The collar popped open and a huge head twice the size of a dog's inflated from the neck. The material split again to make room for two more vicious canine skulls, each one gnashing and foaming at the mouth.

"Let me pass," Doug said.

Three salivating mouths bit the air with foul teeth as long legs tore out of the trousers, bending and thickening.

Then it sprang.

Doug stood his ground, holding the torch up and pole-axing the creature in midair. The animal sailed over his head and landed with a howl. Behind him, Doug heard the last scissoring of dripping incisors, the slowing click of talons on cement. But he would not look back.

He climbed the steps and came up into the passage behind the receiving desk.

"Here, sir, what are you doing? You can't—!"

Doug lumbered across the lobby. It was fully activated again. Men in backless smocks and paper shoes shuffled in the hall like automatons. When they saw him they retreated, cringing against the wall, where a red light began to blink. A buzzer bleated along the corridor all the way to the operating room. He kneed the swinging doors and stumbled in. He would get help for Casey first.

But his wife was already inside, strapped to the table, her hands out at her sides, palms up, as if to receive him. I.V. tubes ran from her arms and a respirator covered her nose and mouth. Two doctors looked up from behind cloth masks, eyes bulging. They stopped sewing Casey's wrists, lowered the curved suture needles.

"Who let him in here? Nurse!"

He approached the table, holding Lori out in front of him.

Casey's eyes opened.

The weight he had borne on his shoulder, the weight that he had thought was his wife, was lighter than ever. He leaned forward and dumped it onto the table.

He had been carrying an empty, rotted husk, nothing more. Its jawbone fell open and crumbled to pieces.

Casey sat up, the tubes ripping out of her arms, the mask falling away.

"Give her to me," she said.

He looked down. Lori had become a distended, blue-black sac, gangrenous beyond recognition, ready to explode in his hands.

Casey reached out, the scars on her wrists splitting and tearing open along the lengths of her arms. She smiled.

"Or don't you want me to have her?" she asked, laughing.

He drew back.

"Don't you love me anymore?" she asked. "Why don't you give me a hug, my darling? Come to me—embrace your wife. Can you do that little thing for me? I'll bet you can't. You're too weak, aren't you?"

He came closer. This time he would not pull away.

"Are you sure you want me to have her, darling?" she said. "Are you sure *you* want me now? Why would anyone want us the way we are? Take a good look!"

He lowered himself over her, laying the child between them. He locked one of Casey's hands in Lori's, the other in his own, holding them together so that no one would let go.

"You're not going to get away from me so easily," he said. "I will not have it. Do you understand?"

He opened his lips and kissed her on the mouth.

And at that the bed, the room and everything in it receded from him, drawing away as if he were being rocketed back along the corridor of a soft tunnel throbbing with life. Faces and places whipped by, as a great and vibrant choir filled his head with a sound that rose beyond the limits of human hearing. He was rushing away down a tube and back into an examination room and the body of a man who sat slumped forward in a chair. A doctor he had never seen before was there, tearing the mask away, and a nurse was shooting a hypodermic full of Adrenalin directly into the heart muscle. The pain stabbed between his ribs, waking him. His eyes opened. He was seeing it all now from the point of view of the man in the chair. It seemed right as rain.

"Dr. McClay's coming around," someone said.

"What about the other one?"

"He's breathing again. He's going to make it."

The watch on the desk read 9:26.

thirteen

Sunday morning

"They never got him," Gil was saying. "They're still looking. But nobody knows for sure what happened to the kid in white. He was a runaway from someplace back east. He kicked around L.A., living with people he met on the street. After that it was panhandling in Venice, in Westwood, while he got his first group of followers together. They found the tunnel system, struck a deal to use the nightclub as a meeting place. It meant more business for the owners. I heard the kid's name, but I couldn't tell you what it was."

"That's all right," said Doug. "It's not important."

"Maybe you're right. He could be anywhere. But he'll pop up again sooner or later. His kind always do. And the next time we'll be ready for him."

Will we? thought Doug. Yes, we will. We have to be. It has to be over.

At his feet, Lizzy was hard at work on her school map while trying to watch *Dappy the Duck's Easter Cartoon Special*, hoping that both would be finished before it was time to leave for church. Judy from Beverly Hills Presbyterian had come by to invite them to the early

234

service, but they had been sleeping in again this morning. There was still time to catch the second sermon; somehow that sounded like a nice idea. A bowl of Kwackles was on the coffee table, Lizzy's colored markers were spread out on the rug, dangerously close to the hem of her Alice In Wonderland dress.

"Don't forget to clean up after yourself before we go," he said to her, "okay?"

"Okay."

It was important, he thought, for the family to return as soon as possible to a state approximating normality, for all of their sakes. Lizzy seemed to be doing the best job of it. She appeared remarkably untouched by what had happened. But then she had slept through most of it. That was one of God's special graces. He would try to answer her questions as they came up, but not before. For now, she was absorbed in her drawing. That was as it should be.

"What do you call that?"

The country she had designed looked dark and treacherous, full of trees and mountains, with what Doug took to be a seaport at the edge of a sprawling, undefined region. He might be able to help her with it later. Unless Gil decided to take it with him to psychoanalyze. But no, that wouldn't be necessary. She was doing just fine working it out on her own. Sometimes that was the best way.

"I don't know yet. I'll think of something." She sat up in front of the TV. "Listen! He's going to say it!"

"Say what?"

" 'Trouble just rolls off my back!' "

Gil grinned at her. "It does, does it?"

"No, silly, that's what Dappy says."

"I like the duck's style."

Lori came in, slightly out of breath from the stairs. She was fully recovered, according to the doctors, but she still had to be careful about over-exertion. It had been agreed that she would stay home from school for an extra week just to be on the safe side.

"Um, guess what?"

"Lo-*ri*." Elizabeth started to complain but controlled herself, moving closer to the television speaker.

"I know," said Doug. "That nice lady, Judy-what's-her-name, is waiting for us downstairs. Mom will be ready in a minute. What time's it getting to be?" He glanced at the timer on the VCR below the set and answered his own question. "I'd better go down and tell her it won't be long."

"I need to be moving on, anyway," Gil said.

"Okay, but that's not what I wanted to tell you, Dad." She spoke to him from Gil's knee. "Towser got away."

"How? Didn't you have the chain on?"

"Yes but, well, he chewed through his collar last night. And ran off."

"My doggie!" said Elizabeth. "Where *is* he?"

"Wherever he is, he'll make out," Doug told her. "That old boy knows how to take care of himself."

"You mean trouble rolls off his back?"

"Something like that."

Elizabeth got up and ran from the room. "Mommy, Mommy . . . !"

Doug peered out the window at the hillside, at the partially denuded firetrail and the earth-moving machinery parked on the ridge, where it would remain idle again until tomorrow morning. He tipped an invisible hat to the wayfaring dog, off now chasing sparrows and panting up a storm in a field of sweet grass. You never liked being a watchdog that much, did you? You barked at some, not at others, waiting for a live one. Selective enforcement, that's called. You weren't so dumb. Good luck, old boy, he thought. Godspeed. Eat some clover for me.

Gil rose and set Lori on her feet again. "Like I say, I gotta get gone."

"Where you headed?" Doug asked him.

"Oh, I thought I'd gas up the car and roll on down over the border, catch some r&r in the sun. You know the routine."

"That I do."

"I was thinking UCLA could spare me for a few days. But then, if it's like I remember it, I might not want to come back."

"Please?" said Lori.

"How far?" said Doug. "Not Ensenada, by any chance?"

"A little farther down, maybe Cabo San Lucas."

"Wish I was going with you," said Doug. "I could use some time in the sun. We all could."

"Can we?" said Lori.

"Not this time. I want to be here Tuesday. That's when they're holding the memorial service for Shannon. Maybe we'll catch up with you. I might take some of his ashes down. Remember that spot on the peninsula, out by the point? *La Bufadora*, it was called."

"Nice camping around there." Gil winked.

"Yeah."

"Don't go," said Lori.

Gil dropped down on one knee and embraced her. She didn't want to take her arms away.

"Like I said, I *was* thinking of doing that. But I can't right now. I have too much to do here."

"Don't put it off on our account."

"Are you kidding? You don't need me—you've got each other. No, it's all those lost kids, Buddy's pals. They're going to need some special handling. Right now they're scattered around between MacLaren Hall, Rancho Park, whatever facility has room. I'm trying to set up a kind of halfway house so they can stay together for now. They need a new kind of counselling. And love. Lots of love."

Gil noticed Elizabeth's map on the floor. She had drawn a crude version of the A for Anarchy sign over the brightest, busiest area.

"That reminds me. I figured out what that sign meant. Remember the circle with the three lines?"

"So did I," said Doug. "When Buddy warned us to stay away from the Darkside, he used the Club logo. That's all it means."

"But that wasn't the name of the Club. Look at this."

Gil turned the posterboard over and made a circle. "See this? Draw a straight line down the middle"—he did so—"and what have you got?"

"The Diners Club trademark. So?"

"Remember this?" Gil added two wings:

"The peace sign," said Doug. "What about it?"

"Do you know where it comes from? Originally it was the symbol for a ban-the-bomb group. The straight line is a D in semaphore code. They put the symbol for N on top of it. ND—nuclear disarmament.

"Now look at the symbol invented by the cult." He made another circle, drew three slightly different lines inside it:

"It's a D on top of an S. Get it?"

"DS," said Doug. "Darkside."

"Just thought you might be interested. The other thing, the anarchy sign, is everywhere. Teenage revolutionary romanticism at it again. Anyway, take it easy. I can find my way out."

He started down the hall, past the intense sunlight from the spring day outside. Doug followed. Gil turned back long enough to clasp his arms around Doug in a bear hug. Then he left.

It was years since Doug had been hugged by a man. Now such gestures were rare. In the context of today's standards that sort of thing was considered vaguely embarrassing. But he would have to unlearn the standards all over again. True, he wasn't now the person he once was; with the seventies and eighties there had been a lot of changes. Not all of them were for the better. Some things, some important things, had been lost. He wondered if the children would have giggled to see two grown men with their arms around each other. Maybe not, he thought.

He watched from the skylight as Gil drove away. Then another car drove up, and the doorbell rang.

"I'll get it," said Lori.

"No, you stay here and keep Mom company."

He went down to find that Judy from the church already had the door open. She was chatting amiably with a young man in a three-piece suit. The teenager looked up self-consciously, smoothed down his long mane of Jim Morrison-style hair, and held out his hand.

"I just stopped by. I hope it's all right. I don't want to bother you or anything."

"Not at all." As Doug shook his hand he recognized him as the boy from the funeral, the only young person who had attended.

"I was a friend of Erin's. I can come back later."

"If you'd rather not go this morning, Mr. Carson," said Judy pleasantly, "I can certainly hear that. If your family isn't up to it, we'll try it another time, how's that? It was just an idea."

"It's a good idea," he told her. "Casey's about ready. It won't be long." To the boy he said, "Would you care to sit down?" Maybe he'd like to go with us, he thought. He's dressed for it.

"I was on my way home from church. Over in the Valley. I don't go much. I mean, I haven't gone since I was a little kid. My folks kinda made me, bein' Easter and all. Besides, I sorta wanted to. So I was driving, and I thought I'd kinda stop by. And pay my respects."

"Did you know her very well?"

"No," said the boy quickly. "Yeah. I guess. It wasn't very long. Just for a little while, you might say."

You might say that, thought Doug. Not long at all.

"I just wanted to tell you that Erin was a real fine person," he blurted out. "I liked her. I mean I really liked her. Everybody did that knew her."

The boy's brown eyes welled up. He had long eyelashes and a hangdog, down-at-the-mouth expression, just the sort that would have touched Erin's soft heart.

"I know," said Doug. And you, he thought, you loved her too, didn't you, for a time? I can see that you did. You must have. "Thank you."

The two of them looked at their shoes.

"Would you like anything?" said Doug. "A cup of coffee, something to eat? Lori, her sister, made some wonderful croissants this morning."

"Naw, I can't stay. I just wanted to . . . I don't know."

"Stay a few minutes, at least. You can meet Erin's mother."

"No, I really—"

"I'd like for her to meet you. It would mean a lot."

"I guess that'd be okay."

"Good." He felt better. It seemed to matter. "I'll tell her you're here. Help yourself to what's in the kitchen."

"Thanks."

He started up.

The boy stood there awkwardly, uncertain about what to do with his hands while wearing a suit.

"If you like," said Doug, "you can wait in that room, the one by the stairs. It was Erin's room. I don't think she'd mind."

Doug went upstairs.

"Who was it?" asked Lori.

"A boy. I think he was Erin's boyfriend, or wanted to be."

"*Damon*? She used to talk about him all the time! Can I meet him? Where?"

"I told him to go on into her room." He had an idea. "Why don't you ask him if there's anything of hers he'd like to take? He might appreciate that."

"Her stuff? No way. She promised it all to me. I get her sweaters, her records . . ."

"I'm sure you don't need everything for yourself."

She put her chin down sheepishly. "I know. I'm sorry."

Lori left and he sat down and waited for Casey. Her blow-dryer made bars of electronic interference on the TV screen, skipping like oscilloscope lines across the animated cel drawings of Lizzy's Space Spirits, who were just now lurking around the edges of Dappy's turf, rayguns at the ready. Looking for Bluesberry Cheesecake, no doubt. Boys, he thought, go to it. He heard Lizzy's voice above the white noise from the bathroom, begging for the right to do something with her own unwieldy hair.

Space Spirits, he thought. The Darkside. It all seemed like a bad dream, the most horrible he would ever know, but one which like all others would be put away and forgotten in time.

The bathroom door opened and Casey came out, her hair given at least some semblance of a sheen by the sunlight from the window. She wasn't right yet and knew it; she was badly overdressed to cover her insecurity. Despite the season she had on a long-sleeved dress.

"Ready?" she said.

"Almost. There's someone downstairs I'd like you to meet."

She adjusted her sleeves. "Do the bandages show? Tell me the truth. I can wear something else if they do."

"You look fine. Come here."

"What? We're going to be late. That nice Judy came all this way—"

"We're not going to be late. Sit next to me. I want to talk to you."

She glanced back at Elizabeth, who was posing in front of the mirror and experimenting with her mother's hair dryer, trying to put a wave into her straight ends. "What is it?"

He thought for a moment to find the best words. He decided there was no right or wrong way; either they'd pretend it had never happened, or they would accept it and try to be stronger for the experience. "How are you feeling, Case?" he said. "Really."

"How should I be feeling?"

That was a tough one. "Did you get any rest last night after I went to sleep?"

"No. But I'm not going to take the pills. Sleep isn't the problem. It's the dream. I can't make it stop."

"Tell me."

She looked around at Lizzy on the other side of the open bathroom door.

"She can't hear. Casey, tell me about the dream. I want to know."

"I can't. It's horrible. I don't want you to know."

But I do, he thought. I live it every night, over and over, the corridors, the blood, so much blood. Was it like that for you, too? Or did you go through a different kind of deception?

"That's enough about that. I'm fine. I have to be. Don't worry about me. I'm sorry for all I put you through, Doug. I just want you to know that I know. Without you, I don't know what would have happened. I know what you did for me."

He bent over and kissed her between the jaw line and neck. Her skin was doughy from the makeup and from being indoors for so long, away from the sun. "I didn't have anything to do with it."

"Just love me," she said. "That's enough. Even if it's hard sometimes. It's all I ask of you."

"I do."

"I know. I do know that now." She pulled herself together before the makeup began to run. "I think we should go, don't you?"

"Sure. But first, there's a young man down there I really want you to meet. He's very nice."

"I'm sure he is. Elizabeth, honey? Come on with me. We'll be downstairs. I hope Judy hasn't been bored to distraction. She'll think we don't want to go."

"He left," said Lori from the doorway, out of breath again. "He wouldn't take anything. But he gave me his number. Mom, can we have him over for dinner sometime?"

"I'm sure we can, darling. Are you ready? My, don't you look pretty?"

"Just a minute. I want to talk to Dad first."

"Well, please make it a fast minute. We're late as it is. Lizzy and I will be in the car."

Lori waited for her mother and sister to leave. She sat

next to Doug on the couch and leaned her head on his shoulder. She was crying silently.

"What is it, angel?"

"Nothing."

"Don't you want to go?"

"I don't care."

"Did anything happen down there? Did he say something that made you feel bad?"

"No. I went in Erin's room. I got this blouse to wear. I was afraid Mom would see it and get upset."

"I know. Shh. I know. It's okay to remember. Really, it is."

He held her as the front door opened, closed below. He heard the car start up and idle in the driveway. On TV, Dappy the Duck was mugging like a hebephrenic in a full-color close-up. Next to the set was the videotape of the final cut of the film from Murdoch's office. He still hadn't started on it, would have to run it as soon as they got home. There were a whole lot of things to be worked through, some of them new, some—like *Is Anybody There?*—the same. He didn't know what to do about the picture. It would be a joy and a release to send it back, tear up the contract and tell Murdoch to find another desperate sucker. He might even be doing a favor for some new kid on the way up, looking for his first gig in Hollywood. But then what was Doug's next move to be? And so on. Casey was outside again, waiting for him to get going. Got to get a move on, he thought. In some ways nothing had changed.

He heard the car motor switch off, Casey's heels on the walk. We're coming, he thought. Maybe she forgot something. That was good. Lori wasn't quite ready yet.

"I love you, you know," he said.

Lori held him. "I know. I love you, too."

"If you ever want to talk about anything, like how you feel about what happened, about the bad dream . . ."

"I don't have any bad dreams," she said. "But I had a good one. A very, very good one. It's so good I don't know how to tell anybody about it."

"No, I mean dreams about—about last week."

"I know. That's what I mean. It's about that."

"What do you mean, a good dream? Angel, I . . ." *was there, too,* he almost said. He knew that. Did she? Surely she would remember it for what it was. He didn't want to push her. Perhaps she had been able to forget.

"Don't let it worry you. You're back with us now. It's over."

"I know," she said sadly. "But it was so-o-o beautiful there, in that other place. I saw—"

He held her by the shoulders and stared at her. "What did you see?"

"Oh, you know. I saw Grandma. And Uncle Jerry. And my best friend from third grade, the one who died from the fever, remember? It was like they were all waiting for me. In the tunnel. With the light. They were so nice . . . ."

"What else? Wasn't there anything else?"

"I—I don't know if I should say this. But I saw Erin. She was happy, too. Do you think I should tell Mom?"

Casey came clipping up the stairs.

"I forgot my purse," she said. "Do you have any cash, Doug? We'll need it for the collection, and Judy mentioned going out to eat afterwards. What are you two doing up here?"

"Here I come," said Lori. She whispered to Doug, "I wish you could have seen it."

He suddenly felt leaden, unable to go anywhere. He got up, made it as far as the chair.

Casey swung by the bathroom mirror, caught a glimpse and panicked. "God bless," she said, "I've got eyeliner all over my nose! Why didn't you tell me? And this hair. What's happening to me?"

The conclusion was inescapable. If Lori saw something different . . .

What happened to Casey and to me, we both did that to ourselves. By our own hands.

But not Lori. That other girl, Angie, "helped" her so that Lori didn't have to take her own life.

And Lori saw Erin.

But Erin wasn't there for me, for Casey, not in the place we went to.

And Erin didn't do it to herself, either.

He remembered asking Buddy, If it was so beautiful, why did you leave the cult?

Because sometimes it's bad, so bad . . .

There's always a catch, Buddy had said. *They don't tell you that up front. Everything's got a price . . .*

What I lost I ain't never gettin' back . . .

It wasn't horror . . .

Long as you don't do it to yourself.

Of course it hadn't been the real Buddy talking on the other side. But maybe the kid in white was telling the truth that time. Maybe the trickster tricked himself.

If it was so beautiful, Doug thought, you would be tempted to do it again. And again. On your own. Sooner or later, by yourself.

But then it wouldn't be the same. No one would be doing it to you. You would be doing it to yourself. You would be committing the greatest sin of all.

That's a whole 'nother thing . . .

That way, by your own hand, you went—where? Somewhere else. The somewhere—limbo, purgatory, call it what you will—that I saw. That Casey saw. The place where all suicides go.

That was why they had the pact!

And the price, otherwise? What exactly had Buddy and his friends lost?

Call it a soul, Doug thought. That's as good a word as any.

He dug his hands into the chair to try to hold the world together.

His hand found something between the cushions. He pulled it out to see what it was.

Hair. The swatch of hair that had come out when he and Erin were playing together that morning, the hair that had been aging, losing its vibrancy, deteriorating so rapidly.

Like Buddy's. Like the others'.

Had they talked her into doing it to herself the first

time, like a party game? Did she even remember what she had done?

Was that when it went out of her, the spark? Without it how long would she have lived in any case?

How long do Buddy and his friends have? It can't be long. Do they know that?

They do, they do.

Not Lori. Not those who had no hand in it.

But what of all the others, those who tried for whatever reason to stop their own lives and then came back?

The ones like me. And like Casey.

In the bathroom, Casey made a few weak swipes with her hairbrush.

"Look at me," she said. "My hair's falling out by the roots! It must have been all that medication . . . ."

She cleaned her brush with her comb, drawing away shocking chunks, handfuls of once-beautiful hair. He saw her pale, doughy skin showing through the layered makeup, already sagging and etched with fine stress lines, like the pasty skin of his own face in the mirror.

He put his hands on her waist and pressed his face into her hair, but there were no tears. He would never be able to weep again. Because once he started he might not be able to stop.

Everything has its price, he thought.

He wrapped his arms around his wife and held her so that she would not be able to leave him, and when the children ran up in their best Easter clothes to say that the woman from the church had finally gone on without them, he grabbed the girls and held them in the same way, they who would be left so soon to carry on alone through the long, dark night that lay ahead.